MADNESS UNHINGED

ML GUIDA

Enjoy!

ML Guida

Buffalo Mountain Press

H oss, wishing he were anywhere but here, gravely watched the three Fates sisters, rising from the Angarth Citadel's bubbling baptismal pool. Their white robes illuminated the citadel, brighter than the Zalara's two suns. They were spirits, but powerful enough to strike down the most powerful dragon.

Besides Queen Cosima and his best friend's new human mate, Hera, they were the last females on Zalara. Three months ago, the Kamtrinians had annihilated all their women, and to survive, they needed Earth women.

But he refused to mate.

King Greum and Queen Cosima bowed slightly to the Fates. The king and queen were complete opposites. The king had dark hair and dressed in black, while the queen was blonde, and dressed in white. The bond between them was strong—something that Hoss knew would never be his.

"Greetings," Greum said.

Rillo, the smallest but the strongest Fate, stepped in front of her two sisters. She stretched out her arms. "Another human mate has been chosen, giving us hope that our race will survive."

Hoss winced at her loud voice that sent his nerves on edge. He hoped to hell they weren't going to call his name. There were at least four hundred men crowded in the church—all eager to have their name read. They all believed the myth that mating was for eternity—an unbreakable bond.

He knew differently.

The myth was a lie.

He clenched and unclenched his fists, trying to relax. Odds were against his name being called. He gave Rillo a hard stare, trying to will her to call anyone's name but his.

"The human mates will all be murdered!" Queen Cosima screamed and covered her ears before falling onto her knees on the altar.

"Cosima!" Greum wrapped his arm around her shoulders.

Sunlight came through the stained glass window of two intertwining dragons. Suddenly, the light dimmed as if a blanket of dread had doused both suns.

Rillo and her two sisters cried out and put their hands over their chest, as if something had pierced their hearts.

Hoss sucked in his breath. Without the humans, they'd all die.

Rillo touched Cosmia's bent golden head. "You've had a vision, child. Speak now before it is gone. I fear time is of the essence."

Cosmia moaned, "Blood. There was so much red. So vicious. So senseless."

The baptismal pool hissed and steamed, then slowly turned red.

Hoss slowly pulled out his eruptor. He was the chief security officer of the spaceship Orion, and his job was to protect his people from evil. He scanned the church, looking for anything that could have turned the sacred pool red.

Greum took her hand. "Please tell us."

She lifted her head. "Greum, it's the Kamtrinians."

"What will they do?" Rillo asked. "Speak quickly."

"Their plan"—Cosima gasped—"is to slaughter each designated mate one-by-one on Earth, hoping to end our race."

Greum's cheek twitched. "How?"

"They plan to use a mercenary to invade Earth. I can see the intruder. It's a Mistonian. He's here on Zalara."

The crowd gasped in horror.

Greum asked, "Why?"

Cosima gripped his hand. "He needs a humanoid form to carry out his mission."

Unable to keep silent, Hoss stepped out of the pew and knelt on one knee. "Your majesties, one Mistonian could easily wipe out the women of Earth. Humans have no weapons strong enough to defeat the Mistonian. Allow me and my team to hunt down the intruder."

And hopefully escape his name from being called.

"No." Yethi, one of the Fates and keeper of the Mate Stones, shook her head, her red hair coming lose from her bun. "The ceremony must be completed."

Topaz, the captain of the Orion, joined Hoss. "We don't have time for this. Our race depends on keeping the Earth women safe."

"But this mating ceremony is different." Yethi's face was pale, as if she were still in pain. "Without this one, Captain, you and your crew can't possibly defeat the Mistonian."

Rillo clasped her sister's arm. "Yethi, how do you know this?"

"The Mate Stone revealed it to me." She slowly opened her hand, revealing a red ruby stone.

Hoss clasped the captain's arm. "We must leave now before the blasted Mistonian reaches Earth."

Topaz nodded. "Let's move."

"No!" Yethi held up her hand. She looked at Topaz. "This Mistonian is different. It's a mutant, who feeds on fear. The mutant plans to possess one of Topaz's crew, then force him to steal a ship to invade Earth."

3

Hoss and the captain's eyes locked. "Impossible," they muttered at the same time.

Every crew member on board the Orion was loyal to the captain and the Confederation. As if to prove Yethi wrong, the twenty crewmen of the Orion hurried up to the altar and stood at attention behind the captain who looked behind him. Pride flickered in his eyes.

Cosmia shook her head. "It's already here."

"Fan out." Topaz gestured with his eruptor. "Set your weapons to kill."

"Listen to me." Yethi hurried over to the captain. "The mates will all die unless the ceremony is finished."

"There are at least four hundred men in here who are not a member of the Orion. Complete the ceremony if you must," Hoss grumbled.

Yehti gave him a curious look. "Are you so sure the stone hasn't chosen someone on board the Orion?"

Hoss's stomach tightened. "Well, it's sure as hell isn't me."

Yehti's eyes twinkled and she laughed. "You're wrong, Anonghos."

"Hoss. Everyone calls me Hoss. Only my grandmother called me by my full name."

"I'm well aware of this—Anonghos. You have been chosen, and you are the key to our survival as well as your mate."

Someone snorted behind Hoss.

Another muttered, "We're doomed."

Sweat glistened over Hoss. Men turned their gaze away from him or sighed in defeat. Others whispered to each other, but he knew what they were saying—failure, player, weakling...

Or at least he used to be a player before the damn Kamtrinians murdered all their women.

The captain whirled around. "Silence. All of you. Hoss won't fail us."

The whispering and grumbling ceased. No one wanted to take on the captain of the Orion.

But he was wrong. Hoss would fail. He was his father's son.

He braced his shoulders and in his sternest voice, he said, "I was never loyal to any of our women when they were alive. Why would you think I could be loyal to an alien?"

Yehti touched his arm. "I know of your past, Security Officer. The guilt, the horror, the betrayal."

Hoss jerked his arm away. "That's enough, Fate."

"You will need to come to terms with your past. Your mate will be key in healing you."

He stiffened. "I don't need to be healed. I just need women to warm my bed. One will never do." He wasn't his father.

"No, you're wrong. You have been chosen Anonghos," she said. "Without you, we will not succeed. The Mating Stones are never wrong."

Hoss shook his head. "You have the wrong guy."

"Wrong. Like you, your mate is a security officer and will hunt the Mistonian down. Without your help, she will die a horrible death."

He narrowed his eyes. "What do you mean?"

"Give me your hand."

Hoss kept his arms to his sides.

The captain nudged him. "Hoss, stick out your hand. That's an order."

Hoss glared, and for the first time, planned to disobey a direct command.

"I suggest you take it," Greum growled. He'd cradled Cosima against his shoulder. His eyes burned gold.

Disobeying Topaz was one thing, but spurning the king meant certain death. Hoss reluctantly held out his hand. "I'll not fall in love with her."

Yethi slowly raised her eyebrow. "Are you so sure, Security Officer?"

"Yes. Love is fleeting." He towered over the Fate, not caring if she struck him down.

"You don't like women?"

"No, I enjoy women."

"You just don't trust them."

He refused to turn away from her perceptive gaze, but clamped his jaw tight. He'd no intention of reliving his sad, pathetic childhood to her.

"You will find, Security Officer, that without trusting your mate, the Mistonian will slip through your fingers."

"You're wrong."

"I will be there when those words come back to haunt you." She covered his hand with hers, nestling the Mating Stone between them. "And you discover true love."

He snorted. "Then you're going to be waiting a long, long time, Fate."

Warmth and tingles raced up Hoss's arm, shutting off another retort. A vision formed in his mind of a blonde woman with a curvy body. She had a holster with a gun over one shoulder, and she had a smirk that teased at his heart. She entered what looked like a dark alley way. A man twice her size jumped out of the shadows and put his hand over her mouth. In a split second, she flipped him over her shoulder. He landed hard on his back. She grabbed his wrist and rolled him onto his gut. She sat on his buttocks and grabbed his wrists. Before the man knew what was happening, she had clasped on handcuffs—very impressive.

He shook his head. No, he wouldn't let her get under his skin. He clutched the stone tight in his hand, forcing himself not to throw it across the room, but instead slipped the dreaded red stone in his pocket. He refused to be weak like his father, and allow a woman to break his pride. He'd mate, but leave her flat.

Yethi gave him a knowing look that he'd fall under his mate's spell and never let her go. He gritted his teeth. She was sadly mistaken.

"Your majesty." The captain bowed slightly. "Do we have your leave?"

"Yes." Greum nodded.

"Be careful, Captain. All of you." Cosima looked at each of them. "This Mistonian is cunning. I fear he possesses hidden powers. I can't see them. He's very clever."

Greum motioned. "Damon, come forth."

"Yes, your majesty," a tall blond man answered. He was Hoss's best friend, and the queen's personal guard. He quickly escorted his red-headed mate, Hera, to the altar to stand next to the queen.

Greum slowly released Cosima's arm. "Damon will protect you while I guard the entrance."

When he walked away, Cosima gasped and swayed. He turned around, but Hera immediately clasped her arm. "I've got her." She shooed her other hand. "Go guard the entrance."

The captain led all of them outside to the landing. "We need to split up and find this thing, but be careful, it wants to possess one of us. We'll go in pairs so if one's attacked, the other can destroy it. Set your eruptors to kill. I don't want this thing on board my ship."

As they quickly divided into pairs, Greum transformed into a black dragon, forcing them to back away. His body covered the stairs, and he wrapped his tail around himself. His enormous wings sprung out to almost the length of the building. No one could possibly enter the doorway into the citadel. He was the deadliest of all of them. Even a Mistonian would have difficulty defeating Greum. His fire could turn the gaseous cloud to water.

But according to Cosima, this thing had no intention of going after the king.

Hoss was glad to be out of the citadel and ready to do his job again. Unfortunately, he was paired with Daidhl, the Orion's navigator. He was an excellent navigator, but a poor fighter. He didn't possess the cunning or the strength of the other Bravian and

Dominan dragons, but then again, he was a smaller dragon and of the Inquistains, which were more scientists and explorers rather than warriors. He wasn't sure what he could do up against a Mistonian bent on destroying all of their would-be mates.

"Transform," the captain ordered.

They quickly changed into their dragon forms. Daidhl was a skinny red dragon, that like his human form, always looked under-fed. Similar to Greum, Hoss was a black dragon, but he had a green streak from his head down to his tail. He'd always been proud of it, since the streak used to make him stand out and attract women. He was twice as big as Daidhl, but right now, they were partners.

Without a moment's hesitation, they flew into the air and headed toward the space port where the Orion was docked and under repairs. Clouds rippled around them and the glisten of moisture clung to Hoss's body, but he didn't detect anything out of the ordinary. A Mistonian would have tried to suck the energy out of him.

He and Daidhl landed near the station, then transformed back into human form. Usually men would have been working, but all the men had been called to the Citadel to learn if they were the next ones to be chosen for a mate. Out of all of the Zalarains still alive, why did the blasted Mating Stone choose him?

Never mind. He had a job to do.

Daidhl took out his transrecorder. "I'm not getting any unusual readings."

"It's a Mistonian, Daidhl. It has the ability to change its form and hide from our scanners. Come on, we need to investigate the Orion and make sure it's not lurking in there."

Daidhl stuffed the transrecorder back into his belt. "I'm well-aware of the Mistonian's abilities, Hoss. I was merely reporting my findings."

The Orion's hatch door was open and the stairs down, so the workers and mechanics could work on repairs. Hoss slipped in front of Daidhl, not trusting that the Inquistain would fire if the bastard attacked. Inquistains always wanted to study first, then fire. Since this Mistonian possessed other abilities, he suspected Daidhl wouldn't want to kill it right away, since Daidhl was a bleeding-heart over any newly discovered species.

Not the smartest thing to do—some of them would want to eat him for a tasty snack.

Cosmia said this thing had hidden powers. The Mistonian must be very powerful if the queen couldn't detect its abilities.

He glanced over his shoulder. "Stay close."

Daidhl glared. "I'm not helpless, Hoss."

Hoss turned away. He'd obviously pricked the little dragon's pride. The captain should have had him stay behind with Damon and protect the women and the other Zalarians.

They slowly made their way onto the ship. The walls and the floor sparkled. The captain would be pleased.

He sniffed, but couldn't detect anything except disinfectant, which was powerful enough to kill any bacteria and wipe away grime and rust. Something the Inquistains had invented, which he grudgingly admitted was useful.

They walked down the hallway and headed toward the medical wing. Something dinged in sickbay, as if the Orion were trying to warn them there was an intruder on board.

Tryker, the surgeon on board the ship, had a medical board that would have gone off instantly if an alien or Zalarian walked by it. Hoss's senses were on alert. Someone was in sickbay when it should be deserted.

"Do you smell something sour?" Daidhl wrinkled his nose.

"Shhh." But Daidhl was right. He detected a foul odor.

They slowly made their way toward sickbay, neither of them making a sound. The door slid open to a spotless medical room with neatly made beds, clean counters, and supplies put neatly in containers, but no gaseous cloud.

Hoss entered first. A struggled moan made him whirl around to look behind him.

Daidhl was shoved up against a wall. Purple mist poured down his mouth. His body shook uncontrollably. The sickbay's door slammed instantly shut. It all happened so fast that Hoss hadn't had time to fire.

"Daidhl!" Hoss slammed his fist on the door, but it wouldn't open. He instantly transformed into a dragon and used his full strength to open the door.

Daidhl held his eruptor. "Good-bye, Hoss."

His voice was meaner, bolder, cockier. His once golden eyes were now an eerie purple.

Hoss swung his tail, but Daidhl fired. Freezing cold engulfed Hoss, chilling his breath, crystallizing his scales, and congealing his blood. Bitter frostbite seized him. If he hadn't been a dragon, he'd be dead, but he wasn't out of the woods yet. The freeze ray was working its way to his already slowing heart.

Daidhl smiled. "Just to let you know, Zalarian, your precious Orion is disabled along with the other ships. I'll soon be on Earth, and the first mate I plan to kill is yours. I'll leave you with an image on what I plan to do."

He blew a puff of smoke into Hoss's face. An image formed in his mind. A woman had her throat slit and her body cut open, her guts draped over her side. He couldn't see her face, but she had blond hair like the woman that the Fate had shown him earlier. Anger and horror and frost flooded through Hoss. He struggled in vain to escape the freeze ray, which continued to consume his body.

Laughing, Daidhl saluted him, then fled.

Hoss drew on every ounce of energy, trying to bring up the fire inside him. How the blazes did this bastard know who the mates were? It had to be one of his hidden powers.

Hoss concentrated on breathing, fueling the fire inside him. His blood stirred. Frost melted off his scales, and water pooled onto the floor. He managed to move his tail, then his wings. The remaining ice crashed around him. He wouldn't be able to fly, his wings were still too brittle.

He transformed back into a humanoid form and shivered uncontrollably. His telicator beeped. He pulled it out of his belt with stiff fingers.

"Hoss, this is the captain. There's a ship, leaving Zalara. What's happening? I've been trying to reach you."

"Captain, it's Daidhl. He's possessed. Froze me, nearly killing me. He's disabled the Orion. I'm not sure about the Excalibur."

"Wait for us. We're only five minutes away."

"He's getting away."

"That's an order," the captain growled.

At least fifty men were hunting for Daidhl, but they'd never get here before he escaped. For the second time, Hoss disobeyed an order and limped toward the docking bay of the Excalibur. Luckily, the bastard had forgotten about it, or most likely hadn't time to sabotage the ship.

He opened the Excalibur doors with his stiff fingers and managed to navigate it out of the Orion. Yethi had said it was his fate to solve this. Hoss's mate was the one in danger. He might not want to fall in love with her, but she didn't deserve to die a horrible death.

As soon as he cleared the Orion's dock, he scanned for Daidhl's ship.

The communication computer signaled. He sighed. The captain wouldn't take no for an answer.

"Captain," he mumbled.

"I gave you an order."

"I know. I'll contact you when I reach Earth."

Before he could answer, Hoss cut off communication. He tracked Daidhl's course to Earth and recognized the coordinates as being the same one Damon had used to retrieve his mate.

In less than four hours, Daidhl had landed in a field, but hadn't come outside yet. As far as Hoss could tell, they were outside the city limits. There were no trees or houses, only grassy weeds. Hoss landed close by.

The door to Daidhl's ship opened, and he stepped outside.

Hoss quickly turned on the cloaking device that hid the Excalibur and rushed outside to face Daidhl.

"Hello, Hoss." He flashed him a smile and his purple eyes glowed. "Did you have a nice trip?"

Hoss aimed his eruptor. "My name is Anonghos. Only my friends call me Hoss."

"Ah and here I thought we were going to be friends."

"Don't make me shoot. You need to return to Zalara."

Daidhl laughed. "I don't think so. The Kamtrinians are paying me handsomely for each kill."

"The Kamtrinians aren't known for their trustfulness."

"That's what you'd like me to believe, Zalarian. Catch me if you can."

Before Hoss could fire, Daidhl vanished. Hoss turned around in a circle.

"Daidhl, where are you?"

A fist plowed into Hoss's chin and sent him flying onto his back.

"Your mates will die horribly. Good-bye, Security Officer."

Footsteps ran away from Hoss. He aimed his eruptor, but there was no one there. He sniffed and inhaled a sour smell, but it was fleeting.

He whipped out his telicator. "Captain, do you read me?"

"Topaz, here. What's wrong?"

"I just discovered one of the Mistonian's abilities."

"Which is?"

"He can turn Daidhl invisible. I think he also smells like sour blilk." Blilk was a sweet cream produced by the gentle borks. Hoss liked to stir blilk in his tea, but once it soured, its odor was enough to make him gag.

"Be careful, Hoss. He could kill you at any time."

"He could have, Captain, but he didn't. I think he has something worse planned."

"The Orion won't be repaired for at least a week. Unfortunately, we won't be able to assist you."

His voice was grim as if he thought Hoss wasn't going to survive.

"I know. I'll watch my back."

"You better. Cosima said the Mistonian had hidden powers. Invisibility might not be the only one."

Hoss's stomach tightened, and he scanned his surroundings looking for anything moving on its own.

"I'll report to you soon."

He shut off his telicator. The hairs on the back of his neck stood straight up as a sinking feeling settled in his stomach: that might be the last time he spoke to the captain.

2

Agnes Malloy walked into the Arvada Police Department, holding her Pumpkin Spice Latte. It was only September, but her favorite drink was already available. She took a sip, trying to ignore the shivers rustling up the back of her neck that meant something was wrong.

"Good morning, Detective." Evelyn Gomez greeted her from the behind the glass partition. She was always cheerful no matter the circumstances and, even on Agnes's worse days, brightened her mood.

"Every time you say that, I still can't believe I made detective."

"You earned it. Your dad would have been proud of you."

In a split second, Evelyn had doused her morning. Her father would have only been proud of her if she had buried her psychic abilities. Even if she had pretended that she wasn't psychic, she wasn't sure he'd be proud of her. Nothing she had ever done pleased him.

But she brushed the pain behind her and smiled. "Thank you, Evelyn. Is Detective Peters here yet?"

"You're kidding, right? He's late, as always."

Evelyn buzzed her inside.

Agnes smiled. "Have a good day."

"You, too...Detective."

Agnes headed for her desk that held five days of paperwork. Her partner's desk was neat as a pin.

Captain Brian Morgan peeked behind his door. "Malloy, my office."

His gruff voice made her wince. The day hadn't even started yet, and she was already in the dog house.

He sat behind his desk in an overstuffed chair. The overhead light shined off his bald head. The only hair he had was his bushy eyebrows. He took a drink from his cup that had the words captain written on it. Papers and files were scattered across his desk. Organization was not his forte.

He glanced at his computer screen, then wrote something on a piece of paper. She stared at the photograph that hung behind Captain Morgan, one of her father when he was a rookie. He actually looked happy. The captain and her father had been partners for fifteen years, but five years ago, her father had been killed in the line of duty. That day had been the worst day of her life.

Her mother had died of breast cancer a year before her father was murdered, so she was an orphan. Or at least that's what she thought. However, the captain had appointed himself to not only to act as her captain, but her father as well. Not a good combination.

Captain Morgan handed her a piece of paper with an address. Agnes knew the area. It was a new development that had just opened.

"This just came in," he said. "There's been a murder. Tom's already on his way to the crime scene. From the reports, it's pretty grisly. I want this done by the book, Malloy. None of this *feelings* crap."

Her muscles tensed tighter than an overly stretched rubber band. Tom must have been shooting off his mouth again. He'd always admired her older brother, Frank, who had made fun of her abilities since she was a child.

"I understand."

"Good. Tom says that you're relying on feelings rather than evidence. Feelings don't get convictions."

She was so tired of this argument, but she nodded. "I know. Have I ever given a case to the DA that didn't have hard evidence?"

He frowned. "No. I took a big risk in promoting you to detective. You know your brother was against it."

She bristled. How could she forget? Her brother thought she should be a meter-maid and use her so-called abilities to guess which car ran out of time first. He thought his jokes were so funny. Unfortunately, so did her dad. He was the superstar and had been Dad's favorite. "Yes, I know."

"Don't let me regret it."

"You won't."

She left the station as quickly as she entered. When she pulled up to the scene, there were black and whites along with Tom's trusty blue Ford truck. As being senior officer, he was always called in first. They'd only been parters for the last five months. Unfortunately, he'd been her brother Frank's partner before Frank went to Quantico to train to be a FBI agent.

He drank from the same Kool-Aid as everyone else. He thought psychics were crack-pots. If she wanted to be respected, she'd better keep any mumbo-jumbo to herself, or she would be a meter-maid.

She found Tom in the kind of wide-open kitchen that she envied—granite counter tops, an island, double door refrigerator, both a conventional and convection oven. He was bent over examining the dead woman spread out on the floor.

"About time you got here," he muttered. Coolness flashed in his silver eyes.

She refused to play his game of always being one up. "You could have called me."

"I thought you would have sensed the call." He chuckled at his own joke. When she didn't take the bait, he shrugged. "Besides the captain wanted a word with you."

She glared, biting back a retort of calling him a rat-fink, but it would only get her in more hot water. He was well respected in the department, but as far as women's rights went, he hadn't gotten on that bus, which was why his desk was neat. He made her do the paperwork. She wanted to complain, but she had too many strikes against her, thanks to her overbearing older brother telling everyone that she saw ghosts.

She looked at the poor woman spread out on the floor. Blood had seeped down the woman's throat, drenching her pink suit, and had spilled onto the floor.

She took out her iPad.

"Forensics just finished up. They've already taken the crime photos." Tom Peters frowned, his bushy gray caterpillar eyebrows nearly touching each other. "Why do you need that cumbersome thing?"

Agnes laughed. "It's not cumbersome. It's an iPad and with the Apple pencil I can write on it."

He was still old school and didn't like technology. She didn't know why he always insisted on having this hundred-year old argument. But then, he was fifteen years older than her and was counting down the days to retirement, which as far as she could tell, he had another long decade before he'd cross the finish line.

Not wanting to argue, she changed the subject. "Who is she?"

"Name's Sharon Reese. She's an accountant." Tom said, as he scribbled notes on his note pad. He even made a quick sketch of Sharon. Unlike her, his few lines were done remarkably well. He always said drawing out the grim scene imprinted it on his mind.

But she doubted he'd have any problems remembering this horror.

"Someone was really pissed off." Agnes walked around the victim, acid burning her gut at the grisly scene. She took pictures of Sharon with her tablet in different positions, so she could go over them later. "Forensics already been here?"

Three slices of bacon were flattened onto a blackened frying pan. She wrinkled her nose at the smell of burnt coffee and bacon. "Must have been cooking breakfast when he attacked her." Grease was splattered onto the stove. "I wonder if she managed to throw grease onto his face before he killed her. Maybe we should check the nearby hospitals for anyone coming in with grease burns."

"I'll call it in," he said.

Agnes knelt next to the body. "God, whoever did this must really hate women."

Sharon's eyes were frozen in horror. Her throat had been sliced from ear to ear, and her shirt ripped into two. A long ugly cut ran from her belly button to her breast bone. Her intestines draped over her stomach as if they'd been pulled out. Near Sharon's stretched out hand, there was a broken mug and a brown stain of coffee on the tile and wooden cupboard.

"Poor woman." Tom shook his head.

"Her fingernails are clean." Agnes studied Sharon's pale hands. "He must have caught her by surprise. Doesn't appear to be much of a struggle."

"According to the first officers on the scene, neighbors didn't hear anything."

"Who found her?"

"Car pool came to pick her up at seven-thirty this morning like always." Tom tilted his head. "Front door was unlocked."

Agnes lifted her eyebrow. "The killer went outside in broad daylight?"

"Apparently, he's pretty damn brazen."

"I'd like to talk to the first person who found her."

Tom checked through his notes. "It was a woman in the victim's carpool. There were five of them who drove together every morning, according to patrol. A woman named Doris Walters found her. She's pretty shook up. Patrol has them outside near their car...A blue Subaru."

"Forensics done with the rest of the house."

"Yes, it's not a big house. They're working on the backyard now. We think that's how he got inside, since they found footprints in the dirt and grass leading to the patio door."

"I'm going to take a look around the house."

"Going to try and get in touch with the victim?" Tom gave her a dry smile.

Agnes shrugged, pretending his comment hadn't peeled back her wounds. "No. I just have an uncanny knack of knowing the victim by wandering through the crime scene."

He gave her a dubious look. He knew she was lying, but she refused to admit she was psychic. Psychics had no place in the police department. Her father had drilled that into her skull.

Despite what father had said, her ability had helped her solve many cases.

Not that she got any credit for it.

She left Tom who was still sketching the victim while she took pictures of the path from the kitchen to the living room to the entry way. Neither room was very big. For an accountant, Sharon had a modest ranch. Her kitchen and living room were both open, and she had a large screen television set, so obviously robbery wasn't the motive. Or at least, he didn't have time to take it before the car pool arrived.

She leisurely walked into each room, starting with the bathroom, wanting to understand Sharon. She'd been someone's friend, lover, or daughter that had been brutally taken from them. Sharon had been extremely neat—everything was put away—curling iron, hair dryer, make-up all lined up perfectly in the cabinet. Unlike Agnes, whose bathroom looked like an explosion went off. But then again, she hadn't had any house guests for a long time. Her mother used to say she was too consumed with her work. She thought it was because she was a plump homicide detective, who worked twenty-four seven and couldn't stop looking at every man as a potential suspect.

She entered another bedroom, which she suspected was a guest bedroom. There were no clothes hanging in the closet or folded in the antique looking oak dresser. A smaller flat screen television hung on the wall and the remote control was on the nightstand. Another opportunity the killer had missed.

The last room she went into was the master bedroom, where Sharon had a king-size four-poster bed that of course was neatly made. Agnes hadn't had time to make hers—again. She was definitely not a morning person, and struggled to roll out of bed when the alarm sounded, but Sharon told a different story.

Stuffed animals were arranged neatly on the bed. The dresser, nightstand, and entertainment set were all dusted. Sharon had perfume bottles on the dresser that sat on a pristine glass mirror. Her movies were alphabetized on a shelf below another flat screen television. This was definitely a woman who liked everything neat and organized.

Pictures of Sharon in happier times filled her room, as if she wanted those she loved to be close to her. In the corner of the room, she had an oak desk that faced away from the television. Agnes bet Sharon had liked perfect quiet while she was working, but there wasn't a stitch of paper or writing utensil.

She opened one closet door, and as she suspected, shirts were with shirts, sweaters with sweaters, suits with suits, and pants with pants. Even the shoes were lined up based on weather—sandals were all together, high heels all together, boots all together. Sharon didn't like to take anything for chance. She wouldn't be someone who liked to take risks. Order and organization had rated high for her.

So, how did the killer get inside? Sharon would have locked every door and window before she went to work.

Something glowed and flickered out of the corner of her eye.

The ghostly apparition of a woman formed. Sharon Reese. She had the same pink suit on—minus the blood and looked at Agnes with desperation. Refusing to acknowledge her, Agnes stiffened and held out her palm. "No!"

The shimmering apparition faded, and Agnes sighed with relief. Seeing ghosts was definitely against departmental rules—one she refused to break.

Alarm—a voice echoed in her ear.

Agnes groaned. Unfortunately, ghostly voices were harder to ignore, especially if they made sense regarding a crime. Agnes hurried out of the bedroom to see if the voice meant an alarm system. Sharon seemed like a person who would have wanted her home protected. Agnes flicked through the pictures on her iPad to see if she missed anything. Sure enough in the corner of doors were little white motion boxes, but they obviously hadn't gone off.

She hurried back to the kitchen. "Tom, what time did Sharon turn off her alarm system?"

"I don't know. Another thing on our list to do."

"We're going to have a big one."

"Detective Malloy?"

Agnes turned to a female officer who was looking less than happy.

"What's the problem, officer?"

"Officer Patricia Evans." She pointed her thumb toward the front door. "There's a man outside insisting upon seeing you."

Agnes frowned. "Is he one of the witnesses?"

She shook her head. "No. But he swears he has evidence about the case and will only share it with you. He's getting insistent."

By her nervous tone, Agnes thought she'd better go. "I'll be back in a few minutes."

Tom waved his hand. "Go ahead. I'll be out in a few minutes anyway. Agnes?"

"Yeah?"

"Be careful. This guy could be the killer coming back to look at his handiwork."

"I don't think anyone would have missed him," Evans said. "He's kinda hard to overlook."

Intrigued, Agnes followed the officer out of Sharon's home. Evans hadn't had to point the man out. Her heart sped when she glanced at him. She couldn't help but be awed by the sheer size and presence of the persistent man. She had never seen anyone with golden eyes. They were the eyes of a predator.

Definitely out of her league, but man, he turned on all of her libido senses. Whoever he was, he looked like he'd just got done doing a model shoot for Marvel comics. He was at least a head taller than any man there, and his chest and arms could have flattened a sumo wrestler. His neck was rock solid, the jaw blunted under a veiled week's worth of bearding, with a deep cleft shadowing the middle of his chin. "He's the one with the long, black hair?"

She wondered if it was as silky as it looked.

Evans nodded. "That's the guy. Have fun. He doesn't take no for an answer."

"Let me in! I need to talk to her!" He slammed into two officers like a bowling ball crashing into two blue pins.

The officers staggered, but managed to keep him back. The smaller of the two actually reached for his taser.

"Stay back or I'm going to zap your sorry ass."

They were having a devil of a time keeping the man behind the yellow crime tape. If the man couldn't tone down his insistent behavior, he'd find himself sitting in the back of a squad car.

Agnes tucked her iPad underneath her arm. "I'll take it from here."

"I told you that you can't cross the crime scene tape." The taller officer had his hands up as if to prevent the overeager man from breaking it.

Other people were crowded outside and had moved away

from him, so the officers weren't the only ones he was making uncomfortable. She thought about what Tom said and left her libido at the crime scene.

Although he was no slouch of man, his efforts would have proven useless if the Hulk wanted to break inside.

The man pointed. "She's coming toward us. Will you please let me speak with her? It's urgent."

His voice was so husky it made her palms sweat.

This was ridiculous. She was at a murder investigation, not at a bar. She refused to think about her traitorous body tingling at just looking at this man.

"Officer." Agnes lifted the tape over her head. "I'll take it from here."

"I need to see the crime scene," he blurted.

Agnes narrowed her eyes. "No, you don't. You wanted to speak to me?"

"Yes, in private." He glared at the two officers.

An image of what he could do with his lips in private made her squirm uncomfortably. Why was she having hot fantasies about him? She'd never done this before.

Using her sternest voice, she said, "Follow me." She led him across the street where a huge oak tree offered some shade.

He was too close, and she got a whiff of smoke, as if he'd been sitting next to a camp fire.

She whirled around, frustrated at losing control around him. "What is it that you want?"

Her voice was harder than the captain's.

He hadn't even blinked, but she suddenly realized his eyes reminded her of a tiger's, studying her, ready to pounce. His lashes were absurdly long for a man, black as night, framing tiger's eyes that burned with dominance and arrogance. This was a man used to getting his way. He'd better get used to disappointment.

She might find him insanely attractive, but she was a police detective used to setting the stage.

"I have information vital for you."

"First of all, who are you?"

"My name is Anonghos, but everyone calls me Hoss."

"Fine. Anonghos what?"

"That's just it. We don't have surnames like you humans do."

"Humans? So, you dropped your last name?"

So, this was a crazy super hero.

He stopped, then opened his mouth and shut it, as if he realized his mistake.

"I have never had one. Look, I know how insane this is going to sound, but you have to believe me, or more women are going to die."

"I'm listening," she said calmly, ignoring her cramping gut that was always a warning something bad was going to happen. Her grandmother had always said it was a shining gift, but Agnes always attributed it to good police work.

"The man you're looking for is pure evil."

A total understatement.

"Go on." She wasn't sure about him and slowly moved her hand toward her gun, not sure what this man was capable of. Her only concern were the curious onlookers who could get seriously hurt.

"He has a list of women he's going after."

"How do you know this? Have you seen this list?"

"No, but I know one person who is on it."

Uneasiness crept up her spine at his penetrative stare.

"And who is it?"

"You are."

God, he was the killer. She slowly removed her revolver careful not to make any quick moves.

Still trying to remain in control, she asked, "Why do you say this?"

He clasped her shoulders. "Because you're my mate."

A shock shimmered up her arms. Instantly, images flowed

through her mind of intimately embracing this man in exotic poses that made her gasp. She jerked away.

"What did you just do to me?"

"Nothing." He shook his head, but studied the front and back of his hands, as if he'd felt the same thing she did. "I just touched you to get you to listen to me."

Strange images of space ships and dragons popped into her head, replacing the sexy pictures, and she shook her head. They felt real, too real.

She stepped away. "Stay where you are."

Her stomach twisted into tiny knots, and her heart beat wildly in her chest. She shouldn't have come over here alone. He could easily overpower her, but he hadn't made any sudden moves. She whipped out her gun and aimed it at his heart. "Freeze. You're under arrest."

"On what charge?"

"For threatening a police officer."

His mysterious tiger's eyes burned brighter, and she thought she detected a low animal growl. "You don't know what threatening is."

Four police officers surrounded him, their guns drawn.

"Don't make me shoot you." Agnes flicked off the safety.

"I won't. But we're not done yet."

She shoved her gun back into her holster. "Read him his rights." Unfortunately, she was shaking violently.

He had to be the killer, but why did every ounce of her rebel? She couldn't shake the feeling that she was making a deadly mistake.

3

Hoss's hands tingled after briefly clasping Agnes's slender shoulders. He shook with desire, and his nostrils flared. What was happening? He'd never responded to a woman like this before. And he was famous for seducing the women of Zalarian, leaving a trail of broken hearts, before they had been annihilated.

But none of them had been his designated mate.

Determined to stay in control and not end up like his weak father, he took several deep breaths until he was sure he wouldn't transform and kidnap his mate, who looked at him warily.

He stared into her fearless grendor-shaped eyes that mesmerized him. Grendors were fierce predators on Zalara and their eyes were shaped like diamonds. If she weren't careful, her spunk would get herself killed.

He was barely aware of the security officers surrounding and aiming their weapons at him. A puny officer grabbed each of Hoss's arms and clamped handcuffs over his wrists. "You have the right to be silent."

He could easily break free if he wanted to, but it would violate the Confederation's directive—planets with inferior technology were not to know of their existence.

"You have the right to an attorney. If you can't afford an attorney, one will be appointed for you."

He quit paying attention to the officer rattling off more of his rights. How could touching Agnes's shoulders so briefly send him over the edge? She was a dangerous temptation—one he refused to sample.

But even as the thought entered his mind, his gaze was drawn to her blouse that was opened at the top. A glisten of sweat caught his eye, and he glanced at her full breasts, large enough to satisfy the hunger of a man. Her gun was sheathed on a belt that curved around the wide hips of a strong and amble woman. His heartbeat quickened, and he was one step away from doing something really stupid. He gulped deep breaths, trying to remain calm, but every twisted nerve was on the brink of unraveling.

Breathe, just breathe.

He slowly realized she was studying him, as if to see what he would do.

Trying to be his normal debonair self, he flashed her a smile. "Finding any answers?"

"Maybe."

Her confident voice triggered a warning inside him.

"You need to be careful." Hoss's grin faded. "You've no idea of what he's capable of."

The puny officer clasped his arm. "Shut up."

"No." Hoss jerked his arm free. "Listen to me, you're in danger. The bastard's going to keep on killing."

"Wait, officer." Agnes held up her slender hand. "You know who did this?"

Hoss nodded. "He's just begun. The body count is going to rise."

"Is he your partner?" she asked softly.

"No. You're not listening to me."

He couldn't hide the anger in his voice, and it was louder than he wanted. Most of the women he'd been with would have of shrunk from him, but not Agnes. She studied him as if waiting for him to stew in his own juices until he revealed unwanted secrets.

He met her curious gaze. She'd better get used to bitter disappointment. He'd a lifetime of hiding the skeletons rattling in his soul.

Another larger officer came along the other side of him. "He's yanking your chain, Detective."

Agnes winced.

Hoss growled, his dragon threatening to cut loose on the taunting man, daring to ridicule her. The officer's face paled, and he kept his trap shut.

She lifted her chin. "I'll be the judge of that, Officer." She did the strangest thing and pulled out a flat screen out of her jacket, then took a picture of Hoss.

He frowned. "What are you doing?"

"Studying you, of course." She examined the screen rather than looking at him, as if she could discover some of his secrets.

He thought humans only possessed the polygraph machine to discover whether someone was lying, which wasn't reliable. Had humans discovered something he wasn't aware of? He squirmed uncomfortably, his palms growing sweaty, at the idea of her unraveling his past.

She tilted her head at the car. "Take him down to headquarters. I'll question him later."

He had to be imagining it. There was no way the little screen would reveal to her his secrets. Human technology was centuries behind developing such a device.

Before the two security guards led him away, a gray-haired man crowded between them. "Agnes, are you okay?"

"I'm fine, Tom."

He gave Hoss a death glare. "This man's dangerous."

"I realize that, Tom."

Tom jerked his thumb. "Take him to headquarters."

As the officers were leading Hoss away, Tom lowered his voice, but not so low that dragon ears couldn't hear.

"Agnes, your intuition isn't going to tell you a thing. Your brother never would have stooped to relying on mumbo-jumbo."

Hoss glanced over his shoulder.

Agnes's cheeks burned red. "I realize that, Tom."

The self-assuredness in her voice had vanished.

He whirled around, easily breaking free from the two security guards. Fury burned inside Hoss's chest, the dragon threatening to fry the old fool into a crispy critter. "You think you're more equipped to find the killer?"

Hoss didn't bother hiding the scorn in his voice. Tom actually took a step back, his face paling.

The officers seized Hoss's arms again.

As Hoss was being restrained, Tom puffed out his chest. "I am the senior detective, and yes, I am more capable."

His arrogance would only play into the Mistonian's trap. Hoss narrowed his eyes. "Then, you're a fool."

Tom's face turned five shades of purple. "Get him out of here."

The two men led him away.

"Do that again and I'll taser you," the bigger of the two men warned.

Hoss ignored him.

Blast it! He should have held his tongue, but no one here, including Agnes, knew how dangerous Daidhl was. Hell, he didn't even know if *he* had the ability to stop him. The Orion's navigator wasn't his mild self anymore and most likely was dead. The Mistonian controlled his empty shell. Cosima had said the Mistonian possessed hidden powers, but besides being able to turn invisible, he had no idea what else the bastard could do.

When they reached the car, the officer opened the door. "Lower your head."

Hoss practically had to kneel on the ground to get into the

vehicle, which was too cramped for his long legs. His knees were scrunched up to his chest.

He took another look at Agnes, who was concentrating on looking at her screen, which he hoped was just a way of her solving cases. Something was odd about her.

Once again, he'd lost his cool over this woman. He'd never reacted with such anger over Topaz correcting a female crew member he had been involved with. Sleeping with women without a commitment had always been his style, but with Agnes, he'd wanted to fry Tom for ridiculing her.

He froze, remembering how his father used to be so protective over his mother, but his mother had mocked him. No matter what he did, his mother rejected him, breaking his spirit. Hoss refused to end up a broken man. He needed to solve this case, mate with Agnes, then get the hell away from her.

He leaned his head back on the leather seat. Agnes wasn't a match for a possessed Daidhl. He needed to convince her that she was in danger. She said she'd talk to him later. He just hoped it wouldn't be too late. He kept thinking of the murdered woman and wondered whose mate she was designated for. Unless another species magically materialized, the Zalarian would never be mated and his lineage would die.

The security officers started the car. He'd read about these contraptions that were so much slower than their spaceships.

Yellow tape was draped across the front door of the little, white house. Officers milled around in the front yard, while others kept curious on-lookers back. Hoss wished he had the power to see through walls like some of the other aliens, but Zalarians didn't possess this ability. "What happened to the woman inside?"

The smaller of the two glanced in the rear review mirror. "That's none of your concern."

"Oh, so you don't know."

"Yes, we do." The brawny one scowled over his shoulder as he was driving. "The woman was—"

"Keep your mouth shut, Johnson," the other one yelled. "And keep your eyes on the road."

Hoss stopped trying to goad them when neither would bite. They weren't as dumb as he thought. After a short distance, they parked in front of a two-story, red-brick building with a huge glass pane window. A semi-circle stone wall sat in front with a mountain logo and the name Arvada Police Station written on it.

Johnson, the husky officer, opened the car door. "Watch your head."

Hoss didn't bend low enough and smacked his forehead on the rim of the car. Pain blinded him for a minute as dizziness swirled around him. He was roughly drawn out of the car, nearly stumbling onto one knee.

"I told you to watch it."

Johnson's hard voice penetrated the fog in his brain.

"Your compassion is overwhelming," Hoss muttered, trying to control the anger burning inside him.

"That's what you get for attacking an officer," the scrawny one growled.

"I wasn't attacking her."

"That's not what I saw," Johnson grumbled.

Hoss wasn't going to get anywhere with these two self-righteous humans. They'd already made up their mind. "I want to speak to an attorney."

"We'll notify one for you."

By his tone, it wouldn't be anytime soon.

He was escorted to a Plexiglas window where an older brown-skinned woman with glasses sat. Her eyes widened when she looked at Hoss. "What do you have, Simms?"

The skinny man gripped Hoss's forearm. "Attacking a police officer, Evelyn."

Evelyn frowned. "You don't look injured."

"Wasn't me. He attacked Detective Malloy."

"What? Is she okay?"

"She's fine. She foolishly met with him alone."

Evelyn glared. "I'm sure she had a good reason."

Johnson laughed. "She did. She thought she could read his mind. Stupid mistake."

Evelyn boosted her double chin in defiance. "She just investigates differently."

Simms mumbled underneath his breath. "For a fruitcake."

Hoss glowered. "Don't talk about her that way."

Simms rolled his eyes. "Buzz us in, Evelyn."

Evelyn pushed a red button. "Sure thing."

A metal door clicked then slid opened. Johnson and Simms led him through the doors to another front desk.

Johnson unlocked Hoss's handcuffs.

"Take off your Batman utility belt," Johnson said.

Hoss lowered his voice. "No."

He stepped closer. "Do it. Or I'll do it for you."

Hoss would like to see him try, but Topaz would be less than pleased if he cut loose on these two security jerks.

He reluctantly removed the belt and handed it to Johnson, who put it into a plastic bag.

"You'll get your little superheroes belt back when you make bail," he said.

Hoss realized that they thought the weapons were fake, which would hopefully save their lives. Otherwise, they could zap themselves into oblivion.

Johnson tossed the plastic bag roughly onto the counter.

Hoss winced. "Be careful with those."

"Sure, Batman."

Hoss clutched his fists and pressed them to his side to keep from slugging the arrogant officer.

He was finger printed. He smiled to himself, because his prints would not match any human—unless they had dragon shifters on

Earth. Once again, he was photographed. He didn't understand why the humans needed so many photos of him.

He was led through the station, booked, and put in a dreary cell. The large cell had a couple of metal benches, a stained urinal, and steel bars that pressed against a scratched, Plexiglas window. Sunlight struggled to penetrate the caked-on dirt.

But it was his fellow roommates that caught his attention—a scrawny, wiry man, two blood-shot eyed men, who by their smell had drenched themselves in alcohol, and a muscle bound one, who kept cracking his knuckles—definitely Arvada's rejects.

The knuckle-cracker sauntered over to Hoss and flickered his gaze over him, as if he were sizing him up. He stood a couple of inches shorter than Hoss and obviously thought he was a bad-ass. "What are you in here for?"

"Attacking a police officer."

He cracked his neck. "Think you're tough, do ya?"

The others watched warily, as if afraid of what the man would do, and quickly went to the other side of the cell.

Hoss met his hostile gaze. "I don't want any trouble."

"Then, you should have thought about it before you came here—pretty boy."

He'd been called many things, but pretty boy? Never been called that. What an idiot.

The man swung and Hoss easily caught his meaty fist with one hand. The man's eyes widened in surprise. Hoss forced him down onto his knees. "Now, was that very nice?"

He beat on Hoss's arm. "You're breaking my hand."

Hoss roughly shoved him away. "Then, keep your mitts to yourself."

"Asshole." Luckily, the man hobbled to another seat, cradling his hand against his chest, while the other three stayed huddled in the corner, whispering among themselves.

Hoss sat on the bench staring at the pitiful bars. They'd be so easy to melt or break in half. However, escape was out of the question, since it violated the prime directive of keeping their existence a secret.

Irritating diplomats! His people's only means of survival was at risk. Could he convince the stubborn Confederation that Zalarians would die if he didn't break through the cell? Highly doubtful.

The Confederation would have insisted he try a more peaceful approach.

He sighed heavily. All he could do was wait.

Minutes turned into hours.

His roommates dozed or paced back and forth in the cell except for the tough guy, who held his wrist to his chest. Hoss didn't feel sorry for him. He was a jerk-off and, from the shiny bruise on one of the red blurry-eyed men, Hoss assumed he'd been one of his victims.

He remained seated, trying to be patient, but failed miserably. He bounced his leg incessantly, drawing the scowl of the wounded man, who was smart enough to keep his mouth shut.

Hoss couldn't stop worrying about Agnes and Daidhl. If someone didn't let him out of here soon, he'd be doing a lot of explaining to the Confederation.

Footsteps echoed across the tile floor. He held his breath as he moved his leg a mile-a-minute. A guard unlocked the door. "Anonghos?"

"Yeah."

"Come with me."

He exhaled slowly. The others looked up and murmured. He thought he heard the word interrogation.

Hope soared inside him that Agnes would be waiting for him. He hurried over to the guard.

"Turn around and put your hands behind your back."

Hoss obeyed, letting the puny handcuffs be clamped onto his wrists. The guard led him away from the depressing cell and his derelict roommates.

He was escorted to a small room with a table and a few chairs. He unlocked Hoss's handcuffs.

"Sit in the chair."

Hoss complied dutifully. The guard re-chained one of his wrists to a large metal hoop drilled into the table that he could easily break and blow his cover, but he played the good prisoner.

"Detective Malloy will be with you shortly." He quietly exited, leaving Hoss alone.

She was coming. His knee jumped up and down repeatedly, smacking the table. He wished he had a free hand to put on his knee to steady it, because his knee had a mind of its own.

Stay calm. Stay calm.

He gazed at a gigantic, dark window that covered one wall. With his dragon eyes, he could see that it wasn't a window, but a one-way mirror. Men were behind the mirror, but unfortunately, his curvy mate wasn't with them.

The door opened. Any hope that she would listen to him vanished. Her angry face would have frozen Zalara.

She shut the door and slid in the chair across from him. She had dark circles underneath her angry eyes, as if like him, she'd hadn't slept.

"There's been another murder."

"When? Where?"

"Downtown. Outside the movie theater. She was on her way home after watching a movie with her friends. Throat slit, nearly decapitating her just like the last one. Her tongue was cut out of her mouth, and she's missing her liver. Care to speculate?"

He grimaced. "Bastard."

"I want you to listen to me very carefully. I'm the lead investigator on this case, and I want answers." She stood and leaned across the table. "Tell me about your partner."

He needed her to trust him. "I don't have a partner," he said softly. "I'm not a murderer."

He caught a whiff of her feminine scent that inflamed his need to mate with her. He struggled to concentrate on what she was saying and fought against the ancient urges to take a mate. Her finger brushed against his, and another shock zapped through his blood stream, teasing his dragon. An image formed in his mind of her running her smooth hand over his tense muscles.

She snatched back her hand and rubbed it as if it hurt, but luckily there wasn't a blemish on it.

"I want answers."

Her serious tone immediately reminded him of Topaz, who was fiercely protective of his crew and ship. Anyone stalking his crew would have find themselves facing a fierce enemy.

Agnes was no different. She wanted to save those women.

The door opened. A tall woman with curly brown hair wearing a blue suit and holding a briefcase entered. Her heels clicked across the floor.

Agnes groaned, as if her worst enemy had entered the room.

"Interrogation's over, Agnes. I want to have time alone with my client."

"Hi, Kathy. How's it going?"

"Same as always, but enough with the pleasantries. If you'll excuse us...Unless, of course, you plan on charging him."

Agnes didn't look at her, but flashed him a scowl that burned up his soul. "No. We don't have enough evidence...yet." She folded her arms and smiled at Kathy. "But you already knew this, didn't you?"

Kathy winked. "Of course."

Hoss stiffened. "I'm telling you I didn't do it."

"Not another word." Kathy put her brief case on the table, then opened it. "Do you mind, Agnes?"

She motioned with her hand. "He's all yours."

Once again, her spicy feminine scent teased his dragon. He wanted to grab her delicate hand and suck every slender finger until she was panting for more. He drew on his self-control, shoving his passion back. His whole body shook. Damn it. His mating instincts were growing stronger every time he was near Agnes.

Remember the mission.

She quietly opened the door and left.

"Kathy Strong." The dark-haired woman handed him a small card. "You're Anonghos, correct?"

"Yes, but I go by Hoss."

"Okay, Hoss. You didn't admit to anything, did you?"

Hoss shook his head. "No. I didn't do anything."

"Good, then based on their flimsy case, I should be able to get you out in less than two hours." Concern filled her eyes. "Are you all right? Your face is ashen, and you're sweating."

"I'm fine," he lied.

"Don't worry," she said, obviously not believing him. "Everything will be fine."

Kathy Strong had no idea how wrong she was, but she was damn good. She actually got him released in an hour and a half. He walked out of the police station a free man with the stipulation he stay away from Detective Malloy. A stipulation he definitely planned to break.

4

Kill. Kill. Kill.

Daidhl licked his lips. The woman, Laura Nybo, came out of the yoga studio—her face glistened with a shine, her top hung loosely over shoulders, and her pants hugged defined legs. Her red hair was clipped into a neat bun, and she had a yellow scarf around her neck. She slipped into her car. Attractive, but she was a human, and a designated mate for one of those Zalarians.

Today she would die.

The Kamtrinians wanted all of the designated mates wiped out, so the Zalarians would die. But they weren't the only ones who wanted the humans dead. One of his own kind had been murdered by mere humans. Revenge would be his—sweet and savage.

He started the motorcycle and grinned at the sound—a dragon's growl. The name of every mate, their address, and how they would perish were engraved on his black heart. He licked his lips, and shuddered with anticipation of listening to their screams. But tonight would be Laura. Would she gasp, scream, shriek, or freeze? The guesses nearly drove him to attack now.

But he was patient. He could wait.

Laura parked her car in front of her building, then headed to her apartment, which was on the fourth floor. A security guard was in the front of the lobby, and the door was locked. She probably felt safe, but he'd no intention of going through the front door.

No, he'd be waiting for her.

He carefully parked his precious blue motorcycle away from the other cars. If anyone nicked it, they'd wished they'd never been born. He walked over to a nearby tree, spread his arms wide, then closed his eyes, drawing on his power. His body tingled. He dropped his arms and changed into a dragon, his bones crunching, and his muscles stretching and constricting. Wings flared out, and smoke puffed out of his nostrils.

He easily flew up to the balcony and waited for his prey.

From the balcony he could see through the living room to the bedroom. Keys jingled, and he smiled. Laura quickly shut the door, then locked it. She tossed her keys onto a dusty coffee table. She entered the bedroom where clothes, books, and magazines were scattered across the floor. Blankets sat crumpled on the bed. She shut another a door that he suspected led to a bathroom.

He transformed into his human form, then he grabbed the handle and pulled. The glass door was locked, but that wasn't a problem. He drew on his dragon strength, then yanked. A crack ran up and down the lock, then the glass shattered into the shape of a sparkling star. He easily walked through it, and shards flew across the carpet.

"Oh, shit!" Laura raced out of the room, only wearing a bath robe. She wrinkled her nose. "What's that smell?"

"You'll pay for that remark."

She stopped and took a couple steps back. The terror in her eyes made him moan in greedy expectation. He inhaled. Her fear smelled like dead crumpled leaves.

Her eyes widened. "Who are you? How did you get in here?"

He gestured with his arm. "Isn't it obvious?"

Rather than cowering with terror, she glared. "Get out, or I'll scream."

"No, you won't." He pulled out his machete, then rushed her, ready to slice her throat.

He expected her to run, but she swung. His blade sliced through her arm, blood squirting into the room. She screamed. He punched her in the throat, immediately silencing her annoying shriek. Tears welled in her terrified eyes, but she didn't turn tail and run. She kneed him in the groin.

He snarled, then raised the blade. He swung.

She held up her palms. The blade easily cut through her flesh. Blood gushed from the wounds onto her fluffy white bathrobe, then onto the floor. She staggered, lowering her hands for a fraction of second before the blade slashed across her throat, nearly decapitating her. She collapsed onto the floor, dead.

Killing her wasn't enough. He wanted terror.

He wiped the drenched blade onto her robe, then lay it across her gut. He lifted her left arm and placed it across her left breast. He spread her legs wide and bent her knees so her bare feet were resting on the ground.

A message needed to be sent to the Zalarians that mating with these women would not ensure their survival. He'd murder their mates one-by-one.

He picked up the blade, and in a few quick cuts, removed her womb. He turned her head so she could watch him leave. He wrapped her womb up in a towel from her kitchen.

Drawing on his power, he turned invisible to wait for the person who would find Laura so he could feed on their horror.

5

In the last few days, Agnes Malloy had only slept for five hours. Weariness spilled into every muscle, turning her legs and arms into lead. Her gut twisted into a half a dozen knots. She rubbed the bridge between her tired eyes, trying to stay focused. Her body needed sleep, but she didn't have that luxury—not with a blood-thirsty killer on the loose. How could she grab a couple of z's with two grisly murders?

Not only did she have a murderer to catch, but she had a stalker. Or at least she thought she did. Anonghos or Hoss, had been released a couple of days ago, and she'd swore she saw him in the police parking lot lurking in the shadows and at a fast food diner where she and Tom had wolfed down greasy hamburgers and fries.

But when she approached him, he'd vanished. She couldn't vouch it was him. Without definite proof, she was dead in the water.

She sat in the conference room with Tom and Captain Morgan, going over the autopsy and witness reports. The glaring and buzzing overhead light hurt her eyes, the constant noise driving her nuts.

She examined her hand again for the thirteenth time. When she brushed up against Hoss, a shock had zapped her. The shock had actually burned, but there wasn't the slightest mark. He must have felt the same sensation too, because he'd jolted back.

But it was the images of dragons, spaceships, stars, and a dark gaseous cloud flashing in her mind that bothered her, making her think she was losing her mind. Sometimes when she touched people she'd get a glimpse of their life, which always gave her a clue about them—especially suspects. The visions of their childhood or friends gave her a place to start building a case and finding evidence.

But those peeks had always been real.

With Hoss, she saw a flock of dragons flying past two suns. No way was that real. Her lack of sleep was playing tricks on her, or maybe she'd seen one too many Lord of the Ring movies.

She tossed a paper down on the table. "These add up to zip."

Tom put down a report and sneered. "Your instincts not working?"

Agnes gritted her teeth. She was too tired to battle with him. Thanks to Frank, she was constantly having to prove that she was a good, investigative cop and not relying on unworldly abilities to solve cases.

"No." She leaned her head back on the chair and stared up at the ceiling, trying to block the strange images from racing through her mind. This was ridiculous. What was it about Hoss?

Detective Matt Hill entered the conference room, holding a report in his hand. "Like you requested, Captain, I ran a super fast DNA test on Hoss's fingerprints." He had a puzzled look on his face. "I have had suspects' fingerprints not be recognizable due to severe burns or injury or old age or manual labor or even taking certain medications, but I've never seen anything like this. He must have had worn some kind of invisible barrier on his fingertips that fooled the computers."

"Why?" Tom demanded. He ripped the paper out of Matt's hand and scanned the report. "I'll be damned." His voice turned low, and the blood drained from his face.

The Captain looked between Matt and Tom. "One of you better tell me what the report says."

Tingles slid up Agnes's spine, and she shivered. She knew what they were going to say. She didn't want to hear it, didn't want to see it, didn't want to believe it.

Tom and Matt glanced warily at each other, but then Matt blurted, "It wasn't human."

Crap! Agnes broke out in a sleek sweat. For once, her ability had to be wrong. It had to be.

The Captain raised his eyebrow. "Excuse me? What do you mean the prints aren't human?"

Matt shrugged. "I'm not sure exactly, Captain. All I can say is that the criminal database must be on the fritz."

"What the devil did it say?" The captain's voice rose two octaves, which was never good. "The mayor's furious and the press is breathing down my neck, saying we've got a serial killer."

Tom slowly handed the report to the captain. "The report says reptilian."

Agnes shuddered. All she could think about was the dragon image that kept rolling over her mind—a black dragon with a green stripe that ran from the tip of its nose down to its tail, to be exact.

"This is ridiculous." Tom ran his hand through his hair, making strands stand straight up.

"What does it mean," the captain snapped.

Matt shrugged. "It means the computer could only recognize reptilian as not human, but the database couldn't recognize the specific species."

Tom scowled. "You're making it sound like his prints are from outer space. That's ridiculous."

"Run it again," the captain growled. "I want to know who the hell this guy is before another a woman is murdered."

Based on her ability, Agnes couldn't believe Anonghos was a murderer. He definitely wasn't innocent, but he sure as hell wasn't a killer. However, the captain wanted facts. Facts she didn't have.

Tom sighed and put the paper on the table. "We should have put a tail on Hoss. He might lead us to the unsub." He gave Agnes a cool look. "Or at least we'd catch him trying to slice his next victim's throat."

Agnes rolled her eyes, but kept her mouth zipped. Ever since Frank went to Quantico, Tom insisted that they use the term unsub for an unknown subject.

The captain shook his head. "Kathy would have my balls for breakfast. She'll accuse us of harassment and violating her client's rights. We need more to go on." Both he and Tom had been friends until they both took the police captain exam. Tom had failed the orals, while the captain had passed with flying colors.

Agnes was too tired to play peacemaker between the two. "As long as we're doing things by the book, Kathy won't come down on us."

"I know she's your friend," the captain said, "but she can be a real pain-in-the-ass."

As long as Agnes had known her, Kathy was always the champion for the underdog, and she was a pit bull if she thought there was an injustice. In kindergarten, Agnes had been her first client. Not wanting to argue with her scowling captain, she asked, "Is it true the mayor is wanting a task force?"

"Women are calling him terrified, and the damn press is saying Arvada has a serial killer."

"Maybe we do." Agnes's stomach flipped over as she glanced at the bloody crime photos. No one should have to die such a violent death.

The captain glared. "It's imperative you don't rattle that off to the press."

"I'm not a rookie, Captain. I know the proper protocol. It's just so damn frustrating, because we don't have any leads. No fingerprints. No fibers. No hairs. Nothing that will lead us to the unsub."

"We do know something," Tom said gravely. "He's not going to stop. We can warn women to lock their doors, to be aware of their surroundings, and not go anywhere by themselves at night, especially walk to their cars alone."

"We don't know for sure," the captain said, "but I'm afraid you're right."

Agnes's heart hurt. She knew without a doubt there would be another murder. Maybe tonight.

Hoss was the key to the mystery. She had to find him. There was something different about him. He might not be the killer, but he knew something. He was holding crucial details back. "I'd like to ask Hoss a few more questions."

Tom frowned. "Hoss?"

"Anonghos. He prefers to be called Hoss."

Tom snorted. "How?" He raised his hands. "We don't even know where he lives. The address he gave us was a phony one."

"Since he was obsessed talking with me earlier, maybe if I go someplace alone, he'll follow me."

"To your house?" Tom gave her a sharp look. "Without police protection, he could kill you."

"I'm not an idiot. I'll go to a public place. By the way, I'm not defenseless. I can take care of myself."

"This man is sadistic," Tom warned. "You could find yourself with your throat slit."

"I don't think so," she said slowly. "The killer is sadistic. That doesn't mean Hoss is."

The captain gave her a hard look that reminded her of her doubting father's. "Nevertheless, you need to be careful. You're not basing this on your so-called psychic abilities, are you?"

"No." She sat straighter in her chair. "I'm basing this on good police work."

"Captain, you're not seriously considering letting her do this. She's got no experience being a decoy. She could get her damn self killed."

"I can take care of myself, Tom," she snapped.

The captain ran his hand over his cue-ball head. "Do you have any other ideas?"

"No," Tom said glumly. "So, what do we do now?"

"Nothing." She shrugged. "I think he'll find me."

Tom's cheek quivered. "You're taking a big chance, Agnes."

"Maybe. But I can't sit around and do nothing."

"That's exactly what you're going to be doing if you're a decoy, Detective," Tom smirked.

A gush of heat swished over Agnes like a hot shower. "Okay, fine. But someone is going to die tonight."

"You don't know that," the captain said, but his worried eyes told a different story.

She tilted her chin. "Yes, I do."

The captain frowned. "You just got through telling me you're not basing this on being a psychic. You're testing my patience."

"Don't worry," she blurted. "I have great cop instincts."

Tom snorted in disgust, and Matt pretended to be studying the report that he'd obviously read forty-two times.

He glared. "Agnes, you have this position, because you've proven yourself to be a good investigator—not a damn nut job."

"I know," she said softly. His condemning voice echoed her father's and brother's. He brought back all his disbarring remarks that had tugged at her heart. She forced her face to be hard, pushing back the hurt.

Tom and the captain glanced at each other. She hated that look. It was the you're-a-crazy psychic look. Her biggest mistake was not requesting a different partner, but then again, her brother was a legend.

She wasn't sure if there was a detective who didn't look at her like she was Madame Weirdo. Sometimes she heard the snickers behind her back. It was hard being a curvy detective in an all-male unit, but adding nutty psychic made it eight times worse.

"Think positive, Malloy." The captain stood. "Don't disappoint me, just get me the facts. Feelings don't have any place here."

She winced.

Tom tapped her elbow with the tip of his pen. "He's just worried. Doesn't want to end up writing traffic tickets if this all goes sour. So, what do we now, Nostradamus?"

She forced herself not to react. "We go along like everything is normal...As normal as you can be with Jack the Ripper hunting for sport in Arvada."

Her voice sounded surprisingly normal, hiding the anger seething inside her heart.

He seized her wrist. "What do you mean by normal?"

She jerked free. "Tom, don't give me that crap. Even you've used guesswork to solve cases."

Her voice trembled with fury.

He put his hands up. "Calm down, woman. I didn't mean to get your dander up." He shoved his hands underneath the table, as if he was struggling not to wring her neck for doing something stupid. "Just to be safe, I'll have an unmarked car outside your house."

"No." She shook her head. "Hoss is too smart for that. I promise I'll be safe. I'll keep in constant contact with you, and I'll be waiting for you."

"Honestly?"

She saluted him with two fingers. "Absolutely." She put her hand down and touched his arm. "Seriously, I don't believe he plans to hurt me."

"Why do you think this?"

Agnes hesitated. "Because I think I have seen him hiding in the parking lot once and last night at dinner."

"And you didn't report this?"

She winced. "I wasn't sure, Tom. You said you wanted facts."

He sighed and shook his head as if he was a disappointed Detective Joe Friday.

"Look." She put both her hands on the table. "I didn't say anything at the restaurant, because I wasn't sure. He was outside, hiding in the shadows." She tilted her head. "He did the same thing in the police parking lot. You've made it perfectly clear I needed concrete evidence. So I'm following both yours and the captain's orders, *Capisci*?"

"It's your funeral," he mumbled underneath his breath. "Are you going to leave now?"

"I told you that everything needs to be normal. On a case like this, I'd only go home to grab a bite to eat, then catch a few hours of sleep."

"Suit yourself. At least now it's broad daylight, and you'd have a fighting chance to see this guy."

"I told you I'll be fine." She just hoped she wasn't lying to herself. "I need some coffee."

"Lead coffee?"

"No, I thought I'd just run over to Starbucks. I need some time to think. Do you want anything?"

He reached into his back pocket for his wallet. "Sure. Get me a latte."

"I've got it. Don't worry about it."

Tom went over and looked up at the bulletin board that had both victim's pictures. Underneath the pictures was the occupation of each victim, and a list of activities they'd each done that day, but they'd nothing in common. Next to the bulletin board was a map of Arvada with a pin, locating where their bodies had been found. Unfortunately, they weren't even close together. Two didn't make a pattern.

But this killer wasn't done yet. If they didn't catch him soon, they'd have a pattern.

She closed the door and headed for her routine of getting her addiction. In the middle of a case, she needed some quick caffeine and drinking the department's tar coffee made her stomach uneasy.

She kept going over the murders and Hoss in her mind as she drove to the nearest Starbucks. Her cell phone rang, and she glanced at the number and winced. It was her brother Frank. Damn, Tom must have called him.

She thought about not answering, but her brother would be persistent like he was in everything he did.

"Hello, Frank."

"What the hell do you think you're doing?"

Her gut curdled at his angry voice. "So, Tom called you."

"Obviously. Look sis, you've just made detective. You're not ready for this."

She frowned. "How would you know? The captain must think otherwise."

"Morgan made a mistake in promoting you this fast."

"Thanks for your support."

"This isn't a game. Your mumbo jumbo isn't going to help you deal with a serial killer."

"I know what I'm doing, Frank."

"Yeah, getting yourself killed."

"Good-bye, Frank."

"Agnes, wait—"

But she didn't. She hung up and shoved the phone back into her purse. She'd heard enough of his lectures and putdowns for a life-time. Ever since Dad died, Frank had taken over his job of trying to mold her into what they both thought she should be—a meter maid. Meter maids had no need to use psychic abilities.

Luckily, Captain Morgan saw something different in her. Something she could never repay him for.

There was a long line in the drive through, and she didn't feel like sitting in her Ford Focus. She got out and headed inside.

The smell of roasting coffee, cinnamon, and steaming milk greeted her as she walked inside. Only a few people were ahead of her, and she smiled. People always thought the drive-through was faster, but she'd found that this wasn't always true. She studied the yummy pastries lined up in the glass. Going home to make dinner was out of the question, and she was torn from a piece of banana bread or a blueberry scone when she caught the smell of a smoldering fire behind her.

Chills glossed over the back of her neck. She froze, cursing herself for not being more alert.

"Hello, Detective Malloy," a husky voice said behind her.

Agnes tried to remain calm, but her heart ignited into a fierce drum roll. Her breath snagged in her lungs. She slowly turned to look into those mesmerizing tiger's eyes that sent tingles down her back. Her gaze shifted to his broad chest, the long muscular arms, the strong, square-tipped hands that would have the power to easily over-power the helpless victims and savagely murder them. He could easily seduce them with his handsome looks and a lethal potency that they wouldn't be able to resist coming under his spell, leading them to their gruesome deaths.

But she could resist. She was under no fainthearted delusions of the capabilities a serial killer possessed. Ted Bundy had been a clean-cut handsome man that had fooled his victims. Despite Hoss's devilish handsomeness, she wasn't a rookie. She called upon her fiercest policewoman voice. "Are you following me?"

He shrugged. "Obviously."

She raised her eyebrow. "You've been waiting outside the police station for me?"

"I think that's evident."

"Your attorney won't be pleased."

"You don't like her?"

"Actually, Kathy's one of my best friends. We've known each other since grade school, but at work, she's all business."

"Interesting."

She frowned, wondering why their surveillance cameras hadn't alerted them to his presence. He'd be hard to miss. Not only was he extremely tall, but his handsome looks would stop any woman in her tracks.

"What do you want?"

"To talk to you." He looked around. "This is a public place. You're safe... For now."

"For now?" Instincts told her not to panic and be aware of her surroundings. She carefully moved her hand across her jacket to caress the butt of her revolver. She scanned the café—three people behind the counter, nine inside.

"I told you. You're in danger."

One man sat on a stool that faced the window, drinking his coffee and reading a newspaper. He'd had a bright flowered bag with tissue paper as if it was someone's birthday. He was a broad shouldered man, and definitely appeared to have the strength to kill those women.

"Is your partner by the window?"

"The killer's not my partner, and no, I've never seen that man before."

"Ma'am, what can I get started for you?"

A perky saleswoman with her hair pulled back and a bright smile waited for her order.

If she didn't get back with Tom's order, he'd worry, but she had a chance to prove herself. "I'll have a non-fat coffee latte."

"And you sir?"

"I'll have a cup of coffee."

"I'll get it." Agnes pulled out her wallet.

"I don't usually let women pay for anything–"

"But you have no money?"

His cheeks actually flared red. "Yes."

"Don't worry about it." She quickly paid. "Follow me." She chose a table and slid into the chair, her back facing the wall.

He sat opposite of her, but based on his large size, he blocked out her view of the café, which was not a good thing. His partner could slip inside without her knowing it.

He took a sip of the coffee.

She twirled her cup around in her hands. "So, you've been following me. Talk."

"The man you're hunting is extremely dangerous."

"I know this."

"No, you don't understand. It's not just the killing, but it's the terror."

"How do you know this?"

"I've dealt with his kind before."

She frowned. "What do you mean his kind? Is he part of a gang? I've always suspected the unsub was a loner."

"He is. He's a mercenary."

Every muscle tensed inside her. "Are you suggesting terrorists are involved?"

"Not like you think." His eyes widened, and he studied the paper cup. "This is actually really good."

"Don't play games with me, Anonghos. I need to know who and what is involved in this."

He put his coffee down and then leaned back in his chair. "Call me Hoss. How open minded are you?"

His tone was low and hesitant.

"What do you mean? I don't like games."

"This isn't a game. Unfortunately, it's very real. This man you're hunting isn't a man. He's not from your world."

"Jeez," she muttered. She had thought Hoss may have been many different things, but bug-eyed crazy wasn't one of them.

"You don't believe me." He took another a sip of coffee, as if her disdain didn't worry him.

"No, I don't. Are you supposed to be taking medication?"

His lips turned up into a sexy smile. "I'm not crazy. I can prove it."

"Excuse me?" The same perky barrister that had taken their order approached them with the flowered bag Agnes had seen earlier. She glanced at the window where the man had been sitting. He was gone, but he'd left his newspaper.

"A man asked me to give this to you." She handed it to Hoss. "He said it was a surprise."

Hoss slowly took the bag. "Thank you."

Agnes folded her arms across her chest. "I thought you said you didn't know him."

His eyes locked with hers.

"I don't. I've never seen him before."

His hard voice made her uneasy.

Something transparent flickered out of the corner of Agnes's eye, and she groaned inwardly.

Not here.

Not now.

She drew on her ability to push the vision out of her mind, but the spirit pushed back hard. Lightning pain shot through her, and she gasped.

Hoss frowned. "Are you okay?"

Chills spread over Agnes like wild-fire. "I'm fine," she lied.

A blond woman slowly materialized, looking at the bag. "He took it from me." She pointed at Agnes. "He wants to kill all of us. He wants all of you dead." Her voice was so sad.

Agnes's heart thumped into turbo speed. The woman slowly faded. Crap! It had to be a new victim.

Sometimes these apparitions weren't always clear, but what if she was telling the truth? Kill all of them? Damn, an explosive.

Hoss parted the yellow tissue paper.

She held up her hand. "Wait. Don't take the tissue out. It could trigger a bomb."

She waited for the panic to flash in his eyes or sweat to trickle down his temple. But instead, he scanned the café. "You want to keep it here and take a chance of killing all these people?"

There wasn't even a hint of fear.

"No. But we don't want to start a panic, either." She pulled out her phone, trying to be calm.

Tom answered immediately. "Peters."

"Tom. I'm in trouble."

"Where are you?"

"I'm at Starbucks with Hoss."

"Who?"

"Anonghos."

"What? You're kidding."

His loud voice hurt her ears, and by Hoss's smirk, he'd heard every word.

Agnes glanced at the people in Starbucks, which were all potential victims. "We have a situation. I think we may have a bomb, and I need you to call the bomb squad. We need to get these people out of here."

"Stay calm. I'll take care of it."

"I will." She closed her phone, not taking her eyes off Hoss. "We need to be cool."

"I'm fine. This isn't my first mission."

"You were in the armed forces?"

"Not any of yours."

She hadn't detected an accent. "Then whose?"

He grinned. "You won't believe me."

She didn't have time to play his game. "People's lives are at stake. This isn't the time to play twenty questions."

"Okay, I'm a member of the United Planet Confederation."

"You mean outer space?"

"I told you that you wouldn't believe me."

She slowly stood, trying not to bump the table and risk setting the bomb off. She pulled out her badge and held it up over her head.

"Listen to me," she said in a loud, commanding voice. "I'm Detective Malloy of the Arvada Police Department. I need you to quietly leave Starbucks. We have a report that there is a suspicious device here. I need you to move outside quietly."

"I don't see anything," an elderly man grumbled. He went back to talking to two of his cronies.

She bristled. They dismissed her like men had done all her life.

A woman picked up her purse and closed her laptop, her eyes wider than chicken little. "Is this for real?"

Agnes nodded. "The police are on their way."

The woman vacated Starbucks faster than the Flash.

"Whatever." A bleach-blonde teen-age girl took a long sip from her chocolate Frappuccino, and then slid into a booth. She immediately surfed on her phone.

Agnes wanted to grab her by her pink-tinted lips and toss her outside.

Her red-headed friend grabbed her arm. "Come on, Jen, you're pissing her off."

Sirens screamed, then grew louder. Police cars skidded into the parking lot, followed by a firetruck, and the SWAT transport van.

Jen's face paled. "OMG." The two girls headed outside lickety-split.

The same grouchy man grabbed his coffee and headed for the front door. "I'll be darned, this is for real." His friends snagged their tall coffees and scuffled behind him.

Hoss snapped his fingers at the frozen barristers behind the counter. "You need to exit."

They looked at each other and abandoned their steamy concoctions.

Hoss put his hands on the back of a chair. "Everyone's gone. But you have a bigger problem, Detective."

She studied the mysterious bag. "What could be bigger than a bomb?"

"I didn't recognize the man sitting at the window."

"So."

"You're hunting an alien with powers that could destroy your world."

Crap, her number one person-of-interest was loonier than Norman Bates.

🐉 6 🐉

Hoss's dragon ears detected screaming police cars and fire trucks. He groaned inwardly. He'd be back in jail soon again with Arvada's rejects.

The police darted out of their cars. The side door of a black van slid opened, and men, wearing helmets and a heavy suit of body armor, poured out of it armed with tactical rifles. They fanned around the café, pointing their weapons. A red dot fell onto Hoss's chest. His lungs sucked in air rapidly as if trying to escape from being a target. He stood perfectly still, not wanting to make a single, threatening move. If he were a dragon, the bullets wouldn't be able to penetrate his thick hide, but in this form, they'd rip through his flesh.

Damn, he couldn't risk going for his eruptor without drawing their rapid fire.

"I'm not the enemy," he said, but she looked at him as if he had four heads. He cursed himself for blurting out that Daidhl was an alien. She was too by-the-book to believe in the impossible.

"Maybe," she murmured. She studied the bag, completely dismissing him. Her lips were pursed shut tight and her skin taut.

A tremor rippled in his cheek. Rather than winning Agnes's trust, he'd just earned her skepticism.

When he entered the café, he hadn't smelled any sourness, but then again, the cafe was filled with delightful aromas that could have masked it. He had to admit he was distracted by Agnes with her curvy body and her sexy scent.

He frowned. The first time he got a whiff of Daidhl's odor it had been very faint. Had the Mistonian discovered a way to hide its stench?

Two men wearing green body armor and helmets entered the café, while the others spread their arms wide to force people back.

One of them gestured toward Hoss. "Hands in the air."

Once again, Hoss forced himself to comply.

"The bag." Agnes pointed. "A man asked one of the barristers to give it to Hoss, who claims he's never met the man. I just have a gut feeling about it."

Hoss lifted his eyebrow. "Claims?"

"Gut feeling?" one of the armed men asked.

She ignored his quizzical face and concentrated on the suspicious bag. "There's something terribly wrong with the bag. I know it."

Two of the armored men looked at each other as if they thought she was short of brain cells. Hoss didn't think a bomb was inside, but if it was from the creature, it couldn't be good.

"Detective," he said. "I don't think it's a bomb, but if the bag is from the creature, it's something awful."

"Creature?" one of the men asked.

Hoss cursed his stupidity.

"Is this some kind of joke?"

"No." Agnes motioned toward the bag. "Peter, I think it's from the Arvada killer."

Peter tilted his head into a tiny radio that was attached to his uniform. "We need to know what's in a bag."

"Ten-four. We'll send in Simon."

"Just to let you know, Captain Morgan's on his way, so I hope you're right about this."

"I am. My suspicions haven't been wrong yet." Her face paled a little, but she squared her stance like a warrior.

"There's always a first time," he muttered.

Agnes wiped her sweaty palms on her pants.

Hoss glared at Tom, who averted his gaze.

A third man entered that Hoss supposed was Simon, carrying a metal box. "You need to move away in case it goes off."

A brown sedan with a siren on top rolled into the parking lot. Two men jumped out–Agnes' scowling partner, Tom, and a tall bald man with crunched thick eyebrows. They rushed toward them. Hoss groaned. He definitely was going back to the dreary cell.

Agnes clasped his arm, and another spark made him jerk, but it wasn't painful. This time, it was pleasurable, igniting lust between his legs. Images of him seducing Agnes and doing wild things to her flashed in his mind, making his cock grow hard. Sweat glistened over him, and he squirmed underneath his clothes. He fought the urge to kidnap her and make do on those images. Damon had said mating was like nothing he'd ever experience, but he'd never watched his father crumple with grief, either.

By her squirming in her clothes like he did, he knew she felt it too, but neither said a word. They moved outside while Simon set up a tripod and put the metal box on top. He screwed and locked it, then aimed the box at the flowery bag. It was cruder and bulkier than anything they had on board the Orion. If Hoss could have pulled out his transrecorder, he could have discovered the contents of the box, but he doubted anyone would give him half a chance.

The bald man demanded, "What's happening, Malloy?"

"Captain, there's a suspicious package inside Starbucks. I was interrogating a person of interest–"

Hoss gritted his teeth and turned away, annoyed she still considered him the enemy.

"When an unidentified man delivered a package to Hoss–I mean Anonghos, he reported that he didn't know him. I had a feeling–"

Her captain glowered. "You brought out the SWAT team and the fire department and escorted all these terrified people out of a public place over a damn feeling?"

His voice chirped high like a screeching bingle.

She met his hostile glare and tilted her chin. "Yes, sir, I did."

"You better be right on this," he warned.

Simon came outside, holding a twelve-inch flat screen device.

"Simon." The captain motioned. "Tell me what you've got."

"Yes, sir," he said.

The captain glanced at the screen. "Well, is it a bomb or not?"

Simon shook his head. "No, it's not a bomb. Some red blobby thing is in a plastic bag. Based on this, I can't tell what it is."

Tom crowded next to the captain. "I swear that almost looks like a piece of meat."

Bitterness burned Hoss's belly. Something dreadful was inside. Something that would create terror.

Agnes shivered next to him and dug her fingernails into his flesh.

He flinched, but didn't look at her. He wanted to comfort her, but knowing the little bit he knew of her, she wouldn't want to look like a helpless female in front of these scowling men. He bet when she was alone is when she broke down. When no one could see the toll the job put on her—the frustration, the terror, the helplessness... He knew those feelings all too well.

She slowly released the fingers that had dug into his arm.

"So, Simon, is it safe to go inside?"

Her voice was back to the hardened detective. Even if she were reluctant to go inside, like him, she wouldn't allow her fear to keep her from doing her duty.

He nodded. "Yes."

She motioned with her arm. "Captain?"

"Check it out." He pulled a radio off his belt.

Hoss followed her. She whirled around on her heels so fast he ran into her.

"You, stay outside." She tilted her head.

The captain snapped his fingers. "Watch him."

Five armored police surrounded him. He could easily see over their heads as he watched Tom and Agnes enter the café. He should be with her, not the old man. She was his mate, and it was his job to protect her.

The murmuring crowd had grown quiet. Only the zooming cars driving passed the café broke the silence.

Hoss held his breath and clenched his fists tight.

Agnes reached the brightly colored bag first, her face grim. She slowly pulled out the tissue paper, then immediately put her hand over her mouth. Tom turned his head away, his face gray.

She slowly reached into her jacket and pulled out a portable walkie-talkie—such a primitive device.

"Captain, we need forensics in here."

The captain spoke softly into his radio. "What is it?"

"I think it's an organ."

"I'll send in a team. In the meantime, we need statements from all the people that had been in Starbucks."

Tom and Agnes came out immediately, both their faces pale.

"What about him?" Tom motioned toward Anonghos.

His narrowed eyes and growling tone left little doubt that he thought Anonghos knew more than he was letting on.

"Arrest him and take him to headquarters."

"On what charge?" Anonghos refused to cower from the scowling captain.

"We're not charging you with anything...yet. You're a person of interest and we have questions. Lots of questions."

"Do I get to call my attorney?"

"In good time."

Agnes's eyes widened. "Kathy will be pissed if she's not notified immediately."

"Don't lecture me, Detective. I said he'd get to talk to her soon. Don't you have some witnesses to interrogate?"

Unfortunately, Hoss was quickly handcuffed again and led away before he could say anything to her. He was shoved in a squad car and taken to headquarters. His weapon and transrecorder were confiscated, but instead of being put in a cell, he was taken to another interrogation room and handcuffed to a table.

The room was stark white, and he faced the infamous one-way mirror, so whoever was inside could examine him as if he were one of Zalara's tiny purple scets under a microscope.

After an hour, he'd been permitted to contact his attorney, who would undoubtedly get him released again or at least be present during questioning. But all he could think about was Agnes.

Whether she knew it or not, she needed him. The man who had given him the bag definitely hadn't been Daidhl. Either he'd convinced the man to give it to him or it had been Daidhl in disguise. But how? Daidhl was a thin navigator. That man looked like he could have been one of Hoss's guards.

The door quietly opened and Agnes stepped inside. Her face was still ashen and weariness reflected in her eyes. She slid into a chair across from him.

"You look exhausted."

"Your attorney will be here shortly."

"Did you find out what was in the bag?"

"Yes," she said wearily as she flicked her hair back. "And who it belonged to."

Her voice was so soft he barely heard her.

Kathy Strong barged in the room. This time her hair was pulled into a neat bun. She had her same trusty brief case and wore the same crisp blue suit. "Agnes, you know better than to ask my client questions without his attorney being present. Just because we're friends, doesn't give you the right to take advantage of the situation."

Agnes glared. "I wasn't, Kathy. I wouldn't do anything to jeopardize my case, and you know it."

Hoss raised his hands to stop the two from getting into a nasty grendor fight. "She hasn't asked me anything yet. Let's not come to blows, ladies."

They both gave him a scowl that made him want to go into the corner with his tail between his legs.

Kathy opened her brief case and pulled out a yellow notepad. "Good. Proceed, Agnes."

Agnes put her hands on the table and folded them. "Did you know what was in the bag?"

Kathy nodded. "Go ahead and answer."

Hoss shook his head. "No. Not exactly."

Agnes leaned closer. "What do you mean not exactly?"

"I was at the crime scene, Agnes."

"It's Detective Malloy," she corrected him. "Only my friends call me Agnes."

Damn, back to formalities again.

"I overheard that it was an organ and not a bomb."

"Do you know what kind of an organ it was?"

"No."

"Do you know whose organ it was?"

"No."

"Do you know the man who gave you the bag?"

"No."

"Did you tell anyone that you were going to be at Starbucks?"

"No."

He frowned. His gut twisted into a ball. That was a good point. The man was there before Agnes and him. How had Daidhl known they would have been there?

"Detective," Kathy interrupted. "Do you have any evidence tying my client to the organ or the obvious murder of the victim?"

Agnes hung her head. "No, I don't."

"Unless you plan on charging my client, we're done here. Release him."

Agnes pulled a key out of her pocket and unlocked Hoss's handcuffs. "I suggest you not be at any more crime scenes."

"If you'll excuse us, Agnes," Kathy said. "I'd like to be alone with my client in another room. One without a one-way mirror."

Agnes stood and motioned toward the door. "This way, Kathy."

Even though the two were on the opposite sides of the law, Agnes's voice had softened when she spoke to her friend—unlike when she'd spoken to him.

They were such a sharp contrast to each other. Kathy was a slender, muscular attorney, while Agnes was chubbier, the kind of woman who a man could be himself with. With her, he wouldn't have to prove anything. But the old hurt returned, worming into his melting heart. His father had felt that way about his mother, and she betrayed him, breaking him.

He followed them behind, not being able to take his eyes off Agnes's curvy ass. He'd seen too many perfect asses like Kathy's. He grew hot thinking about caressing her behind, then digging his fingers into her flesh as he slammed into her. He bet he could squeeze her tight, and she'd wouldn't cry out in pain like the others. He hadn't meant to hurt them, but sometimes he forgot about his strength and gripped their butts too hard.

What was he thinking? Love only caused heartbreak. He had to remember that, but every time he was around Agnes, he wanted to take her into his arms and kiss her worries away. Sex wasn't love. Every time he took a woman, he repeated that. No matter how he felt. It had to be the same with Agnes. He refused to be a broken dragon like his father.

Agnes opened a door to a small interrogation room with no

one-way mirror. Kathy entered first. When Hoss swept past Agnes, he inhaled her flowery feminine scent that reminded him of the purple chisery fields back home that melted away his stress.

"I'll leave you two alone," she said as she closed the door.

He slid in a chair across from his attorney.

She lifted her eyebrow. "This is becoming a pattern, don't you think?"

"Possibly."

She put her hands flat on the table. "You need to talk to me."

He leaned back in his chair, folding his arms across his chest. "Why? So, I can be locked up in one of their little cells?"

"We have client-attorney privilege. You can trust me. What you tell me stays in here."

She seemed in earnest and so far, talking with Agnes had gotten him nowhere. Maybe he needed another tactic and be more direct. "She's in danger."

"Who?"

"Detective Malloy."

"Agnes?" She narrowed her eyes. "Are you threatening her? I won't let you hurt her. She's been hurt enough."

Unfortunately, he didn't have time to pursue this tidbit, but tucked it in the back of his mind. "I am trying to save her."

"Why do you say that?"

"Because the killer is going to come after her."

Uneasiness flittered in her eyes. "What makes you so sure?"

"Because she's my mate and the killer plans to kill every mate destined for Zalarians. Daidhl wants to wipe out our race."

"I'm not sure I understand," she said slowly.

"No, I'm not human. I am from the planet Zalara."

She hung her head. "So, you think you're from outer space?"

"You can't tell anyone what I say?"

"I just said that."

"Yes, I am from outer space."

She put her hands on the table and looked at him as if he

needed to be locked away. "Hoss, you're delusional. You need help."

"I don't. I can prove it." Or at least he hoped he could. He looked around the small space. It'd be cramped, but he could transform.

"How?"

"You need to move away from the table."

She scowled. "Why? What are you going to do?"

He opened his jacket. "They took all my weapons. I'm not going to hurt you, but I need someone to believe me. Agnes isn't listening. She's in danger, and I have to protect her before she gets herself killed."

"If I do this, will you promise to let me help you?"

"Sure. Move against the wall."

She rolled her eyes, but did as he asked. Like Agnes, she thought he was nuts. Humans really did believe they were the only life in the universe. Their arrogance never ceased to amaze him.

He carefully placed the table and chairs alongside her, blocking her escape. Not very smart on her part if he were a killer, but then again, she'd no reason to believe him.

He blocked the door, then pulled on his dragon powers. His bones and muscles crunched and stretched. He transformed into a dragon, but he could barely fit in the tiny room. His tail was scrunched underneath him. His wings were wedged against the wall and his shoulders touched the ceiling. He'd had to bend his head so low that the tip of his nose was right in front of Kathy's terrified face. He inhaled her fear that was mixed with a spicy perfume.

She screamed, her eyes twice as big as a saucer. "You're... You're a dragon!"

Pounding feet raced outside, then someone slammed their fists against the door repeatedly. The doorknob clicked, but didn't open.

"Kathy, are you all right? Open the door."

Hoss cringed. It was Agnes.

The door pressed against his back-side, but his body was squished against it, preventing it from moving further than an inch.

He quickly transformed back into a man. "Obviously. Still think I'm crazy?"

"No, I am." Sweat glistened off Kathy's forehead.

The door busted open, and Agnes and two other officers entered, their guns drawn.

Agnes glared at him. "What the hell is going on in here?"

Kathy shook her head. "Nothing. There was a big spider, and Hoss stepped on it."

Agnes still had her gun pointed at Hoss, but she looked at Kathy. "Are you sure? You're white as a ghost."

"I'm fine." Kathy sat in a chair, her hands trembling. "I have a...a....fear of spiders."

Agnes lifted her eyebrow. "Really? That's a new one. Ever since I've known you, you've tried to scooped them up on a piece of paper and released them outside. When did you develop this phobia?"

"This was one was really big."

Her voice squeaked like a creaky door.

"Why don't I believe you?"

Kathy lifted her chin. "Please, leave us."

Agnes slowly put her gun back into her sheath as the two other officers left grumbling out the door. She put her hand on Kathy's shoulder. "I'll be right down the hall if you need me."

Her warning voice was meant for Hoss as she patted her gun.

He wasn't sure how he was going to convince Agnes to trust him. Every time he tried to make her believe, he pushed her farther away.

Kathy pulled a tissue out of her purse and dabbed her forehead with her shaking hand. "Believe me, I'll yell if I need you."

"Would you like a glass of water?"

Kathy nodded. "Actually, I would." She was breathing hard and her face was still pasty.

"I'll be right back." Agnes kept the door open, as if to make sure that Hoss wouldn't do anything stupid.

Hoss stood against the wall, not moving, not wanting to scare Kathy again.

Kathy glanced at him. "Just give me a few minutes."

"Take your time."

Agnes returned with the glass of water. "Here, Kathy."

"Thank you."

She gave Hoss a warily look. "Do you want me to stay here?"

Kathy shook her head. "No, I need to talk with my client."

"Are you sure?" She rubbed her back. "You still look like a ghost."

Kathy braced her shoulders. "You're interfering with attorney client privilege."

Agnes hesitated, but she left. Obviously, her trust meter for him was minus twelve.

"Please sit down," Kathy urged. "You're making me a little nervous."

"I won't transform." He held up two fingers. "I promise." He put the table in front of her and set the other chair on the other side. He sat slowly. "So, do you want to hear my story?"

"Well, you've proved you're not human."

He glanced up at the clock. Time was wasting away and who knew what his little detective was planning. But he forced himself to be patient. He needed Kathy's help. "Like I said, I'm a Zalarian. We don't mean you any harm, and the United Planet Confederation has charged us with protecting Earth."

"From whom?"

"The Kamtrinians. They want to destroy all life on Earth and claim your planet."

She took another sip of the water, her hand shaking. "Is that who is killing the women?"

"No. We have a protective shield that goes around your planet that they can't penetrate. The killer is a possessed Zalarian. He used to be our peaceful navigator, but now another alien—a Mistonian—has taken over his body, forcing him to murder. I believe Daidhl is dead and only his empty shell is left behind. This creature not only kills, but feeds on fear."

She put her shaking fingers on her temples and rubbed them. "I don't understand."

"Its food is emotions, and unfortunately, this one prefers fear."

"This sounds like something out of Star Trek."

The minutes dragged on, and he tired of this. He needed to get to Agnes, not sit glued in this chair. "I don't know what that is."

He couldn't hide the impatience in his voice.

Kathy scooted her chair further away from the table. "Never mind. Why is it here?"

He forced himself to keep the frustration out of his voice. "The Kamtrinians wiped out all of the women on Zalara. We're dying as a race unless we mate with our designated mates. The Fates—our Goddesses—know who our mates are. We can't mate with just any human."

"Agnes is yours?"

"Yes."

"This is just too strange. I'm having a hard time absorbing what you're telling me."

"If you don't help me, the Mistonian will go after her. I won't be able to mate with anyone else."

"I'm not worried about you. I'm worried about Agnes."

"I didn't mean to sound callous."

She leaned back in her chair. "Let me get this straight. The two women who have been murdered were someone's intended mate on Zalara?"

"Unfortunately, yes. Somehow the Kamtrinians have figured out how to determine our mates. Or they've discovered a species that can do it for them, which is disturbing. We don't even know who our mates are until the ceremony. But our Queen said that the Mistonian had hidden abilities. I fear one is predicting the future. One he definitely has is invisibility."

Her face turned whiter than the walls. "You're kidding? So, you can't track him?"

"It's almost impossible. The only thing I've discovered is that he has a distinct smell of sourness. Here, I believe it would be like sour milk, but it's very faint."

"Great, that's not helpful."

He shrugged. "It's the best I've got. I need you to convince Agnes to trust me. When I've touched her, I've sensed a power within her. Or maybe it's between us. But if she doesn't trust me, he's going to hunt her."

Kathy studied him. "That's strange you sensed a power within her. She's psychic."

"Meaning?"

"She can see the undead."

"That must come in handy as a cop."

"You would think, but definitely not here. Her brother and dad never accepted her gift. They were both cops. The police don't believe in her ability. In fact, she gets shunned if she even mentions it. She's very sensitive about what she can do."

"Humans are strange. On Zalara, this would be considered a valuable gift."

She turned up a corner of her mouth. "We're not on Zalara, are we?"

"Nope, we're not."

"What do you want me to do?"

He glanced up at the ticking clock, warning him that time was of the essence. His knee bounced to the annoying rhythm. "I need to get Agnes alone with me. Will you help me?"

"You promise not to hurt her?"

He took her shaking hand in his and squeezed gently. "I'd never do anything to hurt her. She's my mate."

She stared at him as if she were trying to decide whether he were innocent or guilty. He held his breath.

She didn't answer right away. The clicking clock banged away at his nerves.

"I'll hold you to that, Zalarian."

He exhaled loudly.

She wiggled her hand out of his. "I'll see what I can do."

"Am I free to go then?" He stood so fast he knocked the chair over. She gasped and jumped nearly six-inches out of her seat. The empty glass of water fell off the table.

"God, you scared a year off me." She put her trembling hand over her heart.

"Sorry." He nervously tapped his foot. "So, can I go?"

She nodded. "Absolutely. Where are you staying?"

He smiled. "I'm around."

"How will you contact me?"

Her small voice betrayed that she wasn't the self-assured attorney anymore, but she also wasn't running screaming. He had to admit he respected her. He winked. "Don't worry. I'll find you."

"I was afraid of that."

He hated not opening his secret to Agnes first, but she forced him to play his hand. If he couldn't get her directly, he'd get her through the back door.

7

Time's up.

Daidhl sat comfortably in Kathy Strong's car. The fool, Anonghos, walked her out of the police station and escorted her toward him. The moonless night darkened the shadows except for the glowing street lights that glistened off the car windows. But he wouldn't need to hide in the dark.

No one could see him.

He was invincible.

He licked his lips, anticipating both her fear and watching the life slowly leave her eyes. He ran his thumb over his newly sharpened blade.

Hoss opened the door for Kathy, who slid onto the leather seat.

Daidhl inhaled her spicy scent that would soon change to fear, but then Hoss stiffened; his nostrils flared.

"Kathy, get out of the car."

She frowned. "What are you talking about?"

Before Daidhl could feed, Hoss grabbed Kathy's arm and hauled her out. "He's in the car. Run!"

Daidhl hissed in fury.

Kathy screamed, running toward the police station. Ten police officers raced out, guns drawn.

Hoss pulled out a silver box from his belt.

Daidhl's heart froze. Damn it—an entrapment cage.

Hoss aimed the cage at him. Fear jerked through Daidhl. He'd been captured once before. He picked up Kathy's purse and threw it at Hoss. Luckily, Hoss dropped the cage.

Daidhl jumped out of the car. He flew into the night, screaming over his shoulder. "You'll pay for that, Zalarian! When I kill your mate, I will feast on her beating heart."

Unfortunately, heavy footsteps pursued him. His little trick had bought him little time. Hoss followed him like a Pack Ranger, who were the best hunters in the universe. The bastard swept back and forth, getting closer and closer. A stinging beam hit Daidhl in the leg. He gasped at the throbbing pain. A tracker ray pulled Daidhl toward the Zalarian. Gritting his teeth, he skidded his heels into the ground. The surge of energy glossed over his skin, making every hair on his head stand on edge. A glisten of sweat broke all over his body. If he hadn't been in this form, he'd have been sucked into the dreaded cage.

Drawing on every ounce of power he possessed, his body trembled as he slowly edged away from Hoss.

Not good enough.

He managed to run around the corner of a building, which lessened the ray, giving him time to transform. In a split second, he changed into a bag lady. His body was bent over, his hands gnarled, and he released a human stench of not bathing for weeks.

Hoss skidded to a halt, shutting the dreaded entrapment box. He barely gave Daidhl a glance. Daidhl couldn't help but pat himself for his clever disguise.

Hoss sniffed the air. "Ma'am, did you see anyone run past here?"

Daidhl shook his head. "No." He stretched out his palm. "Do you have any money to help an old woman to stay warm?"

Hoss reached into his jacket and pulled out some coins. "These are all I have."

He gave him two silver coins, two silver coins that Daidhl would use to cover Kathy Strong's dead eyes.

The Zalarian ran down the street without a clue.

Daidhl smiled a toothless grin—just like in the café with all the scent of brewing coffee and steaming milk, Hoss couldn't detect him.

Daidhl could be a young man, a homeless woman, or Hoss's worst nightmare.

8

Agnes sat next to Kathy, who held her trembling hand tightly. She'd never seen her so shaken. Her eyes were wide, and she struggled to breathe.

"Kathy, take a deep breath."

Tom and several officers interrogated Hoss again while others, along with the captain, surrounded Kathy.

"Tell us what happened," the captain demanded. "What did the bastard do to you?"

Kathy raised her head. "He...he...saved my life. The killer was...in my car." Tears slid down her ashen cheeks, and she gasped for air.

Agnes put her hand over Kathy's. "Did you see what he looked like?"

"No," she sobbed. "If Hoss hadn't been there..."

She choked on the words and struggled to gain her composure.

The captain looked up at his men. "Spread out and look for anyone suspicious."

She squeezed Agnes's hand. "I need...to...talk...to you alone."

"Of course." Agnes looked up. "If you'll excuse us, Captain..."

He gestured with his arm. "By all means."

Agnes wrapped her arm around Kathy's quaking body and slowly escorted her to the same interrogation room that she'd been in earlier with Hoss. Kathy lay her head on Agnes's shoulder. It was as if this hardened woman had turned into a little girl, but then, she might have just survived being the killer's next victim.

Agnes needed to inspect Kathy's car before forensics got there to see if she could pick up any images.

Kathy slowly unraveled her hands from Agnes's. "Close the door."

Agnes complied, then sat across from her. "Can you tell me what happened?"

Kathy wiped her wet cheeks with a tissue from her purse. "First, do you think I'm sane?"

Agnes frowned. "Excuse me?"

She blew her nose. "You heard me."

"I've known you all of my life. Yes, I think you're totally sane. Why?"

She laughed, then stuffed the tissue into her purse. "Well, I'm...about to blow...your mind." Her voice cracked.

Between them, Kathy had always been the strong one, but her demeanor put Agnes's every nerve on edge. "So, tell me?"

"I'm breaking attorney and client confidentiality in what I'm about to tell you."

Even though they were good friends, she'd never known Kathy to do this before. "I'm listening."

"The killer isn't human."

"Okay," she said slowly, wondering what the hell Hoss had done to Kathy. "Then what is he?"

"He's a Mistonian possessing another alien. Look, I know it sounds crazy."

Agnes silenced her tongue. Kathy had never made fun of her whenever she saw a ghost. It was her turn to listen.

"In this very room, my client transformed into a fifteen-foot dragon."

"What?" Agnes narrowed her eyes. Kathy's pupils weren't dilated, but her skin glistened with sweat. "Did he put something in your drink?"

Kathy held up her trembling hand. "No. I'm not on anything. In fact, you can test my blood, if you want. I'm telling you the truth, Agnes."

"You're telling me Hoss is a dragon."

"From Zalara. Their women were wiped out by the Kamtrinians, their deadly enemy, and he's here to retrieve his mate."

A gnawing suspicion bit into Agnes's insides. "So, who is his mate?"

Kathy looked around the room as if she was deciding how to decorate the crammed brown room. She finally set her gaze on Agnes. "You."

This time, Agnes burst out laughing. She could barely breathe, her face burned hot, and tears swelled in her eyes.

"Agnes, it's true. Shit, I know it sounds bat-crazy."

Agnes struggled to stop. She took a big breath. "I'm sorry. But really Kathy? Aliens? Outer space? First of all, men like Hoss don't go after women like me. He looks like something out of a super marvel movie, and I'm a plump little detective that constantly has to watch her weight."

Kathy sat straighter. "Fine. Ask him." Her tough exterior attorney voice was back.

"Don't worry. I will."

"Oh, by the way," Kathy said. "Hoss told me something else about the killer."

"What? He's got x-ray vision?"

"No, he smells like sour milk."

Agnes turned sober. "Did you smell it?"

"I did. Right before Hoss yanked me out of the car. It was faint." Her lower lip trembled. "I'll never forget that smell."

"I need you to stay here."

"Don't worry. I'm not going anywhere. I want to be surrounded by Arvada's finest."

Agnes quietly left the interview room where the captain paced the floor. He stopped. "Well, what did you learn?"

She wasn't going to throw Kathy under the bus. At least not yet. "She remembers a distinct smell."

"What?"

"The killer smelled like sour milk. She said it was very faint, but it was there."

He rubbed his hand over his bald head. "That's it. That's all she remembers." Frustration rippled through his tight voice.

"She's pretty shaken up. I think she needs twenty-four-hour protection. She's obviously the killer's next target."

He lowered his hand. "Fine. It's all we've got to go on."

"What about Hoss? Did he have any useful information?"

"No. He said he chased the killer, but lost him. There was some homeless woman that might have seen more. Hoss gave us a description. We're going to search the streets. Forensics is about to turn Kathy's car upside down."

"If you'll excuse me, Captain."

He grabbed her arm. "Where are you going?"

She tilted her chin. "I want to see Kathy's car."

"Don't mess anything up, Detective. I want facts not feelings. Understood?"

She gritted her teeth. "Yes."

He slowly released her. "I'm sorry. This has me on edge, and now the bastard is getting close to one of our own."

Kathy Strong might be a thorn in the captain's side, but he'd always respected her and considered her a friend. She was like that. Kathy might drive you batty, but she was loyal and someone you could always account on.

"I know," Agnes said softly. "She's my friend. I'm really worried about her."

Agnes quickly headed over to Kathy's red Volkswagen bug. She'd just been in it last weekend. Unlike her car, Kathy kept her little bug immaculate, even after they went hiking.

Officers were standing around it. She put her palms in front of her and closed her eyes. She inhaled a deep breath, then drew on her abilities to see if she could get any impressions.

No images rolled over in her mind, but she detected a smell... sour milk. Shit, Kathy was telling the truth about that.

"Get anything?"

A husky voice startled her.

She jumped. Hoss studied her intently.

"I need to talk to you." She glanced at the other officers, who were watching her curiously. "Alone."

"By all means."

She led him away from police quarters to the back of the parking lot. "I'm not going to beat around the bush. Kathy told me everything."

"And you don't believe her?"

"This isn't Star Trek or Star Wars. Women are being murdered."

"And more will die if you don't let me help you."

His grave voice sent goose bumps running up her arm.

But she was done with his cryptic warnings. Her anger got the best of her. She jammed her finger into his broad chest. "I want the truth from you, and I want it now. Did you put something in Kathy's drink to make her hallucinate?"

"No. I guess the only way to prove it to you is to show you."

Before she knew what was happening, he grabbed her, pinning her arms to her sides and putting his hand over her mouth, muffling her screams. God, he was strong. He was tall and muscular, but she'd no idea of his strength. He easily lifted her off the ground and hauled her to a nearby park that was empty except for the street lights that glowed on the edge of the park. He released her at a grove of pines that blocked her view from the police station.

She reached for her gun, but then froze.

In a split second, Hoss released her. His body contorted and stretched. Skin was replaced with scales. His face elongated, and his mouth revealed long pointed teeth. A tail slid around her and wings sprung out of his back.

"Oh, shit," she whispered, as she held her gun tighter. Her rattling heart ricocheted off her ribs like a ping-pong ball.

She couldn't stop staring at his smoldering golden eyes. He snorted, and smoke escaped from his flaring nostrils. Oh, god, was he going to fry her alive?

She gasped for air, and her knees knocked together so hard she thought she'd have bruises tomorrow. "You're…you're…"

He transformed back into her handsome kidnapper. He winked. "A dragon."

She hung onto her gun to anchor her sanity. "This is too weird. Kathy wasn't lying."

"Has she ever lied to you before?"

Her mouth dried up, and she puffed out the answer. "No."

His eyes twinkled. "Then why didn't you believe her?"

She broke out in a hot sweat beneath those laughing eyes. Her heart beat wildly, and her breath wheezed as is she was having an asthma attack. "Because…you're a… freaking…dragon."

"Planning on shooting me?"

Her wits slowly came back to her one-by-one. She sheathed her gun. "No. Not yet at least."

"Good. Mates aren't supposed to go around shooting each other."

She shoved the revolver back into its sheath. "We're not mates."

"Whether you like it or not, we are. But don't worry, mating doesn't mean love."

She jerked to attention. What did she expect? He was a Aragorn, and she was a plump dwarf. "Oh, really."

"My father taught me that, and it's a lesson I'll never forget."

His bitterness softened her stiff spine. He reminded her of the tough-as-nails juvenile delinquents, who scorned love, because they didn't think they deserved it. "You don't believe in love?"

"No. I can be attractive to you without loving you."

Her tenderness went up in smoke, and she glared. "Sorry, not interested."

"When we've accidentally touched, haven't you felt a tingling spark?"

"I don't know what you're talking about." She refused to admit anything—especially to a man, who just wanted to use her body.

Heat rushed to her cheeks. Warmth rushed through her body at the thought of his hands and mouth on her skin. She was glad for the darkness, because she didn't want him to see how the thought affected her.

"I'll prove it to you." He grabbed her shoulders and pulled her toward his massive chest. He raked his hands into her hair and forcibly tilted her head up, and flashed her a challenging grin. He lowered his mouth brutally crushing her lips beneath his.

She tilted her head to break away. "Wait. No."

But his mouth cut off her protest.

Her senses exploded with anger. Her hands were trapped against his granite chest, and although she was no slouch of a woman, she hadn't the strength to break free. She opened her mouth to call for help, but he was one step ahead of her and filled her mouth with his tongue, thrusting with deep hard strokes that were as overwhelming as they were exciting. His grip was firm as his fingers curled into her hair. His mouth was brutal and possessive, crushing each cry or protest.

She slowly realized the same electrical charge that had that had touched her was pulsing through her as his tongue pushed open her tight mouth. She thought about biting his tongue, but his kiss was overpowering, as if he was branding her. Every instinct to push away from him slowly died as his tongue explored the recesses of her mouth.

No man had ever kissed her this way—as if he had a right to be there. She clung to him and molded herself to his hard chest. His heart beat as wild as hers. Images slammed into her mind of a distinct planet of spaceships and dragons—lots of dragons—of a castle of a spaceport, but it wasn't just the images... Desperation, fear, and terror flowed through her. An explosion of gas hit the planet, then women and girls of all ages screamed in agony.

She arched her back and pressed her hands on his chest. "Stop, please. It's too much."

He slowly released her. "I'm sorry."

"I saw images in my mind. I saw... I saw..." Tears filled her eyes. Sadness overwhelmed her, and she clutched his arm. "I saw your women and girls, even babies die. It was awful. I can still hear their screams. Who would do such a thing?"

His eyes turned hard. "The Kamtrinians. They used a dioxide torpedo that targeted only the females. We were powerless to stop it." Regret edged into his voice.

"I'm sorry, Hoss." She squeezed his hand. "I truly am."

"It's not just us that the Kamtrinians want. They want Earth and are determined to seize it. They invade planets and kill all life forms, then suck dry the resources. They enjoy the suffering of men. They're damn parasites."

"I must be losing my mind, but how do we catch the killer?"

He pulled out a silver box the size of a cell phone. "Usually with an entrapment box."

"That's big enough to catch our killer?"

He grimaced at her disbelief. "Mistonian are usually gaseous creatures, and the entrapment box will pull them inside, preventing them from escaping." He shoved it back on his belt. "But unfortunately, this didn't work. This Mistonian is powerful enough to resist it. It may be due to because he's possessing a

Zalarian. If we can force him to release Daidhl's corpse, I might be able to capture him. The only way I've been able to track him is his faint scent of—"

"Sour milk." She wrinkled her nose.

He smiled. "Right." He put his hand on her chin. "I sense something within you... A hidden power."

"How do you know?"

"When I kissed you, I could see what you saw. You have the gift of sight. My queen possesses this same gift."

She smirked. "Gift? I've never consider it a gift. I've always had to down-play what I saw."

She thought of the captain's and Tom's doubting faces, her father's and brother's rejections, the smirks behind her back at the police station, the teasing as a child, and how she was always alone. A freak.

He frowned. "Why? I would think in security work that this would help you protect your kind."

She bristled, refusing to divulge the past twenty-eight years of misery. "The disdain doesn't matter. I've learned to cope with it." She paused, not sure whether she'd get the truth or not, but she had to ask. "Is Kathy someone's designated mate?"

"If she wasn't, he wouldn't be after her."

His voice was grave, making her gut tighten. She and Kathy had been through so much together. She refused to her lose her to some psychotic alien.

She pulled out her radio. "Captain?"

"Malloy, where the hell are you?"

She winced. "We need to put Kathy in protective custody. She's a target."

"That's obvious. She wants to go home. We can have a patrol outside."

Hoss's eyes burned brighter. "Tell him if she doesn't have a police escort, he'll find her."

Every instinct inside her screamed he was right. "Captain,

letting her go home is a mistake. We need to put her in a safe house."

"She's your friend. You know how Kathy is. She feels that super high rise she lives in with the guard is impermeable. I can't force her. We can have an officer in the lobby and a patrol outside, but that's all she'll agree to. She's pretty insistent about it."

Hoss shook his dark head.

She shut off her radio. "Crap. Why does she have to be so damn stubborn?"

"No way to change her mind?"

"You've met her."

He ran his hand down her arm. "We need to try."

Ignoring the chills running up her flesh, Agnes tried to concentrate on what he was saying rather than how bruised her lips were after he'd kissed her, or how the dusting of his beard had chaffed her skin. "Once Kathy has an idea in her head, it would take heaven and earth to change her mind."

He headed toward the police station. "Let's go see her."

She reluctantly followed him, straightening her messed up hair and tucked her rumpled shirt in her pants.

Tom was talking to several officers.

Hoss flashed ahead of her as if he were a speeding running back, leaving her in the end zone.

"Wait!" Agnes put out her palm and ran as fast as she could. "They'll shoot if you're not with me."

Hoss stopped at the edge of the parking lot. "Then, hurry!"

His scolding voice reminded her of the Neanderthals at the police obstacle course that thought women police officers were better off behind the desk than in the field—especially chubby ones.

He stood aside. "After you." His tone hinted at disapproval.

She may be heavy, but she ran every day and could press over a hundred and fifty pounds. But by his scowling face, he was just as overbearing as the other barbarian officers. She stormed in front of him, refusing to comment.

Tom glared. "Malloy, where have you been?"

But he wasn't looking at her. He was looking over her head. A long shadow spread in front of her, and the scent of a smoldering camp fire made her insides melt. Hoss was behind her.

Putting on her detective mask, she met Tom's and the captain's gaze. "Where is Kathy? I need to talk to her."

He flicked his hand. "She's being escorted by a black and white, and there will be an officer standing guard in front of her apartment. Don't look at me like that. Her apartment's less than five minutes away. We can get there in a heartbeat."

She glanced at Hoss. Unless the officers had developed the ability to penetrate invisibility, then Kathy was a sitting duck.

The captain glared. "Don't you have some paperwork to do, Detective?"

She shook her head. "No, I need to talk to Kathy now."

Tom glanced at the captain. "All right–"

Agnes clasped his arm. "No, stay here. I'll be right back."

He looked at Hoss and comprehension spread across his face. "She'll never let either one of you in."

Agnes shrugged. "Yes, she will. I'm one of her best friends. I have a feeling that—"

He seized her arm. "A feeling? The captain won't be pleased."

Hoss released a low growl.

Tom's eyes widened, and he slowly released her.

"Nothing else is working, Tom. Feelings may be the only thing we have to go on."

She turned, and Hoss firmly but gently put his hand on her lower back. She led him toward her Escort. Taking a police car was out of the question since she wasn't necessarily following the captain's order.

Suddenly, an image pierced her mind of Kathy's apartment

building. A man stood outside in the shadows. She couldn't see his face, but evil permeated from him, cutting off her breath.

She stopped, placing her hand on her chest. Hoss knocked her over, but before she hit the ground, he seized her arm, easily putting her back on her feet.

"Agnes, what's wrong?"

His voice was distant, as if she was floating away from him.

She gasped for air, wanting to scream for Hoss, but the vision strangled her voice.

She floated into an apartment that she'd been in a hundred times. The living room had rich hard wood floors, exquisite wooden antiques, marble Greek statues, and expensive paintings, including one of a naked Venus standing in a shell with attendants on either side of her. Kathy never spared an expense on her home. She always said it was her escape.

In the kitchen, Kathy had every possible convenience that Agnes wished she had—a purple Kitchen Aide mixer, a double side stainless steel refrigerator with a matching stove and dishwasher. Agnes didn't even have a mixer, and none of her appliances matched.

On the black marble counter, an open bottle of red was slowly pouring into the sink. Kathy only bought expensive vintage wines and would never waste a single drop.

Panic swelled inside her. She called for Kathy, but her stiff lips refused to move.

Get a hold of herself.

If she didn't concentrate, the vision would vanish.

She took a deep breath and walked past the kitchen into the hallway. She froze.

A wine glass was toppled over, spilling red wine onto the light hardwood floor. Kathy was sprawled out on the hallway. Her throat was savagely slashed, blood drenched the front of her chest. She clutched something in her fist. Tears slid down Agnes's cheeks, her chest could barely contain the sorrow bursting inside her. She forced herself to kneel and put her hand on Kathy's stiff cold one. Before she could unwind Kathy's brittle fingers, a dark shadow fell across her.

"You're too late, Detective." The same man, who had been watching the apartment, held a blade soaked with blood up to the hilt. She still couldn't get a good glimpse of his face. He licked the blood off, smearing it on his chin.

She recoiled.

He laughed, sending anger gushing through her.

Then just as suddenly, the image vanished. Wind whisked around her as she was slammed back into her body, and she trembled violently.

"Agnes! Answer me."

She slowly realized that Hoss was gripping her shoulders, and fear shone in his eyes.

"Hoss, I saw Kathy." She found her voice, but she could only whisper. "He's there. I saw him."

"You had a vision?"

She nodded, her teeth chattering. "I've never experienced anything like that before. It was as if I were actually there. I am so cold."

He wrapped his arms around her, his body warming her. "She's...she's dead." Unwanted tears fell down her cheeks. "I should have been with her."

Hoss stroked her hair. "No, he would have killed you, too."

He held her until she stopped shaking.

"I'm a homicide detective." Agnes lifted her head. "I can take care of myself. But Kathy's only a lawyer. My job was to protect her. She was my friend." She slowly untangled herself from his protective arms.

"Are you feeling better?"

She straightened her shirt. "No, but we need to get to Kathy's immediately."

He tilted his head toward the police department. "Do you want to call it in?"

She laughed bitterly. "On a feeling? No. They wouldn't believe me. Only Kathy did. She never laughed at me." She wiped her tears on her sleeve, smearing mascara on her jacket.

He gently clasped her arm, pity filling his gold eyes. "I'm sorry."

Agnes jerked away. "I'll get over it," she lied. How could anyone get used to losing a good friend? She pulled out her keys. "We need to go."

Her voice was back to being the no nonsense detective. Her tears dried up.

He stuck out his thumb. "Get on my back."

"What? No, my car's faster."

"Not dragon fast." He glanced over his shoulder, then dipped into a thicket of trees away from the street light and security cameras. In an instant, he transformed from a handsome man back into a fierce black dragon with a glowing green stripe down his back. She stepped away, her heart threatening to jump out of her throat. He tilted his neck as if motioning for her to climb onto his back. This was stranger than a fairy tale, but Kathy deserved justice. It was time for Agnes to be strong. Kathy needed a champion.

She forced herself to climb onto his back. She clutched his neck hard. He leaned on his haunches, then jumped into the sky. She bit back a scream and pressed her knees against his thick hide. He flapped out his wings, and they soared into the cool midnight sky. Her hair flew around her, and she sucked down air faster and faster. The midnight sky, bright stars, and dark clouds buzzed around her as if she were on a spinning tilt-a-whirl. She clutched Hoss's neck tightly, determined not to let go.

"I am sorry, Kathy. We're coming. We'll make him pay for what he did to you."

❧ 9 ❧

Daidhl easily walked past the guards in the lobby. The fools hadn't even noticed him.

"Did you smell that?" one of them asked.

He stilled, his finger hovering over the elevator button.

The other frowned. "Smell what?"

"The captain said the killer gave off an order of sourness." He unleashed his pistol. "He's here."

"I don't see anyone. You're imagining it."

"No, I'm not." He clicked on his radio. "Captain, this is Rogers."

"What's happening?"

"I detected the odor of spoiled milk."

"Get to Kathy immediately."

"Yes, sir."

Curses, he should have changed into something else. He quickly left the lobby, uneasiness twisting in his gut. He ducked in the shadowy alley. Sirens screamed in the distance, but that wasn't what sent the hair on his arms standing straight up.

A black dragon with a glowing green stripe down the middle of his back flew in between the dark clouds. Anonghos had found him. He quickly drew on his powers, transforming into the homeless foul smelling lady. He grinned. The Zalarian was becoming too much of a liability and needed to stop his persistent meddling. Soon, he'd be dead.

Daidhl hobbled past the building, not fearing the security cameras or the police cruisers skidding in front of the apartment building. Humans ignored the homeless.

Time for him to send the idiots another message.

Officers raced out of their cars and shoved past him, not giving the homeless lady a second glance. He grabbed his shawl and pulled it tighter around him, as if to block out the cold. He forced himself not to smile. Fools, they'd never guess they missed their suspect.

He was about to escape when an officer stepped in front of him.

"Excuse me, Ma'am, but the detective would like to have a word with you." He turned to see an older gray-haired man approaching him. He'd often been with the Zalarian's mate, pursuing him. Time to have some fun.

"I've done nothin' wrong," he snapped. He rubbed his hands together. "Just tryin' to keep warm."

"I'm sorry," the gray haired man said. He pulled out his badge, then sucked in his breath as if not to inhale his stench. "I'm Detective Peters of the Arvada Police Department. This is very important. Did you see anyone come in or out of the building?"

"I was in the alley."

"Please, it's important."

"I seen the cops go inside. And an extremely tall man came here earlier. He was a giant he was. Scared the breeches off me."

The officer and detective glanced knowingly at each other.

"What time was this?" he demanded.

"I don't have a watch, but the moon hadn't shown her face yet."

"Thank you." That should keep the Zalarian busy for awhile.

"Get her information," Detective Peters said.

He left them alone as Daidhl rattled off more tales to the gullible officer.

The attorney may have escaped tonight, but tomorrow, she'd be dead.

Tonight, he had another woman to kill.

🦂 10 🦂

Hoss landed on the balcony, squeezing his large frame onto the ledge barely big enough for the glass table and two metal chairs. He moved, and his tail knocked over the table, which slammed the chairs into the patio door. The porch light shattered. A loud crack made him wince. His handiwork left the frosted glass shattered.

Agnes slid off his back and fell on her ass.

"Ow," she murmured. "That was subtle."

He quickly transformed back into a man and helped her to her feet. "Sorry. I'm not used to fitting into tight spaces."

She grinned. "I would think you're becoming an expert with changing in the interview room and now here."

He frowned, but it melted away as he stared into her big eyes. Despite the rising terror around them, she remained sane and could even make a jest. He'd never met a woman like her.

She moved the chairs away from the window. Shards of glass fell across her hand.

"Let me do that." He frowned. "You could cut yourself."

She flicked her hand, sending bits of glass falling onto the cement. "I'm fine."

Someone screamed inside.

"He's still here," he growled.

"Kathy," Agnes yelled as she pulled out her gun. "It's me! Let me in!"

Kathy peeked out of the hallway, dressed in a robe, and holding a gun in her shaking hands. "Stay where you are! The police are coming!"

"She's alive," Agnes gasped. "Kathy, it's me! Agnes!"

The door busted open, and an officer barged in gun drawn. "Miss, are you all right?"

Kathy pointed at the balcony. "He's out there."

"Time to go!" Hoss said.

"No, wait." Agnes tried to the door again, but it wouldn't budge. "She doesn't know it's us."

"Stop or I'll shoot!" The officer aimed his pistol.

Not wanting to argue, Hoss transformed back into a dragon, smashing the furniture again. One of the chair's legs pierced the glass.

A shot rang out. Agnes gasped. He inhaled the scent of metallic human blood. Fear seized Hoss's heart. He clasped Agnes with his talons and flew into the air, more shots pursuing them.

Agnes went limp, and his worst horror was realized. She'd been shot. Blood gushed down her temple, then filled her eyes. He knew where her home was since he'd followed her there once, but he needed to get her to a hospital. He flew faster than he thought possible.

Don't die. Don't die. Don't die.

Within a few minutes, he landed out of sight from a hospital. He wished he could have taken her on board to the Orion, but he was forced to use their primitive practices.

He laid her on the grass, and she moaned. He quickly transformed back into a humanoid, then lifted her into his arms and raced to the front doors.

He burst inside to a bright white room containing chairs filled with sick people.

"She's been shot. She's an Arvada detective."

A man in a white gown and woman flew into action. They helped him put Agnes in a wheel chair and ushered her out of the room. He glanced down at his shirt, and it was drenched with her blood. He should have been faster.

Helpless to do anything, he sat in a chair and waited. He was soaked with fear. On the Orion, Tryker would have been able to heal her within minutes, but Earth's medical technology was light years behind him. The clock ticked slowly overhead, if it moved at all. People filtered in and out of the room while he heard nothing. After what seemed like hours, the woman came over.

"She was unconscious from the shock, but she's awake now. She's lost some of her hair and a chunk of skin. Her wound has been cleaned and stitched. The doctor gave her a sedative for the pain. You can see her now."

He followed her quickly down a corridor that had drapes shielding rooms on one side and open rooms on the other side. Agnes sat in a bed, holding her head.

A doctor had his arms crossed and had a scowl on his face. "You need to stay here for observations, Detective."

Agnes stubbornly shook her head. "No. This is nothing. I just need some rest in my own bed."

Pain crossed her face, and she gritted her teeth. She'd a nasty zipper down her right temple.

Cursing the medieval care under his breath, Hoss walked into the room. "So, you think she should stay here, Doctor?"

"Absolutely."

"Well, I'm not," Agnes said. "And neither of you can stop me. Hoss take me home. Now."

Her glare would have melted the Earth's North Pole.

"You can't make her stay?" The doctor looked helplessly at Hoss as if he wanted to him to do something, but Hoss hadn't known Agnes for long and had no illusions, he'd lose this argument.

"No, he can't," Agnes answered.

She slid out of the bed and swayed, but Hoss caught her arm.

"Maybe you should stay."

"I'm not staying. I hate these stupid gowns. I hate hospitals."

The doctor frowned. "We're only trying to help."

"I said no. Where are my clothes?"

"Under your bed."

"Hoss, will you get them?"

"Sure." He grabbed the plastic bag, which had her bloodied clothes. "Are you sure you want to wear these?"

She pulled the oversize blue gown away from her chest. "Well, I'm sure as hell not wearing this."

The doctor shook his head. "I'll have a nurse help you get dressed."

Hoss stepped out as a nurse entered the room. He leaned against the wall, wondering how he got such a stubborn-ass mate.

In a few minutes, the nurse opened the door. "Will you please tell her she can't walk and needs a wheelchair?"

Agnes stuck out her chin. "I can walk."

Hoss gave her a hard stare. "You're taking the chair."

Agnes opened her mouth, but quickly shut it. Surprisingly, she obediently got into the wheel chair and allowed the nurse to roll her out of the emergency room. But before they could leave, Agnes had to sign of mountain paperwork. Another strange human habit. On Zalara, once you were healed, you left, but Zalarians didn't sue their doctors for malpractice, either.

When she was finally finished, the nurse said, "I'll wait here with her, while you go and get the car."

Hoss blinked. Now, what the hell was he going to do?

"We don't have a car," Agnes said.

The nurse whirled the wheel chair around to go back inside. "Then I can't—"

"She's confused. We have a truck."

Agnes opened her mouth to argue, but clamped her jaw tight.

Hoss ran to the back of the parking lot until he found an over-size truck that he could squeeze into comfortably. Using dragon strength, he forced open the door, then ripped out the wires to start the truck. He smiled. Human technology was so primitive and stealing a car was easy.

After the nurse closed the door, instead of Agnes thanking him, she leaned her head back. "We're not keeping this truck. Dump it."

He was about to argue, but she was his mate and a cop. He begrudging parked the truck in the back of another lot. Not waiting for her to argue, he changed back into a dragon and lifted Agnes into his arms, then flew into the sky.

He landed at her cozy townhouse or at least that was what he thought the humans called it. Luckily it was dark and all the lights were off in the other homes. He closed his wings and dropped her gently. She sprawled out on the lawn like a lifeless rag doll. His heart was in his throat. Blazes, he should have been quicker. Why couldn't the bullets have hit him?

He transformed back into a humanoid, then picked Agnes up, cradling her in his arms. Blood trickled down her temple and onto her jacket. He sucked in his gut. What was he going to do? He knew nothing of human anatomy. If only the Orion were here, he could take her to Tryker. But he was on his own.

"I should take you back to the hospital," he muttered.

"No," she groaned, prompting him to move.

Not caring who heard, he kicked her door, the wood splintering.

"Key...in...my jacket."

He thought he'd shout for joy. She was alive! However, the door wasn't so lucky.

"Sorry a little late."

"You'll...fix it." She swayed as she stared at her splintered door. He held her shoulder.

"You need to see a doctor." He cringed.

She glanced warily at him. "Don't worry. I don't want to go to the hospital. Quit making a big deal about this. It's not like I've never had a bullet graze my temple before. I'll survive." Despite her pale face, she flashed him a smirk. "I...promise. I just...need to...rest."

Her voice faded away. Her eyes fluttered, and she collapsed.

He caught her. "Stubborn mate." He gently kissed her forehead.

With his dragon eyes, he could see through the darkness and carried her up the stairs to a bedroom with clothes, books, and magazines thrown onto the floor. He glimpsed one of the covers of the books, which was a man naked from the waist up.

So, his little hardened detective did think of romance. He tenderly laid her on an unmade bed. She released a shaky sigh.

He hurried into a bathroom that had hair spray, mousse, and all kinds of different lotions. Dried toothpaste was stuck to the sink mixed with strands of blond hair. In the cabinet, she had all kinds of pills and bottles, but he had no idea which one to use.

He took out his telicator. "Captain?"

"What's happening?"

"I still haven't located Daidhl. My mate's been shot. I need to talk with Tryker."

He couldn't hide the panic rising inside him.

"Tryker, here."

"Tryker." Anonghos held on tight to his telicator. "My mates been shot. She says she doesn't want to go to a hospital. What do I do?"

"Remain calm. Is there a lot of blood?"

"Yes, but she doesn't want to go back to the hospital."

"Clean the wound, then put antiseptic on it. If the doctors examined her and allowed her to leave, she should be fine."

"But the doctor wanted her to stay for observation, and she refused."

"If you're worried, use your transrecorder to determine if there's any shrapnel, if there is or if the wound keeps bleeding, whether or not she wants to or not, she has to go to the hospital."

He found a clean washcloth inside a cabinet, then wet it with warm water. His hands were shaking so bad he could barely hold onto the slippery cloth. He found a bottle of antiseptic below the sink along with some bandages. He hurried back to the bedroom, then carefully dabbed her forehead with the cloth.

She winced.

He jerked back his hand. "I'm sorry. Are you in pain?"

"Just have a bad headache, but I'll be fine."

"I radioed the ship and—"

"You radioed a ship?"

"The Orion. Our doctor Tryker said that I needed to put antiseptic on your wound, but first I need to check you out with our transrecorder."

She opened one eye. "Excuse me?"

He removed the transrecorder. "It won't hurt. I just need to know if you have any shrapnel."

Hoss gritted his teeth, waiting for the damn transrecorder to analyze her. The green light flashed on, and he released a thankful sigh.

"So?"

"No shrapnel."

"I could have told you that."

He stuck it back into his belt. "You'll have to excuse me for not believing you. Your stubborn streak says differently."

She smiled weakly, closing her eyes. "I just need to rest for a minute. I'm not stubborn. I'm determined."

He dabbed the cloth with the antiseptic and wrinkled his nose at the potent smell. "Brace yourself. This is liable to sting."

He slowly patted the side of her temple. She jerked and

sharply hissed, but didn't complain or beg him to stop. This was a woman who must have experienced some of the same battle scars he had. He hadn't met many women who were like her, even when there had been women on Zalaria.

She put her hands on the bed. "I better get up."

He put his hand firmly on her shoulder. "No, you need to rest. If you're weak and injured, you're liable to make mistakes."

"You sound like my brother."

"Your brother is overbearing?"

"You've no idea. I could use a drink," she said. "I have some scotch in my cupboard above my refrigerator. Why don't you grab us some glasses? Or don't you drink alcohol on your planet?"

"We have something similar, norol. It's a little stronger than your Scotch."

"I'll have to try it sometime."

Norol was spicy and smooth, but could knock even the captain on his ass if he drank too much. He gave her a firm look. "Stay here."

She draped her arm across her forehead. "I'm not going anywhere."

Her voice was heavy, and he wasn't sure if she'd be awake by the time he returned. He grabbed two small glasses and the bottle of Scotch, which sat half empty. He sniffed and detected a sweet creamy fruity smell with a hint of spice.

Her arm still covered her forehead. He slowly unscrewed the bottle in case she was asleep, but she lowered her arm.

She struggled to sit up and released a loud hiss. He raced over to her and knelt at the edge of the bed. "Are you in pain?"

She smirked. "Nothing a little Scotch can't fix."

He put his arm around her and helped her to sit, then plopped a pillow behind her. He hurried to retrieve her drink and poured alcohol in both glasses.

He sat on the edge of the bed. "Here."

She clasped it her hand shaking. "Thank you."

He thought she'd sip it, but instead she tossed it back in one gulp. No tears welled in her eyes, but it did give some color to her white cheeks.

"Do you want another?"

"No. I just needed enough to help me sleep. Help me get out of this jacket. It's too constricting."

He helped her shed the jacket then helped her lie down. She closed her eyes. Her blond hair spilled over her pink pillows. For the first time, he noticed that she had a rose printed comforter and pink sheets. She was such a contrast. Hard and determined, but now, he glimpsed a softer side that he'd like to explore further. His gaze drifted down to appreciate every curve and indentation of her body, his hands twitching at running over her flesh and discovering how she'd like to be pleasured, but taking a woman when she was unconscious left him repulsed.

He wanted her awake, telling him what she wanted, begging him to please her.

Her large breasts rose up down as she exhaled softly. He brought in a chair from her kitchen and sat next to her, determined to guard her. He locked her bedroom door in case the blasted Mistonian knew where she lived. He held his eruptor, ready to blast anyone who threatened Agnes.

"Don't you need to sleep too?"

Her tired voice startled him.

"I thought you were asleep."

"It's kind of hard with you holding a weapon."

"I'll sleep when this is over."

She patted the bed. "No, grab a few winks. I promise I won't bite."

"Yeah, but I might."

"I need you bright-eyed and bushy tailed."

"I don't have a bushy tail."

She laughed. "It's just a silly saying." She looked at him with those beautiful eyes. "Please."

He sighed, hoping he could behave himself. He tossed back the Scotch, pleasantly pleased with its smoothness.

"I'll try to behave," he said as he slid next to her.

"Suit yourself."

"But I don't have a suit."

"You don't. I guess you better go buy one."

He frowned. "Where...."

She giggled. "I'm teasing you." She yawned. "Just come to bed."

He lay perfectly still besides her. Her scent was all over the bed, stirring his libido, his flesh pushing against his pants uncomfortably. His clothes stuck to his hot skin and all he could think about was how she'd taste, and how her body would fit softly against his.

But he was a Zalarian and a dragon of honor. Taking women against their will was against their creed. Besides, loving a woman only led to sorrow. Even mates could break a dragon's heart.

She spooned her behind against him, and he groaned. His little mate was temptation on a stick. He lied on his back and put his hands behind his head, locking his fingers tight to keep from ravishing her.

He inhaled and exhaled, trying to relax, but he thought any minute his taut muscles would snap. Sweat rolled down his temples as if a blanket smothered him. He detested these feelings growing inside him. They were too intense, too terrifying, too crippling.

He'd always prided himself as being a ladies man, which kept him from falling for any one woman. Distance was key. He could mate with Agnes and produce an heir, but he refused to lose his heart.

Trust meant vulnerability, and lying next to her was a struggle.

Just relax.

He closed his eyes. If he didn't get at least some sleep, he'd be liable to make a mistake.

Breathe in, breathe out.

Agnes's rhythm breathing rhythm lured him to sleep...

Hoss ripped up a greetings card he'd received from his mother. Every year she sent him one on his birthday, but that was the only time he heard from her.

His father walked into the kitchen. "What are you doing?"

He threw the bits of the card into a trash can under the sink. "I hate her. I just hate her." His voice brimmed with anger. He slammed the cupboard door hard.

"She's still your mother."

"So! I don't care. It's because of you she left. I hate you!"

His dad reached for him. "Son."

"Leave me alone! Don't touch me!"

His father winced, then hung his head.

Hoss ran out of the house. He needed to get away from there, needed to roll off some steam.

He came home sweating after wrestling with Damon. His stomach growled, and he was ready for some of his father's stew, which made him drool. His bruises and scratches ached. After dinner, he'd soak in the hot tub until he was as wrinkled as a horb.

He opened the door, not one light flickered on, and disappointment hit him at not smelling his father's bubbling stew. He practically ran all the way home to fill his belly.

"Dad, where are you?"

There was no answer. The house was unusually dark. Uneasiness crept up his spine. He walked into the kitchen to a bare counter. He opened the freezer and the stew meat hadn't been taken out.

Something was wrong. His sweat turned cold, and he shivered.

Maybe his dad was hurt and couldn't answer him. He raced upstairs and searched the bathrooms and bedrooms, but his father wasn't there. Blasted, what if he'd left Hoss like his mother had? What was wrong with him that neither of his parents loved him?

His father had promised he'd never leave him. Unwanted tears welled in his eyes. No, he wouldn't cry.

Maybe his father was roasting meat outside.

"Dad?"

He hurried outside, but the fire pit was dead. His father's prize garden of glato and vilfe plants and rerry swayed in the wind. The purple, yellow, and pink vegetables were ready to be plucked, but his father had strangely left them alone.

Something swayed under a giant urlus tree in the middle of the garden. The thick vines prevented Hoss from seeing what it was. Chills made him shudder.

"Dad?"

His voice cracked and died in the wind.

Clouds passed over the suns, casting shadows onto the blooming garden. A crack caught his attention.

He forced himself to move. He trembled as he approached. A gust of wind blew the vines, revealing a pair of silver boots, and Hoss stopped. He couldn't breathe. No, he had to be imagining this.

He stretched out his shaking hand and pulled back the thick vines.

His father hung from a thick branch, his lifeless eyes staring at Hoss.

Hoss fell to his knees, screaming.

"Hoss! Hoss! Wake up."

Someone shook his shoulders hard.

He jerked awake to look into Agnes's concerned eyes.

"What's the matter?"

He sucked in air and was drenched in sweat. The unbearable misery seized him. It was his fault his father had died. He should have come home earlier and told him he loved him. He might have been able to stop his dad.

"Hoss, answer me?"

"Sorry. Give me a moment," he muttered. He pushed his hair out of his eyes, his body slick with sweat.

"Were you having a nightmare about your father?"

He looked at her sharply. "Why?"

"You were calling out for him," she said softly. "Then you started screaming."

"Whenever I'm stressed, the damn childhood nightmare returns."

She rubbed his back. "Do you want to talk about it?"

"No." He yanked back the covers. "I need a drink."

"This kind of work brings out our demons."

"Go back to sleep."

He grabbed the bottle of Scotch and took a long swig, hoping to block out the nightmare. He headed down to her living room and sat on the couch. He wasn't going to sleep tonight. He struggled to breathe normally, but his lungs rattled. Adrenaline pumped blood through him, pushing him into flight and fight mode. On Zalara, he'd transform into a dragon and fly until weariness seized him, but he couldn't leave Agnes. Not with the blasted Mistonian hunting her.

He took another drink, trying to forget those childhood memories, but they wouldn't leave.

He'd never forgiven his father for abandoning him, for making him always be the outsider, the kid everyone felt sorry for. The kid no one could love.

"Hoss?" Agnes slowly swayed down the stairs. She put one hand on the railing to steady herself.

"You're still not well."

She slid next to him on the sofa. "Neither are you."

"I'll be fine."

"You don't sound fine."

He refused to get into a debate with her. No, he wasn't fine and wouldn't be until he could forget about the dream.

He drank another sip, hoping his mind would get foggy, but doubted anything on Earth was strong enough.

"Drinking isn't going to help."

He shrugged. The clock ticked loudly. Cars zoomed by, casting shadows into her living room. Strangely, he found this comforting. She didn't bombard him with ten millions questions like other females.

She leaned her head back and drifted back to sleep.

He grabbed a blanket and tossed it over her.

His telicator beeped.

He walked out of the living room onto her porch where pink and purple rays were lighting up the dusky sky. "Hoss."

"This is Tryker. How's your mate?"

"Sleeping. She's still pretty groggy, but doesn't seem to be in pain. Or if she is, she's keeping it to herself."

"Good. Call if you need me. She may still need to go to a medical facility."

Hoss bristled at the thought of primitive methods being applied to his mate. "How are the repairs on the Orion?"

"According to the captain, we've still got another five days before she's ready. Daidhl knew exactly what he was doing when he sabotaged her."

"Daidhl isn't Dadihl anymore."

"Who are you talking to?"

Hoss jumped. Agnes leaned in the doorway with a puzzled look on her sleepy face. Her hair tumbled loosely around her shoulders, and her blouse was unbuttoned, giving him a glimpse of a lacy bra. She was so tempting.

"Anonghos, are you there?" Tryker demanded.

"Something's come up. I'll talk to you later." He closed the telicator. "Ship's doctor."

"Is that a communicator?"

"No, it's a telicator. I can contact my people from here."

"It has a range all the way to another planet?"

He smirked. "Our technology is a little more advanced than yours."

"That's saying it mildly."

"How's your head?"

"Still hurts. I can't sleep."

He took her hand and led her back inside. "Maybe you need to shower and get into some clean clothes." His cock immediately hardened, thinking about her stripping down and her body sleek with drops of water.

"Maybe. Care to join me?"

"Are you sure? You were shot last night."

"This is nothing. I need a distraction."

He slowly smiled. "And I'm your distraction?"

"Obviously." She held out her hand. "Shall we?"

For a split second he was about to refuse, but he thought about what the Fate Yethi had told him. Mating with Agnes was the key to his race's survival. The dream still haunted him. He wanted to stomp it out of his mind and what better way than raw sex.

A gnes led Hoss up the stairs to her bathroom that was relatively clean. At least all the dirty clothes were stuffed into the hamper.

"How big is your shower?" he asked.

She grinned. "It's big enough for two."

Even in her small house, the master bathroom was large enough for two people, even someone Hoss's size.

She dropped his hand, then quickly unbuttoned her blouse. She tossed it onto the floor.

"Wait," he said. "Not so fast."

"Excuse me?"

"I want to undress you."

His voice was husky and flickered his gaze over her, making her squirm in excitement.

"Okay. I was just a little impatient."

He smiled. "I'm definitely worth the wait."

She raised her eyebrow. He was definitely full of himself. He was the most beautiful man she'd ever met, and probably used to starve-stricken models, who thought a full lunch was eating two celery sticks. She liked to eat.

She expected him to flinch from her curves like some of the other men she'd been with, but he put his hands on her shoulder and slowly rolled down her bra. She shivered as his fingers brushed down her arms.

He brushed his thumbs over her nipples, making them bud.

Before she could make another comment, he bent over, then knelt in front of her. His lips took her nipple into his mouth. He suckled her slowly, his tongue running over her flesh, then his mouth latched onto her, sucking hard until she cried out. She threaded her fingers into his thick mane, cradling him to her breast.

He moved his hands down her sides, and she tensed.

He suddenly stopped. "What's wrong? Are you in pain?"

"No." She shook her head. "It's just that you were moving your hands down my rolls…"

"So?"

Heat peaked onto her cheeks. "I know you're used to thin women."

"I am? I like all kinds of women. You have nothing to be ashamed of. I like the way you feel under my hands." He slowly moved his hands to her pants and unbuttoned them. "I want to see all of you."

She sucked in deep gulps of air as he slid her pants down her wide hips. She wished she had worn lacy underwear, but he'd have to be satisfied with her boring cotton ones.

He slid her pants down past her thighs, still leaving her underwear. He kissed her crotch, and she gasped, wanting to feel his lips on her flesh.

"Step out of your pants."

She did as he requested, putting her hands on his massive shoulders to steady herself. He lifted one leg and pulled off her sock, then the other.

She'd never had any man undress her like this, and her heart beat in excitement. He sat back on his haunches and slowly raised his gaze. Agnes put her arms across her waist to hide her belly, but he took her hands and forced them apart. She avoided his gaze not wanting to see the disappointment in them.

She'd just want to have fast, thank-you-ma'am sex and not this slow vulnerable kind.

Hoss kissed her belly button, which nearly had her jumping out of skin. He raised his head to stare into her eyes. "Never hide yourself from me."

She met his possessive gaze, but refused to comment. She wasn't sure what to make of his comment. Most men just used her as a release and often avoided touching her belly, but not Hoss. He continued to lick and kiss her as if she was his favorite lollypop.

"Aren't you going to get naked?"

"Not yet." He moved his hands up and down her trembling legs. "I want you hot for me."

He slipped his hands behind her buttocks and glided her underwear down her thighs. He edged his mouth down her belly until he fastened it onto her flesh. She cried out as he drove his tongue between her thighs. She hung on tight to his shoulders, afraid any minute she'd collapsed.

As if reading her mind, he murmured, "I'll never let you fall."

Her heart pounded faster and faster, sending blood down to her core. His fingers kneaded the back of her buttocks as he greedily feasted on her. She arched her back as the tension left her and the rising of an orgasm filled her. It came swift and fast. She screamed, calling out his name.

He slowly released her. "That's just the beginning." He tossed his head. "Get in the shower."

Her whole body shook from the release, and she numbly obeyed. She slipped into the shower that normally was big enough for her and whatever man she was sleeping with, but for the first time, she wasn't sure if it was big enough for two. Hoss was taller and more muscular then most men. His shoulders were so wide that she wasn't sure they'd both fit. She was no anorexic girl, either.

"Turn on the shower."

His voice was gruff.

What if he was going to turn into a dragon? Having sex with a beast was not going to happen. But as if under a spell, she turned on the faucet. Warm water cascaded down her already heated body.

Appreciation flickered in his eyes. "I like my women wet."

She was about to make a comment, when he shed his clothes so fast that she thought she'd imagined it. Her mouth froze, and her legs shook violently. He was magnificent and his cock was bigger than any she'd seen... And it had ridges. She kept forgetting he wasn't human. He was an alien. Not just an alien—a dragon.

He laughed. "The ridges are to please women."

He joined her, forcing her to lean against the wall. His presence dominated the shower, making the space seem smaller. He smelled of heat and sex. Droplets splattered off his massive shoulders, then dripped down his wide chest, sliding past his flat belly, and onto his erect cock. He pinned her against the wall, his mouth devouring her. Her nipples pressed against his hard flesh. He inserted one finger into her curls, exploring her as if he wanted to discover her secrets. She moaned at the fiery intrusion that left her dizzy with desire.

His mouth moved down her throat, his tongue leaving a curvy trail. The dark shadow on his chin chafed her hot skin. Heat surged through her, building another orgasm. She doubted she'd be able to stand if he'd hadn't been pressing her against the wall.

He removed his finger, and she groaned at the displeasure. "Spread your legs," he whispered into her ear.

Eager to feel him inside her, she widened her stance. Lord, he was right. The ridges created intense friction, more exotic, more intense than any other man. It was if she was skiing down a steep mountain swooshing over moguls at full force at full throttle. He lifted his hips, then thrust his cock deep inside her again and again. She rocked her hips, then locked her legs around his pelvis, matching his fierce rhythm.

Water patted their bodies as if trying to put out the raging inferno, but failed miserably.

Fervor fueled inside her like a raging forest fire, thumping from her heart to her body. Her skin was on hot, even with the water turning cool. She swore steam rose from their passion.

She dug her nails into his shoulders as the intensity grew stronger. Her heart beat out of control, then in one swift movement, her release exploded.

He slammed her against the wall, then his seed gushed into her, leaving her spent with bliss.

"God," she muttered. "I needed that."

"Was I worth the wait?"

She clung to him, still trying to breathe. "So, sure of yourself?"

"Yes, I am."

He kissed her, silencing another quip from her. He still pulsed inside her and she lost herself in his kiss. The frustration of not finding the killer, the dead women, the invasion from evil ET's, slowly slipped from her mind. All that mattered was Anonghos's kiss, his touch, his strength. He was a man that she could come home to and forget about the horrors of work.

A sharp shrill stopped her kissing.

"Hoss." She tried to regain her thoughts. "I have to answer that."

"No, you don't."

"Yes, I do. It's work." She leaned her head against his shoulder, then bit it.

"Why you little grendor!" He pinched her nipple.

"Hoss! Please, I have to take it."

"It better be your damn job." He slowly pulled out of her and stepped aside, giving her a very little path to squeeze past him.

As she did, he moved his hand down her backside and cupped her ass, sending another wave of desire through her.

She ignored the building need and stepped out of the cooling shower. Water splashed on the tile floor. She fumbled for her now silent phone that was in her pants pocket.

She glanced at the number and grimaced.

"Who is it?" Hoss asked. The water turned off.

"My brother." She immediately redialed the number.

"I thought it was work."

She glanced over his shoulder. God, he was magnificent. "If I don't call him back, he'll keep hounding me."

She reluctantly called Frank. He answered on one ring.

"Are you all right? I heard you got shot."

She was surprised at the concern in his voice.

"How did you find out?"

"The hospital contacted Captain Morgan, and he called me."

"Well, I'm fine."

"How did you get shot? The officer said he was on the top floor."

Her stomach tightened. Like she did as her child, she thought quickly of a likable story. "The suspect ran out of Kathy's apartment, and I chased him. He fired back."

"Why didn't you call for back up?"

"It happened too fast."

"According to Tom, not only are you relying on your mumbo-jumbo, but you've been letting a suspect cloud your judgment. You're over your head, sis."

Agnes stiffened. "I know what I'm doing, Frank."

"Yeah, getting yourself killed. This is a serial killer, who's liable to turn on you. I'm going to ask the captain to take you off the case."

"Frank, don't you dare! I don't need you hovering over me like an unwanted umbrella."

"You don't have a choice. You never should have been a cop."

With that, he hung up. Her throat swelled up and heated tears formed in her eyes, blurring her vision. She stared at the phone, fighting not to smash it into zillions of pieces.

Hoss put his hands on his shoulders. "Everything okay? You're trembling."

She blinked her eyes, refusing to cry in front of him. She took a deep breath before answering. "No. My brother is trying to get me taken off the case."

He slowly turned her around. "Because you got shot."

She saw no reason to lie. "Yes and because of you and my abilities."

He ran the back of his hand down her cheek. "I'm sorry."

"Don't be." She braced her shoulders. "I can handle it."

He nuzzled her neck. "So tough. So brave. So alone."

Another wave of passion formed, but she stepped away, wishing she could lose herself with him. "I need to call the captain before Frank does."

Hoss crowded her against the bathroom door, blocking off any escape. His warm breath tickled on her neck.

She almost dropped the phone in her shaking hand. She quickly called the captain.

"Morgan."

"Captain? It's Malloy."

"I heard you got shot."

Bad news traveled fast. "I'm fine."

"You should have reported it," he growled.

"The bullet only grazed my temple. I need to be on this case, Captain."

"You're losing your head over this one."

Hoss kissed her neck, starting another wave of passion. She struggled to stay in control.

"No, I'm not," she gasped as Hoss moved his hand down her belly toward her curls. "Frank wants me off the case."

Silence turned her passion cold.

"You're off the case when I say so. But don't make me regret it. No more mistakes."

"Thank you, sir."

He hung up without another word.

"See everything's all right," he said as he cupped the juncture between her legs.

She slammed her head back as passion gripped her. Pain zipped through her skull.

"Are you okay?"

"I will be if you take me hard and fast." She couldn't shed the thought that the captain was holding something back, but she needed a distraction, needed to forget about her domineering brother.

He grinned. "Okay, we'll do it your way."

She parted her legs, and he thrust deep insider her, pounding hard, his amazing, ridged cock that wished her to a mile-high of ecstasy, erasing all thoughts of her brother, and creating a distraction that rocked the house.

🐉 12 🐉

Daidhl flew over Annie Watkins, who drove her white SUV. He was invisible and a dragon. She never saw him standing outside her home, waiting for her to leave. He could have killed her inside her room like he had Sharon, but he lusted for more sensation—the terror of her scream, the fear rippling through her body, the life leaving her wide eyes.

She parked her SUV in an elementary school's empty parking lot. School wouldn't start for another couple of hours. Good, he'd have some time to slice out her organs, saving a trophy for himself and sending another to the incompetent police force.

A thick, white scarf wrapped around her slender neck that matched her coat, flickering in the wind. Her black hair was pulled back in a simple ponytail. She was so pure...so innocent...

Landing directly behind her, he kept himself invisible and exhaled hard.

As she spun, her green eyes searched the empty space, puzzled. After a moment, she pulled her coat tighter her and turned back toward the school. Pulling out a flat white card, she jogged toward the door.

He transformed into a humanoid and quickly followed her.

A lock clicked as she whisked the flat card over a small black box that was attached to the building. A lock clicked. She slipped inside with him right behind.

She walked down the wall, and his footsteps echoed behind her.

"Who's there?" she demanded. Her eyes widened when she saw no one.

"Hello, Annie." He slowly appeared with a smile on his face.

She screamed, ran down the tiled hallway, and past a dark office. She pulled out her key, her hand shaking, and stuck it in a lock. She opened the door and was about to step inside when he grabbed her scarf and yanked her against him.

"Who...who are you?"

"Your murderer."

Before she could scream, he slashed her throat deeply with a knife. She crumbled against him, blood gushing down her white coat, turning it into a beautiful crimson. She looked at him in terror as her life quickly bled out of her. A stream of blood ran from her throat and seeped under the door into her classroom.

He spread her legs apart, ready to have his way with her corpse.

"Annie?"

A male voice called from down the hall.

Daidhl growled. He wanted no interruptions in his work.

"Annie, are you there?"

Firm footsteps hurried down the hall toward them. He thought about killing the intruder, but there would be no sport. Men didn't possess the same terror as women. He quickly turned invisible.

A man came ran around the corner and skidded to a halt. His face paled and he stared in disbelief. He made the sign of the cross. "My God, Annie."

His voice was barely a whisper.

Daidhl couldn't help but laugh.

"Who's there?" the man cried as he whirled around. "Show yourself."

Daidhl slowly walked over to him, feeding on his fear. Maybe he should kill him, but he wasn't a mate for one of those dreaded Zalarians. Besides, men didn't possess the same delightful, terror as women.

"Be grateful I didn't murder you, too."

The man jumped back and slammed into a wall. His arms stretched out wide.

Daidhl laughed hysterically, then walked down the hall, leaving the man shrieking and soaking up his horror.

13

Agnes lay blissfully exhausted in Hoss's protective arms. He'd taken her fiercely in the bathroom and again in the bed. She liked listening to his pounding heart and his loud snores. She could lie here all night and all day, letting him take her from one pleasure to another, but her desire was denied.

But she couldn't stop thinking of Kathy. What if something happened to Kathy while she was tangled with Hoss? God, she'd never forgive herself.

As if on cue, her phone rang loudly, tugging at her guilt. She unwound from Hoss and answered. "Malloy?"

"Where the hell have you been?" Tom barked.

She winced. "If you remember, I was shot."

"Get your ass over here. There's been another murder."

Guilt swelled inside her chest. Tom had been on the job while she was dilly-dallying with the Alien-of-the-Month club. "Crap. Where are you?"

"At Hodgkins Elementary."

His hard voice fizzled all of her passion and bliss, then her gut tied into double knots.

Don't be a child. Don't be a child.

"What?"

"The principal just found one of his teachers. He's pretty shaken up and not making sense."

Relief flushed through her shivering body. At least it hadn't been a student or Kathy. "Text me the address. I'll be there as soon as I can."

Hoss rubbed her sore behind where he'd dug his fingers into her flesh when he'd taken her hard. "Daidhl struck again."

"Yes." She kicked back the covers. She threaded her fingers through her hair. "This time it was an elementary school teacher. Her principal just found her." She went over to the closet to yank out some clothes.

Hoss climbed out of the bed. "I'm coming with you."

She turned around. "No, you're not. If I show up with you, the captain's liable to take me off the case."

He grabbed her arm. "You can't solve this without me."

"I can't bring you to the crime scene."

"Yes, you can, and you will."

"Listen, Mr. Dragon, you can't tell me what to do. I won't let you jeopardize my case."

He laughed. "You don't actually think you can put this man in jail, do you?"

She braced her shoulders, not caring he was a foot taller. She met his sarcastic glare. "Yes, I do. I'm a police officer. In case you've forgotten, that's my job."

He stopped laughing, his voice turning serious. "There's no prison on Earth that can contain, Daidhl. Your only hope is for me to kill him or capture him. I'll take him back to Zalara where he'll be punished."

"Fine." She broke free from his tight clasp and went back to dragging a sweater and a pair of trousers out of the closet. Within minutes, she was dressed. The last few months being on a call had taught her how to move fast for an emergency. Murders didn't happen eight to five.

She pulled her hair back in a ponytail, but she groaned when she looked at her chafed cheeks. She hoped to god Tom wouldn't know that she'd spent hours having the best sex she'd ever had, instead of hunting down a sadistic killer.

But it was a foolish hope. Tom was a good cop and could put one and one together. If she wasn't careful, he'd report her to the captain, and she'd find herself sitting behind a desk.

Ignoring the throbbing pain, she slowly secured her holster and stuck her revolver in the sheath.

When she walked out of the bedroom, Hoss was waiting for her. "What took you so long?"

"Very funny. I told you. You can't come."

He shrugged. "Then, I'll follow you. You can't fight Daidhl without me. Or are you determined to be slashed open like those other women?"

"Fine. Then you're coming as an observer."

"I'm fine with that."

"Why don't I believe you?"

"Look, I said I would follow your rules. But remember my people's lives are at stake too. While we were having sex, someone else's line just died. Don't expect me to be an idle by-stander."

"I was afraid you'd say something like that."

He smiled and turned to go down the stairs. Dread settled into her as she trailed behind Hoss. What if they couldn't stop Daidhl? Would she be attacked next? Kathy? How many more women would die?

THE SILENT SIREN ON HER DASHBOARD FLASHED RED. AGNES honked the car's horn at a crowd of curious people filling the street. They parted when she turned on the siren. A black-white officer motioned for her to park in front of the school next to the coroner's white van. Police cars were lined up neatly in the west parking lot.

But it was the brown sedan that made her heart fall to her toes. The captain was here and wouldn't be happy when she came strolling to the crime scene with Hoss trailing her like a shadow.

She opened her car door an inch. "Hoss, don't piss off Tom."

"I'll try."

She narrowed her eyes. "Do better than try."

He got out before she did and slammed the door. She immediately climbed out about to send his ass back to jail. Having sex would not change anything. The job came first.

The same officer blocked Hoss's path. "You need to get back."

She flashed out her badge. "He's with me. He's an observer. Where's the body?"

"In a hallway outside her classroom. Forensics is already down there." He stuck out his thumb. "By the way, the feds are here."

"Lovely." That's when she noticed the black car parked in between two squad cars. Her nerves knotted up into tiny tangled balls of strings. Oh, God, please, please, please, don't let it be Frank.

She motioned to Hoss to follow her. "Come on."

He leaned close. "What are feds?"

"Annoying assholes who think they're gods, and we're a bunch of bumpkins."

He smiled. "I've never met a god before."

She couldn't help but shake her head and grin.

They hurried into the faded red brick building that reminded her more of a detention center with security cameras posted in the hallways rather than an elementary school. But maybe the cameras would give them a break on the case. She could only hope.

Tom and the captain were in the window-framed office that looked like any other school office with wire baskets, pens, and papers sitting on a Formica counter. So far, the suits hadn't made an appearance.

But by Tom and the captain's grim faces, she doubted they'd hit pay dirt.

The captain and Tom were talking with a tall thirtyish looking man. His black hair stood on end as if he'd been running his hand through it. His face was whiter than the tile floor.

An officer stood guard in front of one hallway. Agnes could make out a body sprawled out that had been split open like the other victims.

Sadness filled Hoss's eyes. "Another Zalarain's lineage has been severed."

"I'm sorry, Hoss."

He nodded but didn't answer.

Tom impatiently motioned for her to come inside. When she entered, the captain frowned. "Why the hell is he here?"

"We need him." Agnes refused to flinch. "Captain, did you call the feds? I was handling the investigation."

"No. I didn't. But our illustrious mayor panicked."

"Humpf, yeah, I bet," Tom mumbled. "Your brother will be less than pleased."

Air sucked out of Agnes as if she was hit the gut with a bat. "He's here?"

Tom smiled. "Of course. The mayor wanted the best."

"Great." Blood drained from her face, and the tip of her fingers turned numb. This was so not what she needed. "Where is he?"

Hoss looked at her amusingly. "Is he one of the gods?"

"He thinks he is," she mumbled.

Tom shrugged, then cleared his voice. "Principal Myers, this is my partner, Agnes Malloy."

The principal stretched out his hand. "Bob Myers." He had a nice firm handshake. "It's nice to meet you, Detective." He released her hand. "Agent Malloy is your brother?"

Agnes nodded, forcing herself to bite back a retort. "Yes." She gestured toward Hoss and lied. "This is Hoss, and he's a special advisor on the case."

Just as she said that, another suit and her brother, who looked as smart as ever, entered the office. He was the exact opposite of her—tall, dark, muscular, handsome—her father's favorite.

"Really?" Frank put his hands behind his broad back. "I wasn't informed of a special advisor."

Principal Myers frowned. "I thought you were the agent in charge."

Frank strolled over to Agnes. "I am." He glanced at the tall blond man next to him, wearing an almost identical blue suit with a red tie. "This is Agent Jeff Holmes, my partner. We are both in charge of this investigation."

He gave Hoss a cool look. "I suspect, sis, your claim of this civilian being important to this case is based on your so-called abilities." He humiliated her like he used to do when she was a little girl in front of her friends. "Care to explain yourself, Detective?" He lowered his voice. "Or should I say, Carrie?"

Heat flared in her cheeks and in her neck. He and his friends used to call her Carrie White, based on the misfit character in Stephen King's novel, *Carrie*, who was strange and telepathic.

Hoss frowned. "Carrie?"

Frank shrugged. "She was a crazy, psychic like my sister."

"Don't talk about her like that." Hoss glowered and actually towered over Frank.

Frank's face actually paled. He straightened his tie and his Adam's apple moved up and down. Agnes forced herself to hide a smile.

She'd be called on the carpet for that one, but Hoss was an advisor, not that she could tell these two that their number one suspect was from outer space. She'd be off the case and put on leave until a mental health exam said she was sane.

The principal shook Hoss's hand. "It's good to meet you."

He focused on Agnes. "Your partner reports that you have some amazing deductible abilities and can help us find out what happened to...Annie." Tears welled in his eyes. He put out his hand. "Sorry. I just can't believe something like this happened here. I'm still not sure what happened."

She ignored Frank rolling his eyes and concentrated on the principal. "I'm sorry for your loss," Agnes said. His grief appeared to be genuine, and this was a man who obviously cared about his staff.

"He found her at seven this morning," Tom said. "The principal had just missed the murderer."

"Annie liked to get to school before anyone else, including me. She was our MTSS teacher, who was extremely dedicated. Who would do this to her?"

Hoss asked, "What's MTSS?"

"It stands for Multi-tiered System Support, which really means that Annie had lots of reports to fill out," the principal answered. "She liked to get to school early to work on them. Her main focus had always been the students."

"I know you've repeated what happened, but could you tell me what happened, Mr. Myers?" Agnes asked.

The principal flashed Tom a warning look. "I know your partner doesn't believe me."

Agnes led him away from the captain and Tom, who was mumbling under his breath about the principal being off his rocker.

"Would you like to go someplace private?" she asked.

Principal Myers motioned. "My office."

"Of course," Agnes said. Both her and Hoss followed him into a large office with a wooden desk and a conference table with eight chairs. She and Hoss sat on either side of the shaken man.

Hoss was right at her side, thankfully, keeping his mouth shut.

"Please tell me what happened, Mr. Myers."

"I know it sounds crazy."

"Please," Agnes encouraged. "Anything will help."

He damped his face with a handkerchief. "I was just coming into the building when I heard her scream. I ran toward her room. When... I saw her..."

His eyes turned vacant as if he were reliving the scene again.

Agnes gave him a minute to compose himself.

"Sorry," he muttered. "It's just so surreal." He glanced at her face. "Annie was lying on the floor bleeding profusely. I have never seen so much blood."

"Did you see anyone?" Agnes asked.

He shook his head. "No, but I... I heard a voice."

"Go on." Agnes gently touched his trembling arm.

"The voice said...I...was lucky that he...wasn't going to kill me." He frowned. "Why would he say that? What did he mean?"

"He's only interested in killing women," Hoss finally said.

Principal Myers took a deep breath. "You believe me? You don't think I imagined it like your partner or the FBI agents?"

She smiled. "I'm more open-minded. Did you smell anything?"

"Come to think of it, I did. I thought it was strange that I detected spoiled milk."

"Thank you," Agnes said. "You've been a big help."

"You don't...think... You don't think the killer will come back and murder more of my staff, do you?"

Agnes and Hoss glanced at each other. "We hope not," they answered at the same time.

"That's not very reassuring." Principal Myers glanced up at the clock. "If you'll excuse me, my staff will be getting here soon, and I'll need to tell them what happened."

"Sure." Agnes smiled. "Do what you must do."

He quickly left his office and headed down the opposite hallway where a group of nervous women waited for him. He led them into another classroom. Agnes didn't envy what he was about to do.

She and Hoss approached the captain, who stood by himself. He flashed an angry look at Hoss.

"Captain," she asked. "Where did Frank and his partner go?"

"Back to the office. They're planning on working on a profile."

Hoss looked at her. "What's a profile?"

"Based on what they know and the evidence, they will come up with a profile on the suspect."

"Does that actually work?"

"Yes, it does," the captain snapped.

Not wanting those two get into an argument, Agnes asked, "How was she killed?"

"She was wearing a scarf, and according to the coroner, the killer yanked on the scarf from behind, pulling her to the ground. The bastard slashed her throat so deep that he cut through her wind-pipe, silencing any scream. She bled out within two minutes." The captain shook his head. "The poor girl never had a chance."

Agnes noticed the wooden mail slots and wandered over. Annie hadn't picked up her mail. "How did she get in?"

"She had a key fob," the captain said. "The killer must have attacked her as she came inside."

She frowned. "There were no signs of forced entry?"

Hoss interrupted. "What about the security cameras? Did anyone catch any footage on that?"

The captain frowned. "We did, but there must be something wrong with the cameras. It didn't make any damn sense."

Dread hunkered down in Agnes's gut. "What do you mean?"

He motioned for them to follow. "Come on, I'll show you." He led them to the resource officer's office. On one wall were a slew of screens. A young officer sat behind a desk with a perplexed look on his face. He tore himself from the screen and stood when they entered.

"Officer Wilson, this is Detective Malloy, she was the lead investigator on this case."

Agnes bristled at the word *was*, but kept her composure. She gestured toward Hoss. "This is Hoss. He's my advisor."

Office Wilson stretched out his hand and shook hers. It was a strong, firm, grip. "Detective." He then greeted Hoss.

"Please sit," he said. "I've been reviewing the tape of Annie, and I just can't figure what is wrong with the equipment. The video just doesn't make sense."

Agnes and Hoss glanced at each other as they slid into two chairs that faced the screens, while the captain sat on the edge of the officer's desk, folding his arms across his chest.

"Review the footage, Wilson."

"Yes, sir." He pushed some buttons and the tape rewound. "Just doesn't make sense," he muttered.

Annie entered the building on the west side of the building, her pale face was a sharp contrast to her black hair. With her red lips, Agnes thought of Snow White, but no prince was going to wake her from a dead sleep.

Annie kept looking over her shoulder. She held her purse and bag close.

"Do we know what was in her bag?" Agnes asked.

"Papers, notebooks, and an iPad. Nothing that gave us in any information on what happened," the captain said.

"I'd like to look at her things," she said.

The captain cast her a glowering look, as if to warn her not to do anything supernatural. She pretended not to notice but anger seethed inside her. She was so tired of any guesses she made being suspect. No other detective had to work as hard to be logical.

On the tape, Annie walked down the hall, but the she increased her pace, constantly looking over her shoulder. Her eyes were wide, and she was breathing hard. Strangely, there was nothing behind her. The woman's terror touched Agnes.

Annie's mouth opened in a scream as she ran down a hallway that led to her room. She jammed her hand into her purse and pulled out a key ring. She shoved a key into the lock, and the door opened.

Suddenly, her scarf lifted up from behind her as if by magic, then she was yanked hard back. Her throat was viciously cut, blood gushing down her white coat, turning it dark red. She gurgled, then collapsed on the tile floor. A pool of blood spread from underneath her.

She hadn't blinked nor had her chest rose up and down. Her legs moved apart by themselves, or more likely someone forced them to move.

The principal came around the corner and halted to a stop. A look of pure horror flashed across his face. He jumped back against a wall.

"I just don't understand," Officer Wilson said. "Someone killed Annie, but it looked like the suspect was erased from the tape. No one broke into my office. How the hell did this happen? She didn't deserve this. She was a great teacher, loved by her students." His voice shook with frustration.

The captain shrugged. "Hell, if I know."

Agnes cleared her throat. "Do you mind if I go down to the crime scene?"

"Go ahead. Good detective work that's all, Malloy."

Hoss followed her out of the office. "Daidhl wasn't done with her."

"What?"

"The principal interrupted his work. I fear he would have been more violent."

"So, part of his plan is to cut these poor women up?"

"I told you. He feeds on fear. Not just the women's, but ours. I am sure he got a full belly after feeding on that man's fear. We need to find him."

"Obviously, but how?"

"By figuring out how he knows our mates."

"And exactly how we are going to do this?"

"I don't know, but we'd better damn well figure it out. He's getting more brazen and more violent."

Neither of them spoke as they went down the hallway toward Annie's room. Agnes caught three cameras and felt like her every move was being dissected. Maybe they were.

Cold air whooshed around Agnes, and she pretended not to notice. A white light flashed at the end of the hallway. Agnes quickly glanced at Hoss to see if he saw it, but his demeanor hadn't changed. She took a deep breath.

The light reappeared and formed into Annie Watkins, but she had difficulty maintaining her form and flickered in and out. She looked down at her dead body that was now covered with a tarp. Forensics was still inside taking photographs. Luckily, neither Frank nor his partner were inside.

Agnes slowed as her and Hoss approached the ghost. She leaned closer to Hoss, inhaling his masculine scent. "She's here."

He frowned. "Who?"

"Annie Watkins. I can see her."

He raised his eyebrow. "You can."

"Yes, if I try talking to her, the cameras will see, and I'll be off the case."

"Your kind is foolish to not appreciate your gift."

It was the second time he'd called her abilities a gift and rather than arguing, she smiled, wishing she could kiss him. But this wasn't the time or place.

"I need you to stand next to her, so it looks like I'm talking with you."

"Why?"

"Because we're being watched." She tilted her head toward a camera that was high up in a corner overhead.

"Can't they hear us?"

"No, based on what we saw in Officer Wilson's office, the cameras are only visual and don't have the capacity for auditory. Stand on the other side of the body."

He winked. "Sure, beautiful."

Annie raised her head. "I can't believe I'm dead."

Agnes pulled out her iPad and took a picture. "I know. I'm sorry." She proceeded to take several pictures of Annie's body.

"My students will be sad. We're very close." A tear leaked down onto her cheek. "He was so vicious. I could feel the evil within him. He's not done yet."

"Can you tell me anything else?"

"He's obsessed. I could...read...his mind."

Her fading voice unzipped an uneasiness inside Agnes. Goosebumps slowly edged up her arm.

Annie faded, but her voice was loud enough for Agnes to hear.

"He's going after your friend, then you. You can't stop him. He's too powerful."

❧ 14 ❧

Hoss looked around the hallway for any clues of Daidhl's next move. Besides the metallic stench, he detected foul milk.

Hoss led Agnes out of the elementary school. She'd been quiet. Too quiet.

"You haven't said anything since you saw the ghost. What did Annie say?"

She walked over to her car. "Both Kathy and I are in danger."

"We already knew that."

"But it gives me an idea." She quickly got into the car.

He didn't like her tone and slid inside. "What does that mean?"

"Look Hoss, you've said repeatedly that you and the so-called Fates can't determine who are the mates, but this bastard can. As far as I can see, we're always going to be one step behind."

"Go on."

"Annie said he's obsessed with both me and Kathy. This is our advantage."

"What are you saying?" he asked slowly, knowing he wasn't going to like the answer.

She started the car. "We could set up a trap. Kathy and I could be the bait."

"That's the dumbest thing you've come up with."

She glared. "Don't talk to me like that."

He fought not to lash out at her, but it brimmed slowly out of his voice"How the hell do you want me to talk to you? When you're determined to walk into a wike's den."

She frowned. "What's a wike?"

"A ferocious beast on Zalara with a mouth full of teeth, a spiky tail, and long talons. But it pales to this creature. This isn't a human, Agnes. This is a Mistonian. One of the deadliest creatures in the universe."

"Hoss, this is my job. I swore an oath to serve and protect. If I can stop the killing, I'm going to do it."

"I can't let you do this."

She cast him a look that froze his tongue. "You don't have a choice. This is what I do."

He nervously tapped his hands on his thighs. "Where are we going?"

"Back to headquarters."

He stopped tapping and scowled. "Why?"

"I need to do a time line to see if there is a pattern of any kind."

Her tight face looked like she was a million miles away and she needed to be looped back into reality. "He only goes after mates."

"I realize that, but maybe they're not at random."

He opened his mouth, but shut it. Frustration roasted inside him like a piece of meat. He was about to argue, but it would be pointless. Why was he getting so upset? She was just another woman—a stubborn woman—that he enjoyed, and if she were walking into danger, he shouldn't care. There were always more women—at least tons on Earth.

His fingers turned numbed and his skin chilled at losing her. He'd gone through women on Zalara like water, just to prove he wasn't like his father. Why did the thought of her being killed leave him ice cold? The concern had to be because his lineage would end. He refused to admit it was anything else.

She parked the SUV in police headquarters and got out of the car. She stretched her back then quickly headed toward the front door without waiting for him. Stubborn wench.

The last place he wanted to be was here. Every time, he always ended up in a cell that he could easily escape, but was under orders not to. Pushing aside his unease, he easily over took her. She barely glanced at him, but didn't block him from coming.

"So, you're not speaking to me?"

She stopped and glared. "I don't play games. I just don't want to argue. I learned a long time ago that it's useless to try and change the mind of stubborn over-bearing men."

"Is that what you think I am?" he asked softly.

She turned, her back stiff. "All men are."

Hoss wanted to take her back into his arms and show her that not all men were enemies, but he doubted she'd believe him. Based on the men in her life, she had no reason to trust him.

They were quickly near the interrogations rooms, that he unfortunately knew too well. She led him past the rooms to a large glass office with leather chairs, a long table, and bulletin boards. Crime photos were pinned on the bulletin.

Several men sat around the table, including Agnes's brother, Frank. When they walked into the conference room, Frank stood and headed toward them.

"Agnes, what are you doing here? We are in the middle of doing real police work." He sneered. "I thought you would still be using your psychic powers to figure out how to find the killer."

Hoss narrowed his eyes. "Why are you so disrespectful to your sister?"

Frank straightened his tie. "Because she's been a disgrace to our family for years. There is no magic in police work."

"That hasn't been my experience," Hoss muttered. The dragon

within him burned with fury, and Hoss shook, struggling not to fry the man alive.

Agnes held up her hands and stepped between them. "Stop. I can take care of myself." She faced her brother. "Until the captain takes me off this case, I'm still on it."

Her voice was surprisingly strong.

"For now," her brother muttered.

She glanced at the photographs of the victims' stark faces that were pinned to the bulletin-boards. "There has to be a pattern with these women... Something we have missed."

Frank gestured toward the same pictures. "We are close to developing a profile on him, and we were going to call a briefing to go over it with your team."

She followed her brother. "Good. It's a start." She flashed Hoss a warning look to keep his mouth shut.

He obediently followed her into a room that resembled a classroom. There was a podium and chairs lined up in rows. Police officers started filing into the room, taking the chairs, while Frank and his colleagues stood at the front of the line.

Agnes slipped behind the podium. When the last officer took his seat, she said, "The FBI has come up with a profile on our would-be serial killer." She gestured. "Agent Malloy."

The officers clapped enthusiastically. Obviously, her brother was a favorite among them. Hoss couldn't understand why. Frank was an arrogant putz and liked to bully his sister. A behavior that would not have been tolerated on board the Orion.

Frank lifted his hands. "Thank you. We're honored to be here working with the finest police department in Colorado."

"We're glad to have you," someone called out from the back.

Frank smiled. "I have missed all of you and am glad to be back, but we have a job to do."

The captain entered from the back and came to stand next to Hoss. His face was grim except for his eyes that looked were bleary as if he hadn't slept for days.

Hoss understood. Daidhl was out of control, determined to kill every last mate. If he was successful killing the women here, he'd move on until all the mates were exterminated. They had to stop him before it was too late.

"Captain Morgan," Frank nodded. "Thanks for inviting my team."

The captain sighed heavily and folded his arms across his chest. Hoss got the feeling he was less than pleased having this team here, but was smart enough to keep his thoughts to himself.

"We have a profile," Frank said. "The unsub is Caucasian and between the ages of twenty-eight and thirty-four years old. He's educated and holds a position that requires planning and execution. He's patient and works alone. However, he's charismatic enough to get close to these women. He's filled with anger and hates women, but there has been no evidence of sexual assault prior to the murder. He has had some medical training or perhaps a butcher since he had a knowledge of human anatomy based on his precision in cutting out the organs."

Some of the officer's faces paled, but no one made a comment.

Hoss thought Frank's profile wasn't describing the Orion's competent navigator at all. Daidhl hadn't had any medical training. In fact, he used to faint at the sight of blood. No, it was the Mistonian who had the knowledge, but he kept silent.

Frank's partner, James Holmes, chimed in. "The unsub kills his victims swiftly, and he is in complete control during the attacks. Mutilation occurs postmortem. He's arrogant and brazen, likes to create terror before he murders his victims. He's had training in using a knife."

Frank interrupted. "We know he probably works a swing shift, because the victims were killed in the early morning hours or prior to midnight. He lives in this area, because his victims up until now have all been confined to this area.

Hoss snorted and earned hostile stares from the rest of the

men. But what could he say? The smug FBI agents were as accurate as navigating through a wormhole.

"These are lust murders, which don't have anything to do with love or sexual meaning. The unsub attacks the genitalia of his victims. In this case, the vagina and breasts are the focal points of his attacks. Generally males who are perform such attacks, are involved in a homosexual relationship."

Hoss bit back a smirk. Definitely wrong on that account.

The captain mumbled under his breath, "Something you found amusing?"

"No." Hoss managed to keep his laughter contained. Humans referred everything back to sex.

An officer raised his hand. "This sounds like a profile on Jack the Ripper. Is this man copying the murders?"

Frank shook his head. "No. Jack the Ripper was an opportunist killer. He only attacked outdoors except for the last victim. He also only attacked prostitutes. Our unsub has killed an accountant and a school teacher. We still have not identified the second victim, but I doubt that the victim was a prostitute. Jack the Ripper also had worked a day job Monday through Friday, because all of his murders had occurred on Friday, Saturday, or Sunday in the early morning hours.

However, there are similarities between the two. Both killers would have come from dysfunctional families. They both would have been raised by a domineering mother and a weak and passive father, or an absent one. His mother would have drank heavily and enjoyed the company of many men. Consequentially, both men would have become detached socially and emotionally from people. In their younger years, they would have expressed this anger by setting fires and torturing animals."

Hoss watched Agnes. She furiously moved her fingers over her iPad and excitement flickered in her eyes. He wished he were standing next to her to figure out what she was doing.

"By perpetrating these acts," Frank said. "The unsub would

have discovered dominance, power, and control, and found a way not to get caught. Based on this profile, we know one thing for certain. He likes when he's doing. He's gotten away with it. And he's not going to stop."

The captain headed up to the podium. "Thank you, Agent Malloy." He faced the officers still sitting in their seats. "Now, you've heard the profile. We're dealing with a dangerous serial killer. Be on the look out for anything suspicious."

The men got up talking and murmuring to themselves, but Hoss wasn't listening. All he cared about was getting to Agnes. She got to him first. The same excitement reflected in her eyes.

"Come with me." She pulled her iPad out of her bag and hurried past him. "We need to get back to the conference room."

Hoss followed her, knowing he wasn't going to like what she was going to say.

"What's going on?"

"It hit me when Frank was talking about the comparison between the killer and Jack the Ripper."

"Much of what he said wasn't right. Daidhl wasn't a homosexual, and he came from a loving family."

"Okay, but the murders, they're the same."

"What?"

"Your navigator is mimicking the Jack the Ripper murders. I know he is."

"Of course. Jack the Ripper was one of Earth's most notorious serial killers and still strikes fear in people."

"Exactly. What better way to generate fear."

They entered the empty conference room. "But I need to be sure." She pulled up a website. "Look. Mary Nichols was Jack the Ripper's first victim. Her neck was cut with a strong bladed knife. She had a deep cut that ran along her abdomen and her intestines were draped out of her body, just like Sharon Reese."

"The Ripper's third victim, Elizabeth Stride, had her throat savagely cut from behind, but he didn't have time to mutilate the body, because someone was coming."

"Like Annie Watkins," he muttered.

"Yes, Principal Myers walked in on him."

"What happened to the Ripper's second victim?"

"That was Annie Chapman. She was horribly mutilated. Her womb was surgically removed."

"But we haven't found the second victim. We only have her womb."

"Exactly. My guess is that she must live alone, and no one's reported her missing."

As if on cue, the captain entered the conference room. "Malloy."

His voice was grave.

Agnes put down her iPad.

The captain slid into the chair across from her. "There's another body."

Hoss's stomach tightened. "Where?"

"A high rise. The victim had shown up for her mother's birthday party. Her mother was worried and got the superintendent to open the door for her."

"Oh, God." Agnes covered her mouth. "That poor woman."

For such a tough detective, she had a soft heart. The woman was such a contradiction.

"I don't understand it." The captain ran his hand over his bald head. "How's the bastard getting inside? There's no sign of forced entry."

Agnes and Hoss glanced at each other knowingly. Not being able to answer the captain, they rushed out of headquarters and got into her car. Agnes put a siren on top of the roof. The loud scream stretched Hoss's nerves.

"Agnes," he said. "It's not just the victims he wants to create terror. It's the police. He's toying with all of you."

"He's doing a damn good job," she muttered. "If he follows his pattern, the victim will have her left arm laid across her left breast. Her legs will be drawn up, her feet resting on the ground, while her knees are turned outward. Her face will be swollen, her tongue hanging out of her mouth. Her head will be turned on the right side."

Within minutes, they'd arrived at the high rise. Cop cars were parked in front, and once again, police officers were corralling the curious on-lookers back. Agnes and Hoss got out of the car and hurried to the door. He wasn't looking forward to seeing the grisly scene. By Agnes's drawn face, she was dreading it as well.

They entered the painstaking slow elevator that creaked up to the crime scene. When the doors opened, cops were patrolling the floor, but the first thing, Hoss noticed was the stench of decay and offal. It reminded him of a thousand dead vlats next to a stopped up toilet. He gritted his teeth to keep from vomiting. Agnes's face paled, but she quickly made her way to the apartment. Unfortunately, Frank and his men had beaten them to the crime scene.

Frank greeted them at the victim's door. "What took you so long, Detective? Been trying to use your visions?"

"Excuse me, Agent." She whooshed past him.

Hoss had to walk down the hallway to keep from throttling Frank. He was Agnes's older brother and should be trying to protect her, not humiliate her. Usually he would have taken deep breaths, but the odor was so bad, he thought it would stick to his lungs and dust over his lips.

But he wouldn't abandon his mate. His eyes watered from the smell. He was the chief security officer of the Orion, but he'd never experienced anything so foul.

Agents were taking pictures, including Agnes. He came along side her and his heart froze. The victim was dismayed exactly as Agnes had described. All he could think about was that Agnes wanted to act as bait. How could he ever let her do this? He'd already failed to protect three other designated mates.

She kept glancing over at the balcony, and he followed her gaze, wondering if she was seeing the victim's ghost. He whispered his question in Agnes's ear.

Agnes nodded. "Her name was Laura Nybo. She was a social worker. Worked with middle school students. If you'll excuse me, I need to wander through the house."

He didn't argue with her. Maybe the ghost was talking to her. He wandered over to the balcony. Obviously, it was the way that Daidhl was getting inside. Beyond the glass door on the next building, a pair of gold eyes were glaring at him.

Daidhl—it was a challenge.

Hoss tensed, and his nostrils flared, releasing a puff of angry smoke.

"Hey, no smoking in here." Someone growled over his shoulder.

He ignored him and quickly headed for the balcony. Not caring if anyone saw him, he opened it and went outside.

As he shut it, someone yelled, "Hey!"

He thought it was Frank, but he'd no time to lose. He hated doing this to Agnes, but this was a chance to take down Daidhl. He was stronger and faster than an Inquistain dragon. The door opened.

"What the hell are you doing?" Frank demanded.

Hoss didn't glance behind him. Instead, he dove off the balcony.

"Jesus Christ!" Frank yelled. "Anonghos!"

Hoss did a somersault in mid-air and in a split second, transformed into a dragon. Daidhl jumped off the opposite building and flew into the clouds. Hoss flapped his wings hard and picked up speed. He inhaled and easily picked up the trail of spoiled milk.

A stream of fire burst out of a dark cloud. Hoss shifted to the side, but the tip of his wing was singed. He grimaced, vowing to rip Daidhl into pieces. He inhaled, drawing on the depth of his fire within him. In one large exhale, he sprayed a blazing inferno inside the cloud. His reward was a loud shriek.

Daidhl burst out of his hiding place, his eyes a fiery gold. His scales glowed red along one side and were slowly turning black. But his opponent wasn't done.

He opened his mouth to rows of teeth. He swung around and unleashed his claws. Hoss was ready and easily outmaneuvered him. Daidhl made another pass and this time, he swung his tail that slammed into Hoss's singed wing. Agony gripped him. His wing collapsed, and he spun around toward the ground with Daidhl's flying toward him. Victory shone in the little dragon's eyes.

Hoss forced the pain back to his mind and drew on his dragon strength. He turned over and flapped his wing. He did an about face in midair and blew. Fire caught Daidhl's in the face. He released a terrible howl.

Just when Hoss thought he could destroy him, Daidhl disappeared. He flew straight for the direction that he'd last seen Daidhl, following the stench of burned milk into a dark cloud. It was a mistake.

Out of no where, claws tore into his back side, ripping apart his scales and slashing into his flesh. He bucked repeatedly to get Daidhl off him, but the little dragon clamped his jaw on Hoss's neck. Sharp, jagged teeth tore into his throat, cutting off his air. Panic seized Hoss as he swirled around repeatedly, trying to throw Daidhl off, but the Inquistain hung on tight. He was stronger than normal, thanks to the Mistonian.

Hoss's eyes fluttered shut. Dizziness overtook him. His strength fled from him and his wings collapsed. Daidhl released him.

Hoss fell faster and faster. He tried to flap his wings, but they failed to respond. Moisture from the clouds wet his body, making him shiver. He slammed into a tree, and leaves and twigs scratched and ripped his skin. He landed hard onto the ground. A loud crunch rippled through him—more agony seized his breath. His wings were stretched out and bent awkwardly beneath him. His talons and legs curled up next to his underbelly.

Every time he took a breath, wetness flowed down his chest. He inhaled the scent of metallic. Blood. His blood. He was dying.

All he could think about was Agnes—how sweet her lips were, how sleek she was when he entered her, and how her nails dug into his shoulders when she came, screaming his name. He would have wanted to taken her one more time. But then images of the past victims blocked out her loving memory and terror gripped him as he thought of what that bastard would do to her.

Hoss vowed to come back as a ghost to terrorize Daidhl.

15

"You're mate is in trouble."

Agnes didn't need the ghost to tell her that. He wasn't the only one in trouble.

Frank hurried through the crowd, his wide shoulders, forcing people apart who were jamming around the balcony door. Dread sunk into Agnes's heart. What had Hoss done?

Her brother seized her arm. "What the hell are you keeping from me?"

Her eyes widened. "What?"

He led her into an empty bedroom. "Your boyfriend just jumped off the balcony."

She shook her head in disbelief. "No, you're lying."

"Am I? Then I saw something that couldn't possibly be real."

Her throat turned dry, and she could barely speak. "What was it?" She knew. She knew before he said it.

"He transformed into a fire-breathing dragon. I have to be hallucinating. Dragons aren't real. There must be something in the air vent." His voice was hard, but fear flickered in his eyes. Sweat glistened off his temples.

He knew what he saw, but wouldn't believe it. Just like when they were kids, and she would tell him about ghosts.

"Agnes." Laura's ghost formed on the other side of Frank. "You must leave. Hoss is dying. Only you can save him."

"No, that's not true."

"I know what the hell I saw." Frank ran his fingers through his hair.

Before she could stop herself, Agnes blurted, "I wasn't talking to you."

He frowned. "Then who?" He dropped his shaking hand. "A ghost? Is that who you think you're talking to?"

Agnes tilted her chin, not willing to be drawn back into another humiliating argument.

"Damn it, Agnes. You're determined to dig your own grave."

"Are you going to tell them what you saw?"

He glared. "No. I'm overtired. It doesn't make sense. Unlike you, I'm not willing to flush my career down the crapper and report something that's not real."

She winced.

"Agnes, stop arguing with him. Hoss is dying. He needs you."

Laura's urgent voice pulled her away from the same age battle. Ignoring Frank, she said, "Tell me where he is. I'll call nine-one-one."

"He's a dragon. Only you can save him."

"You're nuts." Frank left and headed straight for the captain.

A tornado of frustration twirled around inside Agnes's gut. "I can't save a dragon." Tears formed in her eyes. She looked through Laura's flimsy form to watch Frank spouting off to the captain. Her career was definitely going to be in the toilet.

"Go now!" Laura urged.

"I can't...save a dragon." Her voice choked.

"Yes, you can. You're his mate."

She wiped a heated tear off her cheek. "How do you know?"

"I am an empath." She pointed. "He's in the park next to the station. Go before it's too late." She faded away, which prompted Agnes into action.

She wouldn't let Hoss die. She didn't know what she could do, but she had to try. She headed for the door, but a cold voice stopped her in her tracks.

"Detective Malloy."

She looked up into Captain Morgan's harsh eyes.

"Yes, Captain?"

He gestured toward the hallway. "A word with you."

"Yes, sir."

"I've been trying to be patient with you, Detective, but this has gone on for long enough. First, you lost our number one suspect."

"What suspect? You mean Hoss?"

"Hoss, is it? You've become very familiar with him."

Agnes braced her shoulders and held his gaze.

"Somehow he escaped from the balcony," he said. "There could be another murder, which would be all your fault."

She flinched. "But Captain?"

"Don't *but Captain* me. Second, Frank tells me you've been talking to a ghost at this very crime scene."

She opened her mouth to blurt out that Frank saw a dragon, but what would be the use? Frank would only deny it, and her accusation would only pound another nail in her coffin.

"I can't keep protecting you, Detective. I gave you a chance, but you blew it. You're officially off the case. Go home."

Years of hard work whooshed around in the garbage disposal. "You can't do that, Captain. I've figured something out. He's copying the Jack the Ripper murders."

"You're sure?"

"Yes. I am." She pulled out her iPad. Her hand shook as she went to the screen. "Here look. I can prove it."

"Captain Morgan, the mayor wants to talk to you." Frank held out his phone.

"I'm sorry, Agnes," the captain said. "We'll look into it. Go home before I have to take your gun and badge."

Frank gave her a triumphant look. She forced the tears back. He'd finally won. Tomorrow, she'd either be handing out parking tickets or typing reports.

"Agnes," Laura whispered in her ear. "Go, now. Hurry."

Not wanting to lose the only man who believed in her, Agnes rushed down the hall and into the elevator. She pushed the button, wishing she could make it go faster. When the elevator opened, she flew out the doors. Several police officers looked at her curiously, but she didn't care. Tears stung her eyes and cheeks. A ball of shame formed in her throat, and she drew on every nerve not to burst into sobs.

She'd fought long and hard for this position, but it was all for nothing. Her captain had totally lost faith in her, and Frank would be back smearing her name. He'd probably claim that she or Hoss put something in the ventilation system to make him hallucinate. Would anyone else even notice that he was the only one?

She ripped open her car door and hauled out of the parking lot, wheels screeching. She had to get to Hoss. She couldn't lose him too.

She didn't remember driving to the park, her mind was so preoccupied with fear, disappointment, and anger. She flew out of the car and hurried. People were gathered around something. She knew right away it was Hoss.

The voices of crowd blurred. "What is it...? It's a dragon... Is it real?"

Agnes rushed past some curious teenagers, who all had excitement flashing in their eyes.

But excitement was the last thing that she felt. Hoss's tongue hung out of the side of his jaw. His eyes were closed. His wings were crumpled underneath him and his legs curled into him like a dead lizard.

She knelt next to him. "Oh, Hoss. I'm so sorry. I should have gotten here sooner."

"Lady, what are you doing?" someone asked.

But she ignored them. The sobs wouldn't be held back. Her shoulders shaking, she stretched on top of him, her tears flowing onto his scales and her fists clenched. She listened for his heartbeat, but only silence echoed in her ears. He was gone. She was too late.

Everything had gone wrong. The Mistonian would keep on killing, and she'd be powerless to stop him. She needed Hoss to help her catch or destroy him. Her heart bounced against her chest as if to make her listen to the truth.

That wasn't the only reason. She needed him as a man. He believed in her when no one else would. With him, she didn't feel like a freak, and now he was gone.

She kissed his still chest. "Hoss, come back to me."

But it was a foolish gesture. He was gone, and he wasn't coming back. Her hair covered her face, hiding the quiet sobs that shook her body, wishing she could have turned back time and done things differently.

A quiet thump-thump-thump broke through her sorrow. She slowly lifted her head. Hoss's eyes fluttered. She held her breath. Was she imagining it? Was the moon playing tricks on her?

"Over here, Officer! Over here! There's a dragon! I swear!"

Red lights flashed as a police cruiser pulled up into the park. Hoss slowly transformed from a dragon into a broken man. His right arm was twisted underneath his back and blood congealed around his throat.

"We need an ambulance right now!" Agnes yelled. She immediately put his head back and started to do CPR. "Don't die on me now." She put both hands over his chest and pumped, hoping to get a pulse. She pinched his nose and exhaled into his mouth.

"Breathe, damn it, breathe."

"The dragon... He's gone," a confused voice said over Agnes's shoulder.

A teenage boy was looking around to see where a dragon limped off. He pointed. "See, that's where he fell."

A bright light shone on Agnes, and she winced, holding her arm out. "Get that light out of my face." She looked down at her sweater, and her stomach churned. Blood coated her jean jacket as if she'd just taken a bath in it.

"What happened?" A police officer moved his flashlight down Hoss's torn up body. "God, it looks like a coyote or a dog ripped him to shreds."

No, a possessed dragon. But Agnes kept the thought to herself. In a clear voice, she said, "I'm Detective Malloy. Send for an ambulance."

"Dispatch," the officer said. "Send for paramedics." He turned around. "Okay, everyone back. Give them some room."

She put her head on his chest, praying for a heartbeat, but was only met with terrifying silence.

"Don't leave me. Help is on the way."

Agnes's voice strained to be heard.

Her palms pressed down again and again on his broad chest. Weariness settled into her arms, and sweat leaked into her eyes.

Live, damn it.

But his stubborn heart refused to respond.

"Come on, Hoss, I need you."

Nothing stirred.

She pinched his nose and breathed into his stiff lips. A warm puff of air rushed into her mouth. Or maybe that was wishful thinking.

A siren screeched in the distance. "They're coming, Hoss. Hang on."

Stormy silence killed her hope. Her frantic rhythm hadn't slowed. Laura had said she was the only one, who could save him.

Her prophesy better damn well be right, or Agnes would hunt her in the afterlife forever.

The pokey paramedics finally drove up onto the grass. They rushed over with a stretcher to where she sat, holding Hoss's lukewarm hand.

"Excuse, ma'am," one of them said. "Let us take over."

She reluctantly stopped pressing onto Hoss's large chest and allowed the paramedics to do their job. They put an oxygen mask over his bruised and scratched up face. One of them cut away Hoss's shirt to hook up a defibrillator. Two pads with electrodes were attached to his large chest.

"Hit it," one of them said.

The paramedic closest to Hoss hit the defibrillator. A charge zapped and Hoss's body arched up.

His partner used a stethoscope to listen for Hoss's heartbeat. He shook his head. "I've got nothing."

Hope died in Agnes's heart.

"Hit him again."

Hoss's body arched up higher again and slammed back down onto the ground. His body still silent.

The paramedic put the stethoscope on Hoss's chest again. "Again."

Hoss lurched high into the air, his arms and legs flailing.

Tears blurred her vision, and she hurriedly wiped them away. She'd seen this many times before—paramedics trying to resuscitate someone who was already gone, but this time, it was personal. She gasped for breath and looked at her blood-stained hands. Dizziness gripped her, but she shook her head, trying to stay focused. She was a hardened detective and should be used to this.

The realization hit her. She cared about Hoss. She cared about him a lot.

"I have got a heartbeat," he said. "Let's get him to the ER."

Agnes thought she'd never heard such sweet words.

A deadly whisper killed her joy. "He'll never survive. I'll finish him and then, I'm coming for you."

Chills rushed down her back. She whirled her around, her gun drawn, but no one was behind her. She trembled uncontrollably, furious she couldn't stop. She hadn't imagined the voice. Daidhl was here, and he planned on murdering Hoss, then her. What if he were here and she couldn't see him?

She couldn't leave Hoss alone. He was barely alive and extremely vulnerable. She looked wildly around the ambulance, afraid Daidhl was already inside, ready to unplug something. She held on tight to Hoss's hand, refusing to let go. Normally, she would have called for a guard, but how could she say that the killer was invisible? Nobody would ever believe her.

She needed help, and the only one who would believe her was her stubborn-ass brother. He had seen Hoss transform. She had to convince him. Without his help, they'd both be dead.

The ambulance pulled into the emergency entrance. She got out first, then a couple of staff wheeled Hoss into the hospital.

"He'll be okay," one of the paramedic said.

His reassuring voice failed to calm her fears.

"I hope so. He's so pale."

She followed the paramedics into the emergency room where an admitting nurse greeted him.

"What happened, Detective?"

"He was attacked. I'm not sure by who," she lied, wringing her hands.

The young nurse escorted her to the waiting room. "As soon as I know anything, I'll report to you."

Agnes nodded. She kept looking over her shoulder afraid she'd hear that same taunting voice. She had no way of knowing whether the bastard was here or not.

A few minutes later, the nurse came out with a bag. "We're not sure what these were, but they seem to be some kind of weapons. We thought you should have them, Detective."

Agnes slowly took the bag. "Thank you. I'll take it from here."

Inside the plastic bag was the belt that Hoss wore around his waist. There was also a weapon that looked like a Star Trek phaser or a Star Wars blaster, and a sophisticated tape recorder with a screen. Anyone else might think they were fake, but Agnes knew better.

She thought about taking them out and examing them, but she had no idea what they could do. Maybe she could use them to convince her brother that dragons were real.

She walked to the back of the corner and prayed that Daidhl wasn't following her. Luckily, she hadn't smelled anything sour. But that didn't mean anything. Hoss hinted that the creature had hidden talents. She quickly dialed Frank's number.

"What do you want, sis?"

"I need to talk with you."

"I'm not going to try and get you back on the case."

His voice was so hard and cruel she almost hung up, but what she had to say involved Hoss, Kathy, and all the other women who were in danger.

"I'm not asking you to."

"Then what? I'm a little busy right now."

"I need you to come to Lutheran Hospital right now."

"Why? Are you hurt?"

At least he had the decency to show some concern in his voice.

"No, but Hoss was attacked. I don't know..." Unfortunately, her voice cracked. She cleared her voice. "Frank, I don't know if he's going to make it."

"I told you that you were too involved in this case."

Trying not to lose her cool and get in a screaming match with her brother, she counted to ten before she answered.

"Are you there?" he demanded.

"Yes. Frank, listen. If you care about me at all, the killer's after me. He said he'll kill Hoss, then me. I need you to come to the hospital. You're the only I can trust."

She held her breath, waiting for him to answer, waiting for him to reject her.

"I'll be there in ten. Don't go anywhere. Understand?"

She exhaled. "Yes. I'm in the waiting with room with lots of people."

They hung up and all she could do was sit like the other worried men, women, and children, eager to get news of loved ones.

She gripped the plastic bag. Every time a nurse would come out, she hoped it was about Hoss, but the nurse would call someone else. Hoss was an alien dragon. What if the doctors were unknowingly killing him?

She studied the weapon and strange equipment in the plastic bag, wondering if any of them had the ability to heal him. She wanted to try, but what if she zapped half the hospital into the netherworld? She couldn't stand waiting any longer.

"Excuse me," she asked a nurse and an orderly sitting at a small desk. "Is there any news of a man brought in here earlier? I'm Detective Malloy and need to talk with him. His name is Hoss."

She clicked on her keyboard. "He's still unconscious. Right, now, the doctor is giving him a blood transfusion."

Agnes's gut tightened. What if a human blood transfusion would kill him? Shit, this was getting worse and worse.

She looked at the bag, trying to figure out what to do. Somehow Hoss had communicated with a ship, but she had no idea how.

The glass doors opened, and Frank walked in with a terrible scowl. He grabbed her by the shoulders. "I got here as fast as I could. Now, tell me what all this nonsense is about."

People in the waiting room, the nurse, and the staff gave them curious glances.

Her face turned hot. "Would you keep your voice down?"

He released her. "How can I?" he whispered. "When you keep digging yourself a hole in believing this mumbo-jumbo crap?"

"Come here. I want to show you something." She led him to the corner of the room where an elderly gentleman slept in a chair.

Frank folded his arms across his chest. "Talk."

She hated when he did this, but she refused to be rattled. She held up the plastic bag. "These are Hoss's weapons."

He raised his eyebrow. "You brought me all the way down here to play Star Wars?"

"Will you listen? You didn't imagine what you saw."

He glanced around nervously as if he were afraid people were listening.

"Yes, I did. I was overtired."

But she could hear hesitation in his voice and in his eyes.

"No, you're not. Hoss is an alien. A dragon from outer space."

"Sis, you're scaring me. I think you've seen one too many space movies." He narrowed his eyes. "You need to be serious. Women are being slaughtered, and you're acting like you're staring in a Star Trek episode."

"Excuse me, miss?" The admitting nurse interrupted. "Hoss is awake. He's asking for you."

She grabbed his arm. "Come on, Frank."

He broke free. "No, I've got to get back to work. I have a murderer to catch."

Suddenly, Agnes inhaled spoiled milk. "He's here. I can smell him."

"What the hell are you babbling about, sis?"

The old man who had been sleeping raised his head. Agnes couldn't move. His eyes were gold, the same color as Hoss's.

He curved his mouth into grin, revealing sharp, jagged teeth. Smoke puffed out of his nose and whooshed into Frank's face. Frank coughed, tears welling in his eyes.

He laughed. "Catch a killer, boy? You couldn't catch a cold if you tried." With that he transformed into a slender younger man, then vanished.

Cold air brushed over them, and the glass doors opened by themselves.

The nurse gasped and put her hand on her chest. "Oh, my god."

The staff and other people in the waiting room stared at them as if they were off their rocker. One woman pulled her two-year-old boy who wandered over toward them. Shit, they hadn't seen the creature.

Frank's face slowly drained until it was ashen. "What just happened? God, I feel sick."

Agnes met his frightened gaze. "That was your killer. He smells like sour milk."

He fixed his tie, his hands trembling. "No, I just imagined it."

"Then I imagined it too," the nurse whispered.

"Neither of you did." Agnes touched the nurse's shaking hand. "You're safe. He won't come after you." She hoped it wasn't a lie. He'd only hunt her if she were someone's mate.

"I think I better go sit down."

Agnes led her back to the front desk where the orderly gave them a curious gaze.

"Is everything all right?" he asked.

"I'm just tired," the nurse said. "I need some coffee." She kept staring at the front doors as if she was terrified the old man would return.

"Frank, we need to go see Hoss now."

Her brother took a deep breath. "Okay, I'm ready to listen."

She expected to find Hoss on death's doorstep, dying from a human transfusion, but when she walked into his room, her mouth dropped. He sat up on his bed, his color had returned, and despite the ugly stitches running along his down his throat, he smiled.

"I thought you would be half-dead," she managed to squeak out.

"Don't you know, a dragon has eleven lives."

Frank entered. "Don't you mean a feline has nine lives?"

Hoss frowned. "I'm not a cat." He glared. "What's he doing here?"

"I called him. Hoss, the killer was in the waiting room."

"What?" He started to get out of bed.

Agnes grabbed his arm. "Wait, there's more."

"Then spit it out."

"I know I'm going to be locked up in a psych ward if anyone hears this," Frank muttered. "But he can physically change his appearance."

"Not only can he become invisible," Agnes said. "But he can transform into another person. He was even able to hide his smell. I didn't know it was him until he changed."

"Then, things just got a lot worse." Hoss rubbed the bridge of his nose. "He wanted you to see him."

"Why?" Frank asked.

"Because this creature feeds on emotions, and in this case, terror. We have to be very careful. He can transform to look like anyone of us at anytime."

Frank looked between both Agnes and Hoss. "How do we know who's who?"

"We don't," Hoss said.

His harsh voice sent chills down Agnes's spine.

Silence overcame them like a dark shroud. The only voices were the ones outside the room. Agnes glanced warily at the door, realizing that any of the doctors, nurses, patients, or visitors might not be who they think they are. The killer could be inside this very room, listening.

Agnes took her iPad out of her bag and motioned for Frank to come closer to Hoss's bed.

"What?"

She put her finger up to her mouth for him to remain quiet. He rolled his eyes, but followed her lead. She quickly typed on her iPad

We need a code word that only the three of us can share. The word is *Jack*.

They all nodded in agreement and just as fast, she deleted the word, praying the killer hadn't been looking over her shoulder, grinning.

❧ 16 ❧

The smug detective would regret telling the nurse that she'd be safe. He waited patiently outside...

Betty Wible couldn't sit still. Every time she typed, her hands shook. All she could think about was the old man and his shiny, pointed teeth. His golden eyes had been filled with hate. Besides the FBI agent and the detective, why had she been the only one who could see him?

She'd seen things before. Shadows out of the corner of her eye that no one else had seen. Once, she saw a glowing mist. But she'd never seen anything like the evil man.

"Betty, are you all right? You haven't stopped shaking for the last hour." Bob Martin, one of the staff, looked at her with overly concern. He was a by-the-book kind of guy, and she had no intention of telling him what she'd seen.

"I'm fine. Too much coffee," she lied.

The next couple of hours dragged on. She was glad when the detective, agent, and the drop-dead-gorgeous patient all left. With them gone, she didn't have to keep remembering what she'd seen.

Her shift ended at midnight and her car was parked on the

other side of the hospital. She thought about asking Bob to walk her to her car, but his shift wasn't over until one, and she wanted to get home and have a glass of wine.

Besides, the detective had said that the killer wasn't coming after her. Had he been Arvada's Ripper? That's what the press was calling him.

She took a deep breath as she stepped out into the night area. Cool air rushed over her, and she pulled her coat tighter around her waist. When she exhaled, she could see her breath. The killer had been targeting women in Arvada. She was in Wheatridge, and she lived in Lakewood.

I'm safe. I'm safe. I'm safe.

She repeated this over and over in her mind, but the words failed to keep her heart from leaping in fear. The less than a five minute walk to her car, but it might as well been miles aways. She jogged a few steps, and then forced herself to a slow walk.

No one else was out there and with everyone leaving, she could see her Chevy truck parked under a street light—a beacon of hope.

She broke out into a run, her breath echoing against her ears, but a loud flapping sound took over. She looked around, and no one was behind her. But the man had turned invisible. He could be right behind her.

The flapping grew louder as if overhead. She looked up into the sky but only cold stars and an eerie moon peered down at her.

She pumped her arms faster and pushed her legs harder, as if Tolkein's ringmasters of Mordor were after her. Her feet pounded against the pavement and her beating heart strained to break through her ribcage. She'd never run this fast. Her breath was heavy and dizziness gripped her.

God, don't have a heart attack.

She fumbled to pull her keyless remote out of her purse. Her hair had fallen out of her ponytail, teasing her mouth. Tears of desperation blurred her eyes. She grabbed her remote, spilling the contents of her purse onto the pavement—her wallet, brush, and car keys.

"Damn it!"

She shoved the contents back into her stupid purse. Slowly, she realized the flapping had stopped. She whirled around.

Only her heavy breathing marred the unusually silent night.

A cloud covered the moon, blocking it out. Only the stark street light lit up the parking lot.

No one was here.

She hit the remote and the loveliest sound of the truck clicking filled her with joy. She'd been imagining the sound. She reached out to open the door, but someone seized her wrist and whirled her around. She stared up into the same hateful, golden eyes.

"Miss me?"

She opened her mouth to scream, but terror died on her lips.

Daidhl smiled. "Detective Malloy claimed you were safe. You'll pay for her insolence."

The killer slashed her throat with a blade, hacking through her windpipe and severing her blood vessels. Blood poured down her throat like a waterfall. She collapsed into a pool of death.

🦂 17 🦂

S tuck at the police station, Hoss sat miserably in a
conference chair going through crime photos. His back
ached where Daidhl had ripped him open, not to mention
his tender neck that felt like it had been Daidhl's favorite chew
bone. With the slightest turn, the crude stitches pulled. At least
the doctors hadn't killed him.

Human blood was close to Zalarian's but not perfect. His
empty stomach churned from the blood transfusion, swishing
around a burning nausea. What he needed was some alone time
with his mate, so he could continue to heal. According to Damon,
mates had the ability to heal each other. He hadn't believed it
until Agnes had touched his hand in the emergency room, sending
a healing spark through him, reducing the agony.

That had only been a caress. What could she have done if she
had kissed him? But all he could do was look at his curvy mate,
who was within grabbing distance. Every instinct pushed him to
take her, but they were in a small glass conference room with her
brother, who watched Hoss warily.

Hoss sighed, forcing the pain and desire back into his mind.
Frank had requested an isolated room away from the other inves-

tigators. And, he'd asked that Agnes be put back on the case. The captain had thought it strange, but granted the request. After all, Frank Malloy was the one asking. If Agnes had asked, she probably would have been turned down. Hoss couldn't understand how the police couldn't see what a smart and gifted investigator they had in Agnes.

Frank studied his team that worked diligently on the other side of the glass wall. "Do you think the unsub could be one of the investigators?"

Hoss followed his gaze. "Possibly. By the way, you can stop calling him an unsub? We know who the killer is."

"I'm still trying to wrap my brain around that he's an alien."

"Deal with it," Hoss growled. "Daidhl is getting bolder. He believes he's unstoppable."

"So far, he's been right," Frank mumbled.

Agnes examined crime photos. "There has to be something we're missing."

Frank tossed another photo on the table. "We've been through these a thousand times. Hell, the FBI computers aren't able to figure out patterns. None of the victims had anything in common."

"I told you that they did," Hoss said.

Frank glared. "Oh, that's right. They're designated mates for your dying planet. Forgive me if I forget that little fact."

Every muscle hurt and weariness bore down on Hoss. The condescending agent spurred his bone-tired dragon. He clenched his fists. "You're trying my patience."

Frank stood and slapped his hands on the table. "And you're trying mine. According to you and my sister, the killer isn't even human and he's slaughtering innocent women."

The captain frowned on the other side of the glass wall and opened the door. "Is everything all right in here?"

Frank lifted his hands. "Yes, we're fine." But his voice shook with anger.

"Captain, we're just all a little tired." Agnes glanced nervously at Frank.

"Fine," the captain said, "but let's keep our cool."

Frank turned his back, obviously trying to gain control.

"Hoss," Agnes asked. "You don't look well. Your face is turning pale." She gingerly put her hand over his.

Another pang of healing shot through him, enough to distract him from his stiff neck. "Just a little hungry," he lied. Or more like a half-truth. What he needed was for her to kiss him or make love to him, but he couldn't blurt this out. Not with her brother only a few feet away and a bunch of law enforcement outside. He'd have to suck it up.

"Would you like something to eat or drink?"

As long as I'm feasting on you.

Hoss shoved the thought behind him and in a strained voice said, "Sure."

She glanced at Frank, who leaned over the table, studying a map of Arvada. "I could order us take-out. Would pizza be okay?"

"Fine," he said absently.

"As long as it has meat on it," Hoss grumbled, wishing instead he could lick every inch of her body.

"I'm sure the other investigators are starving. In the mean time, I could get us some bottled water. Frank, would you like a bottle?"

"Yeah, I would."

She walked out of the room to check with the others. As far as Hoss could tell, no one had eaten in the past four hours. Grisly murders didn't exactly make anyone hungry.

Frank leaned his shoulder against the wall. "My sister shouldn't be here. She's a caregiver. Not a cop."

Hoss got up from the table and walked over to Frank. "You and I are going to have a serious disagreement."

"You're right. When this is over, if we all get out in one piece, you're not taking my sister to your desolate planet."

Hoss flashed his gaze over Frank and smirked. "You're going to stop me?"

"With everything, I got in me."

"Why? You treat her like she's a freak."

"She is a freak."

Hoss crowded him against a wall. "No, she isn't."

"You don't get it, do you? My father and I have tried to make her normal, so she wouldn't get hurt. We were both afraid something would happen to her. That she'd get into some kind of trouble she couldn't get out of." He pushed Hoss back hard.

Pain jolted his neck and put his back in spasms. He'd underestimated Frank's strength. Maybe there was a reason why so many cops respected him.

Frank went nose-to-nose with him, not seeming to care that Hoss was at least six inches taller. "And now, it's come true. If she didn't have this damn ability, none of this would have happened."

"What the hell are you talking about?"

"Things happen to her that don't happen to other people. She attracts weirdness."

Fury burned in Hoss's heart at her brother's disdain for Agnes's ability. He walked away from Frank to keep from strangling his thick neck, but he thought about what the condescending agent had just said. A hunch formed in his mind... Maybe a long shot, but the idea was all that he had to go on.

"What kind of things have been attracted to her?"

"I don't know. Ghosts, psychics, weirdos...*you*."

Throbbing pain shot up Hoss's back. He turned away and slid into a chair to look at the photos one more time. "I'll ignore that last part, but maybe you're on to something."

"Excuse me?"

"Maybe the killer doesn't know who our mates are. Maybe our mates have abilities. Maybe they're the only ones we can mate with. And the Mistonian knows this."

"I thought the unsub, I mean Daidhl, was one of your people?"

"He was. The Orion's navigator." Bitterness swept over him. "He was a good Zalarian, but he's possessed by a Mistonian. Daidhl never would have done these things. He wasn't a violent person."

Frank snorted. "I bet."

Hoss didn't argue. The humans didn't know Daidhl, wouldn't know the kindness in him. Even though he annoyed the hell out of Hoss with his constant sprouting off annoying facts. He never should have been a crewmember of the Orion. He wasn't strong enough to fight off the Mistonian. "Do you know if the other women had a psychic ability?"

"How the devil would I know?"

"Did you ever research it?"

Frank folded his arms across his chest. "No. I would think the FBI computers would come up with that fact."

"Like Agnes, what if the women didn't report their abilities, tried to keep them a secret? Would the computers pick that up?"

The stubbornness in Frank's eyes left, replaced with uncertainty.

Agnes walked into the conference room. Her face pale and tears glistening in her eyes.

Both Hoss and Frank burst out, "What's wrong?"

Agnes opened her mouth, then turned away. When she faced them, her lower lip trembled. "There's been another murder."

"Damn it!" Frank glowered. "Where?"

"Lutheran hospital. The admitting nurse... Betty Wible."

"The same one who was with us when we saw Daidhl?"

Frank's voice trailed off as if he was witnessing the event all over again.

Agnes nodded.

He looked between her and Hoss. "But that's out of his hunting grounds."

Agnes shook. "I told her she'd be safe." She put a shaking hand up to wipe away her wet cheeks. "We should have...put...a guard on her."

Not caring if he offended Frank or the other law enforcement, Hoss wrapped his arms around her quaking body. "It's not your fault."

She didn't try to fight him, her fingers curling into his shirt. "He mutilated her body. It's my fault... It's my fault..."

Just holding her made the stiff pain in his neck decrease. He could turn his head without the stitches pulling on his flesh. The connection between them was growing stronger, moving too fast. He kissed the top of her head. "No, it's not."

He rubbed her back, trying to soothe her. If Frank spouted off another quip, he was liable to forget he was Agnes's brother. But instead, Frank looked down at his shoes.

Agnes took a quivering breath. "I'm okay."

Hoss knew she was far from okay. Her body still trembled uncontrollably, but surprisingly, her voice was strong. She was tough.

Frank cleared his throat. "Where was she found?"

Agnes straightened her shirt. "In the parking lot of Lutheran hospital underneath a pine tree."

"Who called it in?" Frank asked.

"No one," she said slowly. "Betty told me."

Frank narrowed his eyes. "Betty the victim?"

Hoss put his hand on her shoulder, hoping to give her strength.

She braced her shoulders. "You heard me."

Frank spread his arms out wide. "Is she here?"

Agnes hesitated, but then blurted, "She is! She's standing right in front of you."

"Bull shit."

The air turned cold and heavy. The hair on the back of Hoss's neck stood straight up. He looked around the room, but even with his dragon eyes, he couldn't detect anything. Chills blew over his skin. Something was here.

Suddenly, papers flew off the table, turning into a whirlwind, then circling Frank. He staggered back, swinging his arms to ward off the attack.

"What the hell's happening?"

"She's angry. Really angry." Agnes slowly turned her arm over to reveal three long red slashes.

"My Fates!" Hoss carefully examined her arm. Anger erupted inside his gut. "Leave her alone."

Agnes put her hand over his. "Please stop. She's not just angry. She's still frightened. Very frightened."

Frank gathered papers off the floor. "Why? Daidhl can't hurt her anymore."

Agnes pulled down her sleeve, concealing her scratches. "I know, but she can't rest until we catch him."

"You need to get medical attention for those wounds," Hoss said.

"I will later. Right now, we need to go to the crime scene."

Frank put the discarded pictures and paper onto the table. "Wait a minute. You've never said anything about a ghost ever scratching you before."

Hoss frowned. "Is that true?"

"Yes. So?"

"Can you talk to her now?" Hoss asked excitedly.

"Yes, but why?"

Frank organized the papers and photos, then put them back in order. "We have a theory about the victims that we might have missed."

Hoss cast him a warning look. Frank just couldn't admit that he or his law enforcement officers or the computers could have passed over an important clue.

He focused on Agnes. "Frank and I think the women were

psychics or had some kind of special ability. Did Betty possess this?"

"I don't know. I've never encountered a spirit this powerful so soon after their death. I–" She held up her hand as if to silence them. "Betty says sometimes things would fly around when she was angry."

Frank put the photos and reports in a folder. "That's an understatement."

The captain burst into the room. "We found another body."

"Where?" Frank demanded.

"Lutheran Hospital's north parking lot. The body was found underneath a large pine tree near the victim's truck."

The captain hurried out of the room, barking orders. Frank straightened his tie and cracked his neck. He clasped Agnes's arm. "I was wrong. I'm sorry."

Before she answered, he left. Hoss tipped up Agnes's chin. "Maybe your brother's not such a bad guy."

"I never said he was. I just wanted him to believe in me."

"I know." Unable to resist, his lips brushed over hers, allowing himself to indulge in the moment at her sweet taste. The nausea roasting in his stomach lessened.

Agnes put her hands on his chest and pushed him away. "What are you doing? Not now." She breathed hard, and her voice was thick with passion, not anger.

Hoss put his hand on her lower back. "Let's go."

They left together while Frank went with his partner. Agnes insisted on driving and despite his male pride, he allowed her. He wasn't sure how great he would have been at driving a car anyway.

She turned out of the parking lot, the siren on top of her car screaming. "Do you think Frank's apology means he believes what we've been telling him?"

He shrugged. "Maybe."

She gripped the wheel tight, her knuckles turning white. "Figures. I was an idiot in thinking I could trust him." She circled her head around as if trying to get rid of tension.

"Don't write him off yet. Here, let me try." He reached over and rested his hand on the back of her neck. "Your muscles are bunched up tighter than a constricting plake."

"What's a plake? Another creature on your planet?"

"Yes, its an eight-legged creature that can curl up into a tight ball." He massaged his fingers, and she immediately raised her shoulders, as if to ward him off.

"Relax."

"Not going to be able to until we catch the bad guy."

He pressed his fingers deeper into her flesh, trying to work out the bunched up knots. "Listen. While you were gone, I confronted Frank about always putting you down for your abilities."

She glanced at him. "You did?"

"Yes, I'd had enough of him bullying you."

Gratefulness flickered in her eyes, but she didn't say anything.

"You'll be surprised on what he said." The tension in her neck began to unravel. He needed to get her alone and do a deep massage that made her forget everything but his fingers.

"And?"

"He claimed that both he and your dad constantly worried about you. They were worried you'd get hurt by using your ability and that's why they wanted you to stop. In their strange domineering way, both he and your father were trying to protect you."

"I never got that feeling."

"Maybe you weren't listening."

She jerked, knocking his hand off her shoulder. "You weren't there, Hoss. You don't know what it was like... The rejection, the pain, the humiliation..."

He flinched at the anger storming through her voice. She turned the car, the wheels squealing. He had to grip the door handle to keep from bashing his head onto the dashboard, and his heart slammed against his chest.

For the rest of the three minute ride, they were silent. A distant gulf formed between them, and he was powerless to stop it. He thought she'd want to know that her brother and her father had really cared for her, but he'd guessed wrong. He stepped right in the middle of a stinging set's hill.

They drove into a parking lot, swarming with cop cars. She parked the car without saying a word and got out, slamming the door so hard the car shook.

He slowly got out, not sure how to handle her anger, but he immediately inhaled the stench of death. He hurried over to Agnes, who didn't turn his way.

Agnes headed for a group of officers, who were huddled around a truck that was parked next to a large pine tree.

Agnes whipped out her badge. "Detective Malloy. Lead investigator."

The officers parted. A tarp covered a body.

A tall dark officer flicked up his lapel. "Officer Jameson." He tilted his head. "She's over here, Detective. It's pretty gruesome."

"I need to see her," Agnes said.

"Yes, ma'am."

He led them over to the tarp and peeled back the tarp. Hoss's stomach tightened. Agnes released a small gasp.

"Lord of mercy," Agnes whispered.

Hoss reached for her hand, but she jerked it away.

Daidhl must have been in a frenzy of hate. Betty's throat was savagely cut six or seven inches from left to right. She was disemboweled, her intestines lay over her right shoulder. Unfortunately, the intestine was nicked, spilling fecal matter behind her shoulder. Unlike Reese and Nybo, who had straight cuts, Betty's cut were jagged as if Daidhl had released all of his anger. He was getting worse, more vicious, more ruthless.

Betty's face was ghastly. The bastard had cut triangles below each eye, peeling back the flesh. They reminded Hoss of arrows pointing to the eyes. He mumbled underneath his breath, "Was there a significance to this?"

"Devil worship, possibly," Officer Jameson answered. "Never seen anything so barbaric."

Betty also had cuts on her eyelids. The left one was at least a half-inch long.

The ground was soaked with her blood. From the waist down, she was naked.

"Did you find her pants or underwear?" Agnes asked.

Officer Jameson shook his head. "No. We haven't found anything around the body."

Agnes glanced at Hoss. "I'm betting he took some organs."

"Can I talk to you in private?"

She nodded and allowed him to lead her away.

"Did Betty tell you what was missing?" he asked.

"No, but I can see why she's so angry. I wished he'd gone after me rather than her." Her voice was soaked in guilt.

An image of Agnes having her face carved up, organs slashed out of her body, and her throat grisly cut, flashed in his mind, sucking the air out of his lungs. Anger and fear surged through him like an exploding star. He gripped her arms tight, not caring who saw. "Never. Never. Say that." He shook her hard, trying to knock some sense into her guilt ridden soul.

"Hoss, stop."

He growled, the dragon threatening to burst through. "Do you hear me? I won't lose you."

"Hoss, please."

Suddenly, he inhaled the sharp smell of sour milk. He abruptly stopped, but wrapped his arm around her waist pinning her to him. Several officers gave them strange looks.

Officer Jameson approached them. He gave Hoss a dubious look. "Detective, is anything amiss?"

Agnes gritted her teeth. "Hoss, will you release me? You're embarrassing me."

"Sorry." He reluctantly obeyed. The sourness was growing stronger. "Do you smell it?"

"Yes," she nodded. "Daidhl's definitely here. He could be anybody, or he could be invisible."

"Stay close."

Frank and his partner, Jeff Holmes, arrived, and hurried over to the crime scene.

"Oh God, Jeff. I smell spoiled milk." Frank pulled out his gun.

"So?"

"The killer's here."

Jeff looked around, his steely gray eyes scanning the parking lot. "Are you sure? I don't see anyone suspicious."

"I told you, he smells like spoiled milk."

"And I told you you're crazy."

But Frank wasn't looking at Jeff. He was staring over Agnes's head, his face pale.. "Shit, Agnes! Move!"

Officer Jameson's brown eyes turned gold, and he opened his mouth to reveal sharp, jagged teeth. "You're dead, Detective."

The evil voice was loud enough to catch the officers, who all pulled out their police specials.

Jameson lunged for Agnes, his hand turning into a claw. He scratched Agnes, his talons ripping through her shirt and flesh. She cried out, holding her arm. Blood seeped through her fingers.

Hoss yanked Agnes out of the way, shoving her behind him.

Hoss growled. "You'll pay for that, Daidhl."

Jameson released a mechanical laugh, stirring Hoss's rage. Puffs of smoke exhaled out of his flaring nostrils. He tried to transform, sweat rolling down his face, but his muscles and bones wouldn't move. He was trapped in humanoid form. It had to be the damn human blood.

"You're too weak to stop me." Jameson swung, his fist hitting

Hoss square in the jaw. He fell to the ground, smashing his head against the pavement. The world swam around him.

Frank roared, "No!" He ran toward Jameson, firing repeatedly.

"Don't!" Hoss yelled as pushed himself up. "You'll only make him mad."

Frank stepped in front of Agnes, shielding her with his body. Ignoring Hoss, Frank continued blasting Jameson. The noise was deafening, blocking out Hoss's pleas for Frank to stop.

Bullets riddled Jameson's body. He released an angry shriek, then vanished.

"Die, Agent Malloy."

Frank flew back almost twenty feet.

"Frank!" Agnes screamed.

His gun fired into the air, and he crashed into his car. Blood gushed down his nose like a wild river. His eyes fluttered shut.

Realization slammed into Hoss. While everyone else was stunned, including Frank's partner, Frank hadn't panicked and had jumped into action, sacrificing himself to save his sister. He really was a hero.

Hoss managed to pull out his eruptor and aimed it where Jameson had last stood, but if he wasn't there, he'd kill the stunned officers.

Blood drained from Jeff's face. "Holy shit!" He whirled around, waving his gun in search of a visible target.

"Get control of yourself!" Hoss glared, afraid the idiot would start shooting wildly.

Agnes ran over to her brother's crumpled body. "Frank! Frank!"

Her tough exterior shattered into a thousand pieces.

Hoss swayed as he followed her. "Stay calm. Terror is what Daidhl wants." He tightened his grip on his eruptor ready to blast Daidhl into the Netherland if he made another ugly appearance.

Jeff rushed past Hoss and pulled out a radio. "Agent down.

Send the paramedics." He gestured toward the shocked officers. "Fan out."

They came out of their stupor and followed his orders with guns pointed ahead, slowly moving across the perimeter of the parking lot.

Hoss fell next to Agnes. "I'm sorry."

Tears streaked her face. "I can't believe it. He risked his life for me."

"I know." He'd never forget what Frank did for her. He hadn't been lying. He really did care for his sister.

"He can't die. He just can't."

"You need to stay calm. Daidhl could be lurking, ready to attack again."

She shook her head. "Betty says he's gone."

"Why didn't she say something earlier?"

She wiped her cheeks. "I told you. She's frightened, afraid that Daidhl can still hurt her."

Her voice was calm, but frustration flickered in her eyes and her jaw was set taut.

"She damned well could be right," Hoss muttered.

"Frank, Frank! Can you hear me?" Agnes clasped her brother's hand. "Please, don't leave me." She bowed her head.

Although he felt like he'd been just thrown around in a black hole, Hoss's senses were on red alert—his ears keen, his eyes eager, his fists ready... Ready to protect his mate at all cost. What if he couldn't transform into a dragon? Daidhl would be unstoppable. Hoss needed help.

A siren shrieked and rotating red lights lit up the dreary lot.

"The place is secure," Jeff stated, but his voice shook. Obviously, the man wasn't totally convinced.

Hoss hid his bitter laugh. The idiot didn't know how wrong he could be. Daidhl could be watching, despite what Betty's ghost said. Betty wasn't exactly stable.

The paramedics rushed over to Frank with a stretcher, while Agnes was still holding his hand.

"Excuse me, ma'am."

"Yes, of course." She released Frank's hand.

She watched them examine Frank and check his vital signs with a sorrowful gaze. Hoss wanted to tell her words of comfort, but none came to mind. She clasped Hoss's hand with her shaking one. He squeezed hers, hoping to send her comfort.

She raised her chin. Tears and anger glistened in her eyes. "We need to end this."

"I promise you we will."

He frowned. There was no weapon on Earth that could kill a Mistonian. He needed to contact Taog. He recalled another Mistonian invading Earth and mere humans had destroyed it, but he couldn't remember how they had done it. Studying history wasn't his forte. The creature hadn't possessed the same great powers of Daidhl, but it would be a start.

Agnes's captain approached them. Hoss didn't remember him being here. Was this the captain or was it Daidhl again?

He spotted the brown sedan and thought perhaps it was the captain's, but wasn't sure. He thought that Frank had been driving that car.

The captain looked down at Frank as the paramedics worked on his still body. "Agnes," he said softly. "Go with Frank." He gestured toward Betty's corpse. "For now, there's nothing else you can do. Go with Frank. He needs you."

Agnes bit her lip. "Thanks, Captain. You'll keep me in contact, especially with what the coroner finds?"

"Of course. And I am sorry, Agnes. Frank was one of the best."

She puffed out her chest. "He's a Malloy. He's not dead yet, Captain."

The captain bowed his head. "Yes, you're right."

Hoss sniffed, but didn't detect anything sour, but then again, he hadn't detected the scent earlier until it was too late. He wasn't sure if this person was the captain. He had get Agnes far away from him.

Daidhl had said she was next.

"Come on, Agnes." Hoss forced himself to keep his voice normal. "We'll follow behind the ambulance."

Agnes glanced over at Betty's exposed body. "If Frank dies, I'll kill the bastard."

Death reflected in her eyes. She meant it. And Hoss would be at her side to rip out the Mistonian's black heart.

❧ 18 ❧

gnes clutched Hoss's hand in the dreary waiting room. The smell of antiseptic and anesthetics nearly choked her lungs. The buzz of the television that nobody watched made her want to scream. People murmured among themselves. The emergency doors opened as more people filed inside. Each time she held her breath, wondering if Daidhl had slipped inside to finish the job of murdering her brother.

He was winning, and they were losing.

The horrific scene in the parking lot replayed over and over in her mind–Jameson's eyes turning gold and opening his mouth to reveal sharp teeth, Hoss being thrown to the ground like a rag doll, Frank rushing to protect her with his life, her being helpless. Now, Frank lay in the hospital struggling to live.

She should have reacted faster and shot Daidhl rather than being a too-dumb-to-live-heroine. It was her fault Frank lay dying.

Pain throbbed in her arm where Jameson had scratched her. He clawed her like a demon, nails ripping into her flesh so deeply they required stitches. She shivered uncontrollably.

Hoss glanced at her. "Are you cold?"

"A little," she lied. Terror had turned her blood to ice.

He wrapped his arm around her, his warm body fighting the fear threatening to take her over. She was a cop like her father, a Malloy—bred to laugh at the enemy.

But not this time.

She hated this place. The hospital only reminded her of death and pain and misery. Hoss had survived the attack, but he was an alien. Frank was strong, but he was only human. He might not make it because of her. Her chest hurt as if it were being crushed.

She looked around the room. Daidhl could be anywhere—a staff member, another admitting nurse, an Hispanic family huddled in one corner, an elderly woman surrounded by two younger women, or a mother with two young children... Any one of them could be Daidhl in disguise, just waiting to look at her with those deadly golden eyes and a mouth full of sharp teeth.

She dragged her iPad out of her purse and flicked through the pictures, trying to figure out a clue. Anything that they'd missed. Usually there was a pattern, but the victims had different color hairs, different positions, different social status. What was the connection?

Hoss hugged her tightly, distracting her. He kissed the top of her head, sending chills down her spine. "Are you okay?"

"Such a silly question. No."

He hung his head, his dark hair hiding his face.

"I'm sorry. For the first time, I feel the killer is slipping through Justice's fingers. And now, he's gone after my family. Frank's all the family I have left..."

Her voice trailed off as a well of pain swelled in her throat.

The victim's hollow pictures and grisly crime scene failed to prickle anything with her. "This is so damn frustrating. I'm not getting anything from these photos. Usually, I do. Why when I need my abilities to work they're on vacation?"

"I don't know." He rubbed her knee. "Frank seems to be a tough agent. He'll pull through."

"Will he? People told me my dad would. They were wrong."

"I'm sorry. It's hard to lose someone you love."

The hardness in his voice caught her attention. She really didn't know much about him except that he was an alien shapeshifter and a member of a space Confederation and had the best six-pack of abs she'd ever seen.

"Have you lost someone you cared about?" she asked softly.

"Hasn't everybody?"

"That's not an answer."

"I don't like to talk about my past. Talking doesn't change anything."

"Sometimes talking will ease the pain."

He shrugged. "Hasn't been my experience."

"Do you have any brothers or sisters?"

He raised an eyebrow. "Not going to let this drop, are you?"

"We're probably going to be here for a while, and I just realized I really don't know anything about you."

"I could say the same for you."

"No, not true. You know about my brother and father, and that my mother's dead. You know I live alone, and I'm not the greatest housekeeper."

He sighed and unwound his arm from around her shoulders. The warmth he'd provided slowly ebbed way. He leaned back in the metal chair that could barely contain his large, muscular body.

"Let's just say my childhood wasn't a happy one."

"So, do you have any brothers or sisters?"

"No, but I consider my best friend to be more like a brother. I don't know what I would have done without him."

She looked carefully around the room, not wanting anyone to hear their conversation. "Is he part of the crew of the Orion?"

He shook his head. "He's the personal guard of our queen."

She opened her mouth to ask another question, when the double doors into the emergency room opened. A tall pretty nurse held a clipboard. "Detective Malloy."

Agnes grabbed Hoss's knee hard to steady herself.. "I'm Detective Malloy."

Her confident voice hid the turmoil rolling around inside her.

As the nurse walked toward them, Agnes thought she was the shadow of death, ready to tell her that her brother had died. Pain severed her heart, pulling it in two.

"The doctor would like to talk to you about your brother."

Hoss put his hand over hers, and she glanced up at him, needing his strength. She couldn't talk, afraid she'd become a blubbering mess.

He helped her out of the chair and locked his arm around her shoulder. She quickly shoved her iPad back into her purse, then forced her trembling legs to move.

"This way," the nurse said.

Dread breathed on the back of Agnes's neck. She was too afraid to pray, too afraid to hope, and too afraid to be alone. She leaned against Hoss, hungering to listen to his beating heart. He'd made it out of here alive.

God, don't let them take Frank.

Damn, she'd prayed. What if her prayers backfired like they had with her father?

The nurse led them to a quiet room down the hall. Their footsteps softly echoed on the cold tile floor. Nurses quietly talked among themselves at the large station. Bells and dings irritated Agnes nerves. The sound of deep breathing of ventilators brought back memories of her father. His face covered by a plastic mask. The doctor telling her that only the machine was keeping him alive.

Both her and Frank had made the decision to end his life. It had been the most difficult thing she'd done, but at least Frank had been there. She hadn't had to make the decision alone.

Her legs betrayed her, her knees buckling.

But she didn't fall. Hoss held her up. "I've got you."

She nodded. He had her.

The nurse opened a door. "The doctor will be with you shortly."

Agnes nodded.

"Thank you," Hoss said as he led her to a chair next to Frank's bed.

She couldn't hide the tears. Frank lay still on the bed with the creepy plastic mask over his face. There was a plastic tube inserted between his ribs. A heart monitor was hooked up to his chest and steadily beeping, but it was so slow. She covered his icy hand with her shaking one.

Black and blue bruises covered his cheeks. He was unrecognizable.

Hoss stood behind her and rested his hands on her shoulders.

"Detective Malloy?" A blond woman entered with her hair pulled back in a neat bun, wearing a white smock. She had a stethoscope around her neck.

Agnes wiped her tears. "I'm Detective Malloy."

Somehow she found her hardened cop voice.

The woman reached out her hand. "I'm Doctor Rush."

Agnes reluctantly let go of Frank's hand and took the doctor's warm one, but it was her sorrowful green eyes that shattered any hope Agnes had.

Hoss stretched his arm over Agnes's head. "I'm Hoss. Detective Malloy's friend."

"Glad you're here for her." Dr. Rush glanced at Frank then back at Agnes. "I'm afraid I don't have good news for you, Detective."

Agnes bit her lip. If she talked, she'd burst into tears. She wanted to shake Frank, wanted to hear his sneering voice, wanted him to scold her for not being a hard-nosed detective. She desperately wanted to tell him how much she loved him.

"Go on," Hoss answered for her.

"Agent Malloy has suffered massive internal injuries. His spleen is severed, and one lung is punctured. He has numerous broken ribs. We've tried using a chest tube to drain the air in his lung, but he's not responding. He's bleeding internally. When he crashed into the car, the force broke his back and his spine may be severed. If he does recover, there's a chance he could be paralyzed."

Agnes gasped. "Oh, my God." Frank confined to a wheelchair. It would kill him. This was all her fault. She should have reacted faster. Why did Frank always have to be a hero?

"What are you suggesting?" Hoss asked.

"We need to operate to stop the bleeding and to repair his lung. I need your consent to operate, since you're the next of kin."

Agnes nodded, unable to speak.

"I'll draw up the necessary papers."

Agnes stared at Frank's ashen face, wishing he would tell her what to do. The ventilator pumped softly matching the ping of the heart monitor. She put her hand on her sweating forehead, trying to decide her brother's fate.

"Agnes," Hoss said.

She jumped, not realizing the doctor had left.

He knelt in front of her. "There's another alternative."

She croaked, "What?"

"The Orion. Our surgeon, Tryker, has far superior abilities than this hospital."

She sniffed. "You going to beam him up like on Star Trek?"

"I don't know what beaming is."

She pulled her iPad out of her bag and found a Star Trek episode. "See, it's an energy pattern when your molecules are scattered one from point and resembled at another point."

He frowned. "No, we don't do that. Sounds like you could end up with your ass between your shoulders and your head between your legs."

She blinked, then burst out laughing. The image shoved her awful decision away. Tears streamed down her face.

He squeezed her shoulder. "Seriously, he could be taken to the Orion or a medical ship could come here."

Somber reality returned and her laughter died. She wiped the wetness off her cheeks, studying Frank's overly still body. "But he's so weak. How could you move him?"

"I wouldn't. Moving a fragile human in need of medical attention isn't my area. It's Tryker's."

"Would Frank be able to walk again?"

"Possibly. But with these crude facilities, he's got no chance."

"Then, how would he get there?"

"By space ship, of course. Let me contact Tryker."

"Why didn't they come earlier?"

"Because Daidhl sabotaged the Orion. If we're lucky, he'd didn't damage the medical ship."

Agnes sat next to Frank, holding his cold hand. Her brother would slowly die in a wheelchair. He was such a proud man. His life was the Bureau. He'd hate being behind a desk. He was all action—always had been. She had to make a decision. There was no one here to make it for her.

Hoss pulled out what looked like a cellular phone and flipped it open. God, this was really like Star Trek.

"This is Hoss to the Orion. Come in, please."

"This is Topaz. What's wrong?"

"My mate's brother is badly wounded. I'm asking permission for him to be taken to the Orion. Can I speak to Tryker?"

"Permission granted."

"Tryker, here. What's your emergency, Hoss?"

"Daidhl attacked Agnes's brother. According to the medical doctor, he's got internal bleeding, lacerated organs, and a severed spine. Can you help him?"

"What are the doctors planning to do?"

"They want to operate."

"By Fates, don't let them!"

Agnes jumped at his angry voice.

Hoss glanced at her and held up his hand as if to silence her. "What do you want me to do?"

"The Orion is still disabled, but I can bring a medical shuttle down to you. But you have to get him out of there before it's too late. If they operate before I get there, I'm not sure there will be much I can do."

Hoss looked at Agnes. "You heard what he said. What do you want to do?"

"I don't know. How can we move him?"

"I can stun everyone here long enough for us to get Frank out of here. The choice is yours."

Not what she wanted to hear. Dr. Rush returned, holding a clipboard. "I need you to sign before we can get started."

Agnes glanced at the clipboard, at Hoss, and at Frank. He grew paler by the minute. He risked his life for her. She'd an opportunity to save him, but what if it went wrong? What if Tryker couldn't save him or made him worse? Frank would never forgive her. But then again, he'd never forgive her if she threw out a way for him to be whole again.

Butterflies flapped against the sides of her gut.

"Detective?" Dr. Rush asked. "Did you hear me? We're preparing for surgery, but I need you to sign these papers before we can do anything."

Betty slowly materialized next to Frank's bed. She looked at him. "If you take him away from here, he'll be safe. You don't know who will be in the operating room. Daidhl needs to feed on your pain and murdering your brother would satisfy his hunger."

Acid burned a hole in Agnes's gut, killing all the fluttering butterflies. She never thought of Daidhl lurking in the operating room ready to slice and dice up her brother. Right or wrong, there was only one answer.

She squeezed Frank's hand. "Please forgive me in what I'm about to do, brother." She looked at Hoss and braced her shoulders. "Send for Tryker."

"Tryker, I'll send you the coordinates to meet us."

"Over and out."

"Also, bring down any files on the Mistonians. I remember hearing there was one on Earth that was destroyed."

"The medical shuttle can only house myself and my staff. I'm sorry, but I'll bring down the files."

Confusion settled in Dr. Rush's eyes. "What are you doing?"

Hoss pulled out his weapon. "Saving Agent Malloy's life."

She put her hands up. "Please, don't."

Hoss fired. A blue ray streamed out of Hoss's gun and hit Dr. Rush. Her eyes rolled back in her head. She collapsed on the floor.

Agnes rushed over to her and put her fingers on her wrist. "There's a pulse."

"Of course. I said I would stun her, not kill her. Don't you think I know the difference?"

She slowly released Dr. Rush's wrist, hoping she hadn't made a terrible mistake. "Will Tryker really know how to save my brother?"

"You're going to have to trust me."

"A scary proposition," she muttered.

"Do you want to do this or not?"

She slowly stood. "I said, yes."

"We need to move now."

She clasped his arm. "I'm putting my brother's life in your hands. Don't make me regret my decision."

"You won't."

Agnes looked at the machines hooked up to her brother. "He needs oxygen so he can breathe."

"Then we take what we can with us." He headed for the door, then glanced over his shoulder. "Wait here."

A bright light burst outside and Agnes nervously paced in the room. God, what was she doing? What if she were making a giant mistake, costing her brother his life?

"You need to trust him," Betty said. "He won't let you down like you did me."

Agnes winced. "I'm sorry."

Betty's eyes faded to all black except for her fiery red pupils. "Sorry is only a word. I'm dead." She flicked her hands down her body. "My corpse horribly disfigured. I can't even look at myself."

Agnes hung her head. "I didn't know he'd come after you. I didn't know you were a mate."

Her puny apology was barely audible.

"Obviously."

She jerked her head up and braced her shoulders. "I promise you I'll find him."

"You'd better. If you don't..." Her blue eyes changed to a fiery red. "I'll haunt you for the rest of your days."

As she faded, the room turned to ice. Goosebumps broke out over Agnes' flesh, and she shivered. She'd never had a ghost threaten her before. But Betty was right. She'd made promises she never should have made. Daidhl was sick and twisted, and wouldn't want anyone saying who he could or couldn't kill.

The door flew open. Hoss's large frame filled the doorway. "Everyone is unconscious for now, but they won't be for long." He frowned. "Why is it so damn cold in here?"

She shrugged. "Betty got mad."

He looked around the room cautiously. "She's not stable."

She dabbed Frank's feverish face with a cloth. "I know. She still blames me for her death."

He rested his hands gently on her shoulders. "It's not your fault. It's Daidhl's. I don't know why she can't see that."

Not believing him, she wrestled free of his gasp. "What do you propose we do?"

Her shrew voice cut any tenderness between them.

He sighed heavily behind her, his breath brushing over the back of her neck.

When he walked over to look out the door, the hurt was gone

and he was back to being a soldier. "We'll wheel Frank into an ambulance and then take him to my ship. "You're kidding right? Don't you think the police and hospital staff will know we stole an ambulance?"

"You got a better solution?"

"No." She frowned. "How come your space ship hasn't been discovered?"

"It's invisible. So, is Daidhl's."

She shook her head. "Of course it is."

He went over and kissed her briefly on the lips, sending warmth through her shivering body. She unscrewed the oxygen tubes that were hooked up to the ventilator. She had just enough medical training to hopefully keep her brother alive.

This was a huge risk. If Tryker didn't get here soon, she'd end up an only child.

They lowered the bars on Frank's hospital bed, the banging put her nerves on edge. For such a larger-than-life man, Frank was so vulnerable. At the police station, he was everyone's hero. And now, he was hers, too.

He couldn't die. He just couldn't. He was Frank Malloy.

If she'd made the wrong decision, she'd never forgive herself.

Hoss pulled the bed away from the wall, while Agnes wheeled the oxygen tank next to Frank's bed. Without the heart monitor, she wasn't sure how strong his heartbeat was. She had to strain to hear his shallow breathing.

When she walked out of the room, she gasped. Men and women were sprawled out on the floor, over the desk, and slumped up against the walls.

"Agnes, I promise they're fine. We need to move before they wake up."

She nodded. "We'll be on video."

"No, we won't. I melted the cameras."

"You don't think they'll notice?"

He smiled mischievously. "That's why we need to move."

They carefully maneuvered Frank's bed through the bodies. Agnes had to move several arms and legs to keep from running over them. In the waiting room, she winced at several children lying over their toys. She was going to hell for this.

The emergency room doors were open and an ambulance waited. Within a few minutes, they had Frank loaded inside.

"You need to drive," she said. "I have no idea where your ship is."

His cheeks flamed crimson. "I'm not very good at driving."

"You don't have to be good." The streets were relatively quiet since the busy morning traffic hadn't started yet. Hopefully, no one would notice a slow jerky ambulance. Besides, she wanted to be by Frank's side.

Hoss shifted from one-foot-to the other like a nervous little boy. "You don't understand. I've never driven before."

She hung on tight to Frank's limp hand. "I'm not leaving Frank alone in here. For all we know, Daidhl could be inside."

"Fine, I'll stay with Frank, while you drive."

His sharp voice and stiff stance made her want to strangle him, but she gave in, since they didn't have time to indulge in a stupid argument. She reluctantly released Frank's hand. "Where the hell am I going?"

"My ship's in a field outside the city."

Frustration built up inside her like a simmering volcano. "Hoss, that doesn't tell me much."

He pointed. "Go northwest."

She rolled her eyes. "Do you remember anything about where you landed?"

He rubbed his lower lip. "There was a bunch of houses. I think I saw a sign that said five parks or five larks or something like that."

"I think that's a housing development." When she'd been on patrol, she responded to a couple of domestic squabbles. The houses and town homes were upscale, and the community pool was nicer than some of the recreation districts'. "It's about a fifteen-minute drive from here."

"I'll set my transrecorder to my ship's coordinates. It will tell us when we're getting close."

"How long will it take for Tryker to get here?"

"Less than four hours."

She tucked Frank's blankets around him and wiped his hair off his ashen face. What if four hours was too long? What if an hour was too long? Helplessness dug into her heart like a pickaxe. "I hope Frank can hang on that long."

"He will." He ran his hands down her arms, making her shiver. He tilted his head. "Let's roll before we're both behind bars."

Hoss lowered his head and crawled into the back of the cab. She had to bite her lip to keep from laughing. He looked like the Hulk, trying to fit comfortably in a refrigerator.

She flashed him a sweet smile. "Comfy?"

"Loads. Dragons always like to be squished into a trash compactor."

She laughed, then closed the doors.

Agnes drove carefully out of the parking lot, making sure to look both ways. More cars zoomed down the street. She hesitantly glanced out the window to see if anyone recognized her. None of the cars slowed down. Satisfied they were safe, she pulled out onto the street.

A police car whizzed past them, and she sucked in her breath. Her fingers clutched the wheel so hard her knuckles threatened to burst through her skin. In the rearview mirror, she watched the car turn toward the crime scene. Worse, the captain and Jeff were walking into the emergency room. Her career just burst into flames, but she didn't care, not if she could save Frank's life.

Taking a deep breath, she kept her eyes on the road, especially since she was stuck behind a public transportation bus. Cars and trucks were bumper-to-bumper in the other lane. Even with her blinker on, no one made room for her. She rolled her shoulders and counted to ten to not lose her cool.

Deal with it.

She wasn't going anywhere.

A billboard of some ambulance-chasing attorney caught her attention. She smiled as she quickly called Kathy. Her phone rang and rang and rang, but no answer. Kathy always answered her phone in case a client was in trouble. Something was wrong.

Agnes slammed her phone down on the seat next to her police special. Normally, she would have called Tom to check on Kathy, but since she was guilty of patient-napping—not possible.

The rocking bus moved slowly but steadily. Agnes put on the brakes, and her gun slid next to her thigh, but her phone fell on the floor. Damn!

Hoss pounded on the window.

"Christ!" Her adrenaline spun out of control. She jumped, her knees bumping on the steering wheel. The wheel jerked out of her hands, and the ambulance drove up on the sidewalk. She swerved it back on the road. Sweat rolled over her. "What! Is Daihl..."

"No. Sorry." He motioned. "Keep going straight on this road."

She glared at him through the rearview mirror and gritted her teeth. He was damn lucky he wasn't sitting next to her. "I know where Five Parks is." She glanced over her shoulder. "How's Frank?"

"Still breathing."

For now, she thought. Still shaking, she gripped the steering wheel and re-checked the speed limit. Oh, crap!

Red lights flashed behind her, and she held her breath as she pulled over to the side. Luckily, they raced past her.

"They're looking for us?"

"Obviously. Definitely a man-hunt. Hopefully, it will take them awhile to discover we stole an ambulance. Tryker better get here soon."

"Even with light speed, it's going to take him a couple of hours."

"Then we need to hide out until he gets here."

"Where? We're in a red and white ambulance."

"Not if we park in an urgent care facility. Plus, if Frank gets bad, we can rush him inside." She drove him to a medical facility near Five Parks. She parked the ambulance in the back.

"You don't think anyone will notice we're out here?"

"Do you have a better idea?"

He shrugged. "No."

She got out of the front seat and joined Hoss in the back of the cab. Frank's face was paler and his breath was shallower. Hoss's knees were jammed up to his chest and his arms pressed to his side. She was squished between him and her brother's bed.

"He's not doing too good." She looked at the urgent care facility where there were doctors and nurses ready to help. "Maybe we should..."

Hoss clasped both her shaking hands. "Do you want your brother to live, to walk again?"

"How could you ask that? Of course, I do."

"Then, trust me."

She blurted, "That's a two-way street, which you keep thinking is only a one-way."

"What the hell does that mean?"

She yanked her hands free. "You keep telling me to believe in you. You even convinced me to risk my brother's life, but I really don't know anything about you except for your mission and the Orion. I need more, Hoss. I need you to be real. To know that I made the right decision with Frank."

"Do you really think this is the time to deal out secrets?"

She crossed her arms over her chest. "According to you, we have a couple of hours before your medical space ship gets here. How else would you want to spend the time?"

He leaned closer and ran a finger down the outline of her breast. "I can think of one way to reduce your stress."

His breath brushed over her, heating her skin and making her squirm. The cab grew smaller and stuffier. She shoved him away hard. "You're not serious, are you?

He bumped his head on the ceiling. "Ow."

She flicked her hand. "I can't even move. It's hotter than hell in here. My brother's half-dead. And you want to have sex?"

At least he had the decency to look sheepish. He rubbed the back of his head, mumbling. "Hey, I was just trying to break the tension."

Not caring one bit, she pulled her thick hair off her neck just to feel a tiny bit of cool air on her sweltering skin. "Can you please contact the doctor to see where he's at?"

He rubbed her back. "He'll get here in time."

She rested her head in her hands. "Easy for you to say."

He whipped open his communication device. "Tryker, how long before you reach us?"

"Three hours."

He closed it.

She jerked her head up. "What do you call that thing anyway?"

"It's a telicator."

She grabbed the device out of his hand. "Looks just like a cellular phone, but lighter."

He carefully removed the telicator from her hands as if she were a small child about to break it. "It's a little more powerful than anything on Earth."

She glared. "I realize that." She slammed her palms on her knees. "This is so frustrating just sitting here sweating. Daidhl could be anywhere stalking his next victims."

"Relax." He gently massaged the back of her neck. "We already know two on the list—you and Kathy."

Her coiled muscles unwound so she could think. She sat straighter. "That reminds me. I need to check on her."

The phone rang. "This is Kathy Strong, attorney at law. Please leave your name and number, and I'll return your call as soon as I can."

Agnes left a message. She brushed her thumb over the screen of her phone. "I hope she's okay."

"Does she always answer her phone?"

"No, not necessarily, especially if she's in court or meeting with a client."

"I thought she was in protective custody."

"She is. That's what worries me. She should have picked up. Wait, you could go change into a dragon and check on her!"

He shook his head. "I can't."

"Why not?"

"In the parking lot, I tried to transform into a dragon, and I couldn't. I think the human blood prevented me from changing." He clasped her hand. "Listen to me. Daidhl is more powerful than me. We have to be damn careful—especially you."

She bristled. "I can…"

"No, you can't." He squeezed her hand. "Promise me you won't do anything stupid."

She narrowed her eyes. "Stupidity is not part of my vocabulary."

He slowly released her hand, but doubt remained in his eyes.

Prickles ran down the back of her neck. Kathy was in trouble. Her gut instinct shot into overtime. "Shit, now, what do we do? I know Kathy's in trouble. She needs our help."

"You need to calm down. What would you normally do?"

She took a deep breath. "Investigate. It's just so hard when people you know are threatened or hurt."

"I know."

"Do you? Sometimes I'm beginning to wonder. Or are you just saying that to make me feel better."

"Back to secrets again. I lost my parents when I was a kid. Does that help?" he snapped.

She winced then reached for his clenched fist. "I'm sorry, Hoss."

"Don't." He yanked it back, bristling up like a cactus. "See, talking doesn't help."

"Okay, I get it. Let's review the case then." She pulled out her iPad.

"What are you doing?"

"Looking at Jack the Ripper's next victim, Mary Kelly. She was found in her apartment gutted like a deer. She was his last known victim."

"Was he caught?"

"No. There's all sorts of speculation on what happened. He got arrested for another crime or he himself was murdered or he left London. This is strange. According to my research, after the 1888 murders, there were two murders that happened a year later. The other two murders were of Alice McKenzie and Frances Cole, but there's arguments on both sides on whether or not these were Jack the Ripper killings."

"The real question is what side is Daidhl on."

"I know. I'm calling Kathy again." She called again. "Answer damn it! Answer!"

"Aren't the police guarding her?"

"Yes, but you saw what happened in the parking lot."

"If you want we could drive there."

She glanced at Frank's pale face. "He could get hurt again." If he did, he wouldn't make it.

"I'll protect your brother, I swear."

His voice was so confident, but Frank's heroism had put him in this position.

"Hoss, Daidhl said he was stronger than you. It's because of the blood transfusion, isn't it?"

"I think so."

"Will Tryker be able to change you back to your normal self?"

"That's the plan."

She drummed her fingers on her knees. "Your doctor isn't going to be here for another three hours. I just can't sit here, either. Not if I can save Kathy's life. Let's go check. Wait. You asked the doctor to bring some files on the Mistonians. Why? I thought there were no weapons here that could kill them."

"There aren't, that I know of, but I remember hearing something about two humans that were able to destroy one. I'm not sure if the story was true or not. I asked Tryker to bring everything we had on the incident."

She moved her shaking hand to her gun, wishing she could pump him full of lead, wiping his sneering smile off his face forever. But so far nothing the department had done effected the bastard. "So, there's a chance we can destroy him."

"Yes, but it's a slim one."

Her hope wavered. Daidhl had the annoying knack of beating them at their own game, but one thing she learned in the field—a suspect's overconfidence led to their downfall. "But it's all we've got. Let's go check on Kathy."

"You'll drive?"

"Obviously. When this is over, you're going to learn how to drive, Mr. Drive-a-phobe."

"I'm not afraid." His stricken face said the exact opposite.

She rolled her eyes. "Oh yeah, I believe you."

"Daidhl could be anyone there—even Kathy."

The thought of Kathy smiling and revealing sharp-pointed teeth made her shiver. "That's a lovely thought."

Another win for Daidhl.

19

Daidhl flew up to Kathy's balcony after Hoss and his mate departed. They'd checked on Kathy and left.

Stupid mistake.

Arvada was slowing down with the setting sun. People were driving home from work. Below, there were two cop cars and most likely cops camped outside her front door. But their little attempts to stop him would be useless.

Tonight, Kathy would not escape him. He was tired of playing these hide and seek with her. He took out a blade out of his jacket and quietly entered the apartment.

He frowned. Damn! A man sat on a leather couch, holding a gun in his hand. He wasn't supposed to be here. Most likely, Hoss's curvy detective had insisted he'd be inside. The cops were moving up their protectiveness of his prey.

He could easily ambush the man, but he wanted time with Kathy. He didn't want to be rushed like he'd been with Annie Watkins. If he killed him, he ran the risk of alerting the other officers.

He needed to be patient and come up with a plan. He sat in

one of Kathy's patio chairs and studied the man through the patio door as a plan formed in his head.

He was about to open the door when the Zalarian's telicator started to beep. A Zalarian ship was entering the Earth's atmosphere, trying to contact the now dead navigator and Hoss.

The man grabbed his gun and slowly got off the couch. He pulled back the blinds with his weapon drawn.

Daidhl smiled as the fool relaxed and headed back to his roost. Before the telicator could beep again, he carefully opened it.

"Hoss, are you there? This is Tryker."

"I read you. Where are you?"

"Less than fifteen minutes from your coordinates. How is your mate's brother?"

"He's still alive, but barely."

Impressive. Not many humans would have survived his attack.

"Do you have the information I wanted on the Mistonian?"

Daidhl's smile faded. Hoss tried to use the entrapment cage on him once before, and it almost worked. What were in those files?

"I do, but if the entrapment cage won't help you, I'm not sure this will."

Daidhl hesitated. Could the incompetent Zalarians have found a way to kill him? They were just a bunch of flying lizards. The Kamtrinians had sworn their technology was inferior.

"We're on our way," Hoss said.

Daidl closed the telicator. Hoss and his mate would be busy trying to save her interfering brother. No one would be able to disturb him. Hunger burned in him to taste fear. It had been delicious. He wanted so much more. Let the Zalarians try to save the human. He needed to feed.

Drawing on the Zalarian super speed, he thrust open the door and slashed the man's throat before he could fire a single shot. He grabbed the cop's radio and cell phone, stuffing them in his jacket.

He whistled as he walked down the hallway to Kathy's bedroom. He opened the door to find her sleeping on her bed, her brown hair tumbling over her face.

He quietly shut the door. "Let the fun begin."

20

Hoss got out of the back of the ambulance. Dusk had centered over the fields, the air turning cooler.

Agnes raced over, looking around wildly. "Where are they? I thought you said they were here."

"They *are* here."

"What? I don't see anything. You said they would be here."

The Orion's medical ship, the Centarus, materialized.

Agnes covered her mouth. "Oh, my God." She looked up at him. "They're here." Tears swelled in her eyes.

He wrapped his arm around her waist. "I told you Tryker wouldn't let you down." He gave her a kiss, wanting to take away her pain until someone cleared his voice.

Tryker looked at him. "You have a patient for me?"

"Yes, yes." Agnes pushed away from Hoss. "He's in here. Please, hurry." She climbed into the ambulance.

Tryker leaned close. "She's quiet beautiful, Hoss. A little curvy for your taste."

Anonghos grunted, not ready to admit anything yet. Too much was at stake to discuss mating. Who was he kidding? The permanence of a true mate terrified him.

198

Hoss slowly followed Tryker, who pulled out his medical tran-srecorder. Tryker aimed the device at Frank. "I'm not going to lie to either of you. It doesn't look good, but let's get him on board the Centarus."

Agnes nodded, but didn't answer. She cast Hoss a look of pure hate. He flinched. If Tryker couldn't heal Frank, she'd never forgive him.

He'd been so confident that Zalarian medicine was far superior from humans, but nothing on this mission had turned out the way he thought. Too many women murdered, an agent down, weapons useless.

On board the Centarus, Tryker motioned for the doctors to take Frank into the operating room.

Agnes cleared her throat. "Doctor, what are my brother's chances?"

"To be honest, he has a fifty fifty chance. His vitals are very weak. Our treatment is more aggressive than yours. I hoped he'd be stronger."

Hoss went to put his arm around her shoulder, and she ducked. "Will he walk?"

"If he survives, he'll walk."

Agnes bit her lip. "If I would have—"

"Let me be straight with you," Tryker said. "The doctors may have saved his life, but he wouldn't have walked."

"Are you so sure about that, Doc? Sounds like to me I've been fed one big tale after another. If you'll excuse me, I have to go and salvage what little career I have left."

She turned to leave.

Hoss clasped her arm. "Agnes?"

She whirled around, like a black hole, slamming her fists onto his chest repeatedly. "You said he'd live."

Her force didn't hurt him physically as much as it hurt his heart. He'd broken her trust. For not wanting to end up like his dad, each time she hit, a crack split on his iron wall.

Tryker grabbed her fists. "Stop. This isn't helping your brother."

"Let go of me." She twisted and stamped on his feet.

"Tryker, let her go," Hoss said wearily.

Agnes jerked her wrists free. She walked away with her shoulders braced. A loud shrill of sirens broke the tension.

She yanked out her cell phone and stared in disbelief. "Kathy? Noooo! You fucking bastard! I'll kill you!"

Hoss rushed over to her. Agnes fell on her knees, but before she hit the floor, Hoss caught her. He ripped the phone out of her hand and his eyes widened at the grisly images. "Daidhl, you plake!"

Agnes clutched his shirt, burying her face. Her body shaking hard.

Daidhl laughed. "I got to take my time with her. Your mate is next."

With that the phone went dead.

Hoss wrapped his arms around her shaking body. "I'm so sorry." He kissed the top of her head, not caring if she cut out his heart with her fingernails.

Between sobs, she managed to say, "He-he-said he gutted her."

His dragon raged for her. Daidhl would pay for his cruelty. "Stay here with your brother. I'll–"

"No!" She pushed away and wiped her tears on her sleeve. "I'm a homicide detective. Kathy was my friend. I"ll be the one to bring him to justice."

Hoss put his hands on her shaking shoulders. "You can't arrest him," he said softly.

Hate flared in her eyes. "Then, I swear I'll kill him."

"Don't be foolish." Hoss clasped her shoulders. "Not even the entrapment cage worked on him. It's the most powerful jail in the universe. So believe me when I tell you there is no weapon on Earth that can kill him."

"Hoss, that isn't exactly true," Tryker said.

Hoss yanked up his head. "What?"

"I've been reading the logs of the first Mistonian who was killed here. The humans used an entrapment cage similar to ours, but theirs had light. In doing further research, I found that the light was the same brightness of the Mistonian's sun. The Mistonian was different than the one possessing Daidhl. Not only did it feed on the victim's fear, it sucked on their blood."

Agnes frowned. "You mean, like a vampire?"

He flicked her silky hair behind her slender neck. "I don't know what a vampire is."

"A creature that sucks your blood."

"Sounds very similar to a Mistonian."

Eagerness flashed in Agnes' eyes. "Wait a minute. How long will it take you to make this entrapment?"

"Once I discovered how the creature was killed, the other medical lab doctors and I have been working on one."

"Is it ready?" Hoss asked.

Tryker looked between Hoss and Agnes. "Yes, but it hasn't been tested. I don't know if the trap will work."

"We have to try." Agnes looked between the men. "It's not just women were saving. We're saving the mates who will continue your race."

"I'll contact the lab to bring you the weapon, but right now, I have to try and save Frank." He clasped Hoss's shoulder. "Be careful. The Mistonians are difficult to kill. May the Fates be with you."

Tryker left them alone.

"Hoss, do you think this thing will work?"

He ran his hand through his hair. "I honestly don't know. The one I used earlier failed miserably."

"Why?"

"For one thing, he was invisible, and the entrapment is designed to hit a suspect in the heart."

She paced back and forth. "I'm just so worried about Frank

and so damn angry about Daidhl that I don't know whether I'm coming or going." She braced her shoulders. "But I can't let this go, Hoss. Daidhl has gone after my friend, my family, and me. He's not going to stop."

"Agnes, this is getting too dangerous. You need to stay in the ship where it's safe and wait for Frank."

"No, I don't. If I stay here, I'll go crazy. If you're my mate, then you know staying behind will kill me."

He groaned. "Fates, you're not making this easy."

She scrunched up her face. "Oh, I'm sooo sorry. I didn't realize this was so hard for you."

"Look, I know you're brother's fighting for his life and your best friend was murdered, but I'm worried about you. I've never felt…" He turned away, not wanting to acknowledge what he was feeling. "I… I don't want to lose you."

"Because you'll lose your breeder."

He whirled around. "Is that what you think?" His angry voice changed into a loud snarl.

Agnes took a step back, putting her hand on her throat.

Crap, what the hell was he doing?

A tall Inquistain dragon in humanoid form came out of the lab, holding an entrapment cage. "Is everything all right here?"

Agnes slowly put her shaking hand down. "Yes. We're fine."

He reached out his hand. "I'm Flask. One of the scientists that helped work on this."

Her gaze focused on the weapon. She hurried over to the doctor. "Is that the ensnarement cage? God, it looks like a compact mirror."

Flask stiffened. "I assure you, this weapon is not a compact mirror."

Disbelief shone in Agnes's eyes. "Can this really capture Daidhl?"

Hoss seized her arm. "You don't know how to use it and could trap yourself inside. Plus, we don't even know if it will work. The Inquistains didn't have a long time to work on it."

Flask glared. "Despite what you think, Bravian, we are not as incompetent as you think."

"I agree," Hoss said. "Daidhl's been making a good show of an Inquistian's abilities."

"That has been unfortunate."

Agnes glared. "Look, we don't have time for a pissing contest between you two." She gestured toward the cage. "How does the thing work?"

Flask's eyes and mouth lost their tenseness, replaced with a beaming smile bigger than a proud new father's. "The light feeds on their radioactive cells."

Confusion replaced the anger in her eyes. "I don't understand."

"Thousands of years ago," Flask said. "The Mistonians had humanoid bodies. They were a peaceful race. However, a rogue comet passed their sun, making it extremely radioactive. The radiation not only destroyed their body's cells beyond repair, but it changed their race. They became more aggressive, more vengeful. Most of the population was wiped out. Those who survived, developed into gaseous forms creating a whole new species. Instead of feeding on solid forms, they feed on emotions."

"What does this have to do with the light in this weapon?"

"The sun was so powerful that they could no longer could go out during the day. The radiation would fizzle, even their gaseous forms. On Mistonia, they can only come out at night, so most of them have dispersed throughout the universe."

Agnes frowned. "Wait a minute. If you unleash this weapon on Earth, what will happen? Will it destroy us?"

Flask shook his head. "No. Since Earthlings have not been exposed to the Mistonian's sun, none of your cells have been damaged. But this light will reactivate the Mistonian's already damaged cells, which will either kill him or make him vulnerable to our weapons."

"Does the Mistonian's sun have an impact on a Zalarian's body?" Agnes asked.

Flask handed it to Hoss. "That's the flaw in this device. Our bodies were also not exposed to their sun, so the light won't harm us."

"Then, this thing's not going to work," Agnes said.

"Not necessarily," Flask said. "If Daidhl is out in the daylight in humanoid form, this could weaken him."

Hoss attached the entrapment cage to his belt. "Enough for me to kill him."

"However, if he's in dragon form..."

"It won't work on him." Agnes finished for him.

"Our dragons are much too powerful for the light," Flask said. "The light can't penetrate our scales."

"The problem is drawing Daidhl out," Hoss said. "The bastard has been lurking in darkness."

"Are you sure?" Eagerness shook in Flask's voice.

Hoss and Agnes looked at each other. "Yes," they answered.

"There's a chance, a small one, that Earth's sun may be having a negative effect on the Mistonian."

Hoss smiled. "Then, he's vulnerable."

"Good," Agnes said. "I know a way to draw him out."

Uneasiness fluttered in Hoss's gut. "How?"

She smirked. "Live bait."

He scowled. "No."

"Listen to me. We have a chance. He came out once in the daylight at Starbucks to give you Laura Nybo's uterus."

Flask rubbed his chin. "I bet that stunt weakened him."

The memory of his mom leaving him flashed in Hoss's mind. He remembered screaming at her to stay, but she hadn't even glanced over her shoulder, hadn't waved, hadn't blown a kiss—just walked out of his life forever.

Unwanted tears threatened to flow again. He cleared his throat, pushing them back. He drew on his strength to ignore those dreaded memories, but they were getting stronger. "It's too dangerous!"

Agnes winced.

Flask frowned. "You don't have to yell. We're both standing right next to you."

Glisten of sweat trickled down Hoss's temples. Fates, he was trying to stay in control. "Sorry, I don't want Agnes to get hurt." His voice shook uncontrollably.

The panic welling through his thoughts and words wasn't him. Logically, Agnes being bait was a sound idea, but he couldn't handle the thought of her being exposed and vulnerable. He'd fought too long to be a stronger dragon than his father.

"You don't have to worry about me. I'm a Malloy. I can do this." Agnes braced her shoulders. The stubborn glint in her eyes meant trouble. He groaned.

Hoss clenched his fists to keep from shaking. "You're going to get yourself killed."

"No, I'm not. You need to show me how to use this thing. Daidhl won't expect me to have it. This gives us a huge advantage."

"Total madness." Hoss put his hand over the cage, afraid that Agnes would try and grab it.

"We're wasting time." Agnes put both her hands on his chest and pushed as if to get him to change his mind.

"See," Hoss said. "You're losing your cool, which is exactly what Daidhl wants."

"Because you're not using your head." She faced Flask. "Who is in charge here?"

"It's still Topaz, even though he's back on Zalara. We report to him."

She narrowed her eyes at Hoss. "Then it's his decision. Contact him."

Flask pulled out his telicator. "Captain, this is Flask. Do you read me?"

"Topaz here."

Hoss grimaced. He knew what Topaz would say. "Flask, she's my mate. It's my decision whether she's put in mortal danger."

"You explain it to the captain."

"What's going on?" Topaz demanded.

Before Hoss could answer, Agnes snagged Flask's telicator. "Captain, this is Detective Malloy of the Arvada Police Department. I'm Hoss's mate."

"I know who you are."

"Agnes, no." Hoss reached for the telicator. "It's not his decision."

"Yes, it is. He's your superior."

The captain interrupted. "Hoss, shut up, so I can hear what's she saying. That's an order."

Hoss threw up his arms in frustration.

Agnes flashed Hoss a superior look then she proceeded to fill the captain in on what was happening.

Anonghos's telicator beeped. He glared at Agnes, who was on the other side of the room, taking deep breaths.

This was ridiculous. He yanked his telicator out. "Hoss, here."

"Is it true what your mate said?"

"It's too dangerous, Captain."

"I asked you a direct question."

Hoss hesitated. He could lie, but what good would it do? "Yes, Captain."

"Then you know what must be done. We can't afford to lose any more mates."

"But I could lose mine."

"I suggest you figure out a way to protect her. Think with your head, not your cock. That's an order, Hoss. If any other mates are murdered, I'll hold you personally responsible. Do we understand one another?"

"Understood," he grimaced.

Agnes handed Flask his telicator. "What will happen if another woman is murdered?"

"It means he could be sentenced to death," Flask said.

"What!"

"We're facing extinction, Detective. Every mate we lose, means our population grows smaller." He clasped Hoss's arm. "I suggest you follow the captain's orders. You're a good chief of security." He bowed slightly at Agnes. "If you'll excuse me, Detective, I better return to the lab to see if Tryker needs any assistance with your brother."

"Yes, of course."

Hoss and Agnes stood studying each other. He still hadn't taken his hand off the cage. Warring emotions threatened to burst through his tight chest.

Agnes broke the silence. "What happens if I die?"

"The captain said all mates. That would include you."

She frowned. "He's serious?"

"Yes. Topaz doesn't have a sense of humor."

"Then, we better find a way to keep me safe. I don't want anything to happen to you, because of me."

"Don't worry. I'm hard to kill." He wrapped his arms around her waist, glad she didn't pull away from him. Her curves fit perfectly against him. "You're determined to do this?"

"Yes, I am."

He framed her face between his hands and whispered her name silently. He captured her stubborn lips, kissing her long and hard, afraid this would be the last time he would taste her. She balled her fingers up in his shirt. He brushed his lips over her temples, her eyes, her cheeks, the corners of her mouth, branding her every feature on his heart. Her lush heat drew him inside. The kiss deepened, turning desperate, bruising, urgent. Their tongues were hungry to claim each other. Agnes threaded her fingers through his hair. He crushed her to him, lifting her toes off the floor, then twirling her around in a final dance.

All Hoss knew was that she was his mate, a chance for him to find some happiness in one bed, rather than a host of empty ones. He'd so long denied falling for any woman, but none of them had been his fiery mate.

Agnes pulled away, panting. "We need to get going. Before he kills again."

Hoss looked down at her flush face, wanting to memorize every line, every curve, every lash. Her parted lips begged to be taken again. What if this was last time he looked at her alive? His heart pounded faster than ultra drive, and he realized hers matched his. She was as terrified as he was, but determined to do her job. She was so brave, so foolish, so stubborn.

"Promise me you won't die," he said.

She sighed and looked toward the lab where her brother had gone. "You know I can't promise that. Any call I respond to as a cop could mean my life. But what I can promise you..." She put both her hands on his cheeks and stood on her tippy toes.

He kissed her again, wishing he could make her forget this foolishness. Let him go after Daidhl.

Once again, she broke off their kiss. She ran her fingers through his hair. "I promise I'll fight to live."

It wasn't what he wanted to hear, but her promise was all she would give him.

❧ 21 ❧

Agnes sat at the same Starbucks where Daidhl had given Hoss the bloody package. Her flat white coffee had no flavor. The café was crowded with a group of chattering teenage girls, a circle of elderly men, and a couple snuggling together on the couch. She couldn't see the woman's face, but the man was very attentive. There were several single people wearing earplugs and typing on their iPads. God, any of these people could be Daidhl in disguise.

Her phone rang. "Detective Malloy."

"Any sign yet?" Hoss asked. He waited across the street in a rented dark window van. Daidhl would be able to spot him if he were flying overhead or seated in the café.

"No," she answered nonchalantly.

Her phone buzzed again—Captain Morgan.

"I'll call you back."

"Wait, Agnes—"

But she hung up. She planned on avoiding Tom's persistent calls, but she couldn't ignore the captain's. Not if she hoped to have a job after the killer was found.

She sat straighter. "Captain?"

"Where the hell have you been?"

She flinched. "Investigating." More people entered the café, including laughing teenagers, a kissy couple, and a single woman. She carefully watched them, wondering if any of them were Daidhl in disguise.

"Did you and Hoss steal an ambulance? One was found out on Indiana and Eighty-sixth Avenue."

She hesitated before answering. "No." Lying to the captain, who had always believed in her, put her at an all new low.

"Your brother is also missing from the hospital."

His accusatory tone pushed her lower than a child kidnapper.

She cleared her throat. "Captain, Frank's safe."

"Where is he?"

She bit her lip and turned her cup around. "I can't tell you." Her lame answer echoed the same excuse former suspects had used that she had scorned.

His response were hard, angry breaths.

She shuddered as she sipped her cold coffee.

"You got ten seconds to tell me where your brother is, or you're off the force."

His belief in her just died.

"Okay," she said slowly. "He's in a private facility that specializes in cases like his. As his only living relative, I had a right to move him."

"What facility?"

Her lies and half-truths tongue-tied her voice. Ignoring his gruffness, she put the phone gently down on the table and stared at Hoss's car. When no one else believed in her, her dragon had faith.

Not wanting to play the coward, she picked up the phone and blurted, "If he makes it, I'll let him tell you."

"You're walking on thin ice, Detective. Where the devil are you?"

"Captain, he went after my family and my best friend."

Silence greeted her on the phone.

"You know about Kathy?"

His voice turned gentle, something she wished he hadn't done.

"Yes, I know." Her eyes blurred for a second, but she blinked back the wetness. She couldn't show weakness, not while searching for Daidhl.

"I'm sorry, Detective. I know she was a good friend."

Betty materialized in front of Agnes, her eyes burning red. "He's here." She pointed toward the couple. "Over there. Are you going to let her die like you did me, Detective?"

Agnes grimaced at the haunting tone.

"Captain, I have to go." She stared at the couple, trying to decipher whether it was Daidhl. When the man looked over, she swirled around in her chair. Her heart pounded louder than the captain's angry voice.

"Damn it, Agnes, tell me what is going on before—"

She hung up. She had a job to do. Not one more woman would fall victim to Daidhl's sick craving.

She glanced at the couple, who had taken a seat near her, and then took another sip of her coffee. The man whisper in the woman's ear, but she'd hadn't moved once.

Now, what was she supposed to do? Agnes refused to have her actions result in losing another innocent woman. She needed to get the woman away from him. The plan was to get Daidhl to follow her outside and away from potential victims, but as usual, he was a step ahead of them.

The entrapment cage only opened based on fingerprints. Hoss had reprogrammed it for human instead of Zalarian. She slowly pulled the device out of her purse. No one gave her a second glance, since it resembled a woman's silver compact. Only Daidhl would know that it was a weapon capable of destroying him. Or at least, she hoped it would.

She turned her body so her back was facing Daidhl. God, she

hoped Betty hadn't been mistaken. So far, the ghost hadn't been wrong.

"Who is the woman with her?" Agnes lowered her voice, hoping no one heard her except for Betty.

"Her name is Stacey Flynn. She's a college student, studying to be an engineer. Daidhl followed you here. When you went inside, he forced her to come with him. He's got a knife hidden in his pocket and promised to slice her throat if she made the slightest move to get away or cry for help."

Fear filled Agnes. She was only a young girl and the bastard was threatening to cut her life short. Agnes couldn't help but wonder if the girl was a mate. If Agnes failed, she wouldn't be the only one who would die. Hoss's life, the girl's life, and an unknown number of other women's lives also hung in the balance.

Agnes took a deep breath until she was in control of her fear. She'd learned too many times that losing her nerves led to deadly mistakes.

"Well, here goes nothing," she muttered under her breath.

Hot breath rolled down the back of her neck. "Take it out, and she dies."

Agnes choked on foul breath, as if teeth hadn't been brushed for years. Chills rolled over her like an icy, arctic wind. She glanced over her shoulder. Daidhl had his arm locked around the terrified girl's throat. Her blue eyes were so huge, Agnes thought any minute they'd pop out of her head. Agnes wasn't going to let the girl die.

"Let her go, Daidhl. It's me you want."

She didn't waver from underneath his deadly gaze.

"Not until you give me that thing."

A slight tremor echoed in his stern voice. For once, he was afraid. The plan could work if she stayed frosty.

"At the same time."

"Why, Detective, you don't trust me?"

His sugary voice made her want to poke out his glimmering eyes with her finger.

"No."

"Then, we have an accord?"

The girl moved her head, her voice muffled underneath his palm.

"One more thing, Daidhl. She'll be alive."

"You're no fun," he smirked.

She met his taunting gaze. "No, I'm not. Now, let the girl go."

"So brave, Detective. We'll see how brave you are when we're alone."

Fear ignited like a fire in Agnes's belly. All the gruesome murders and his almost deadly attack on Hoss flashed in her mind, but she kept her cop-face on and hoped she hid her terror. She narrowed her eyes. "Counting on it."

His arrogant face paled and a vein in one cheek quivered. He hissed loudly.

She raised her eyebrow. He needed her fear, but... His frustration made her wonder if he couldn't sense her own. she wouldn't give it to him. Maybe he could only feed on the surface of emotions, not ones hidden.

She stood. "Back up."

"No," he growled.

She put her hand over the cage. "Then I'll open it."

"You'll pay for your insolence." But the bastard backed up. He loosened his grip on the girl, and she darted around him, but he grabbed her wrist. "Don't."

Agnes stared at the frightened girl. "Let her go. She won't scream."

The girl nodded. "I promise, please, *please*..."

Daidhl leaned closer to the girl. "I can capture you anytime. Don't disappointment me."

Tears ran down her cheeks. She nodded silently, her lower lip trembling.

Agnes lusted to open the cage so bad, but if she did, the girl would die.

Daidhl released the girl, but immediately clamped on to Agnes's wrist. His fingers were like sharp icicles, digging into her flesh. "You'll not be needing this." He ripped the cage out of her hand and stuffed it in his jacket.

The girl ran to the other side of the room, slouching in a corner. She didn't make a sound, but her face was pure white.

"Now, you and I are going to walk out of here real slow," Daidhl said. "Do you understand me?"

Something sharp pricked her back. "Yes, I said I'd go with you."

"You try anything stupid, Detective, and you'll be missing a kidney."

Her heart thudded in her chest. Agnes brought on all her police training to stay calm. Her favorite was thinking of her safe place—the Malloy cabin. She thought of the smell of pine, the thin, clean, air, the peacefulness. Little-by-little the tension pent up inside her muscles unraveled. Daidhl wouldn't kill her here. He'd want someplace private where he could take his time.

He whispered in her ear. "We're going to take a little drive."

His wretched breath made her stomach churn, threatening to lose her coffee. "Where?"

"To your home, of course."

Agnes hid her smile. If their plan didn't work, knowing the captain, he'd have a stakeout outside her home. At least she'd have a chance to escape.

When they walked outside, the sun shone brightly overhead. Daidhl flinched and hissed, but didn't lose his grip. Agnes struggled to contain her excitement. Flask had been right. The Earth's sun did have an effect on him.

A car door opened and shut, but Agnes pretended not to notice. She led Daidhl toward her car.

"That's it," he said. "Nice and slow. You don't want to piss me off."

She turned and smiled. "Actually, I do."

He frowned. "What?"

Hoss stepped around a large truck. "Hello, Daidhl." He aimed the open entrapment cage at Daidhl. Blinding orange rays lit up the parking lot.

Agnes winced.

Daidhl stepped back, snarling. He jerked her in front of him, blocking the ray from his chest, but she could feel him panting behind her. His grip on her arm tightened .

"Agnes, get out of the way." Hoss reached for her.

Daidhl jerked her away and placed the blade under her throat. "Drop it, Hoss, or I'll cut your little mate's throat."

Black smoke flittered around Agnes, making her eyes water.

Betty flittered next to Hoss. "He's losing strength. You'll be able to break free soon."

"Oh, my god. He's got a knife!" a woman screamed.

"Someone help her!" another cried.

"Call the cops," a man yelled.

Hoss wouldn't drop the cage. "It's over, Daidhl."

"It's not over until I say it's over."

His hand slipped where he held the knife under her throat. Agnes jabbed her elbows into his gut and stomped on his foot with every ounce of strength she had. He howled in pain and dropped the knife on the pavement.

Agnes scooped the knife up and slashed it down Daidhl's chest, spilling blood down his shirt.

He roared with rage.

Hoss grabbed her shoulder and hauled her back. Daidhl knocked the entrapment out of Hoss's hand. Hoss lunged for it, but Daidhl's attention was on his next victim.

He grabbed Agnes's wrist and pinched hard, loosing the blade. The weapon was wretched out of her hand, then the world spun around her. When she stopped, hot fear shot through her like a burning bullet. Golden eyes glared at her. A mouth full of sharp teeth greeted her.

Daidhl bit her neck, tearing out her flesh. She screamed.

Blood squirted into the air like an angry fountain.

"Die bitch!" Daidhl stabbed her repeatedly in the stomach.

Agony seized her. Blood gushed up her throat and trickled out of her mouth. Her legs gave out underneath her, and she collapsed on the concrete. She blinked through a haze as Hoss grabbed Daidhl by the throat and fired his weapon.

Daidhl disappeared. Hoss dropped onto his knees next to her. "He's gone." Tears swelled in his eyes. "Agnes, don't leave me."

Blood filled her mouth. "Is it over?" she spit out blood as she spoke.

"Yes." He held onto her hand tightly.

Betty appeared behind Hoss. The anger and hate were gone from her eyes. She smiled. "He's telling the truth. We can all rest in peace."

All of the victims—Sharon Reese, Laura Nybo, Annie Watkins, Lisa Strong—stood behind Betty. Agnes blinked, not sure she was seeing right. Lisa was Kathy's younger sister. She had the same hair, the same color eyes, the same height as Kathy. No wonder Daidhl had killed the wrong woman.

Lisa smiled. "Kathy's alive. Good-bye, Agnes. Tell her I'm at peace."

The ghosts all faded into bright lights and disappeared.

Agnes coughed up blood. "Hoss, Kathy's alive."

"What?"

"An ambulance is coming, buddy." A pale-looking fifty-year-old man stood behind Hoss. "She'll be okay."

But Agnes could see it in Hoss's and the man's eyes. She was dying. The anguish was worth it. The killing was over.

She gripped Hoss's hand. She gasped, choking on blood.

"Before...I die, I need to tell you...before it's too late. I...love...you."

Hoss leaned his head back and roared. "No!"

She closed her eyes, glad the last person she'd see before she past on was Hoss. He let her go of her hand and emptiness soaked in her. He didn't love her.

"Shit, a...a...dragon."

The voice shook with fear and disbelief, but it sounded too far away. Agnes couldn't make out whether it was male or female and didn't care. Hoss was leaving her. Maybe he'd convince Topaz not to kill him.

That was the last thing Agnes thought before she felt air rushing over her as her soul lifted to heaven.

৩৶৩

HOSS PACED IN THE CENTARUS'S WAITING AREA, NEARLY wearing out the floor. Agnes had been in surgery for the last eight hours and still no sign of Tryker or his doctors. When Hoss brought Agnes to the ship, he discovered Frank had made it through surgery and was sleeping comfortably. Topaz was furious he'd changed into a dragon in front of humans, but Hoss didn't care.

Agnes had been dying. He could careless about his own skin. His heart nearly jumped out of his throat when she stabbed Daidhl in the chest, weakening him further. It was enough for him to yank out the bastard's heart and suck out the last of the Mistonian into the cage. Daidhl was dead, but the Mistonian wasn't. At least he couldn't escape.

The foul creature would be handed over to the Confederation for sentencing. But that didn't matter. All that mattered was Agnes.

While he waited, Hoss couldn't breathe, he couldn't eat, he couldn't sleep. His father had complained of the same symptoms before he hung himself. In that moment, Hoss finally understood what his father was going through. His father hadn't been weak. He'd been brokenhearted.

Fates, Hoss would rather be wounded in battle then suffer like this.

The medical lab doors opened, and Tryker walked out wearing scrubs. He rubbed his blood-shot eyes.

"Tryker, is she alive? Can I see her?"

He hung his head. "I'm sorry."

"No!" Hoss picked up a chair and hurled it across the room, jamming into a wall.

"Hoss, you need to calm down." Tryker grabbed both of his arms. "Destroying the Centarus isn't going to help Agnes."

Anonghos broke his grip and flung his arm toward the room where the agent slept peacefully. "But you saved Frank, why the hell can't you save her?"

Tryker folded his arms over his chest. "Because I'm not her mate. I've done all I can for her. The rest is up to you."

Fear punched a whole in his tantrum. "What?"

"Don't act surprised, Anonghos. If you want to save her, you need to claim her. That's the only way she'll survive."

"Why do you think I haven't claimed her?"

"Because she's dying, you idiot."

Tryker's low voice smacked Hoss into motion. He'd been so afraid of ending up like his father, and giving up pride, that he'd left Agnes vulnerable. Even if she hadn't been his mate, he'd want her. Her passion was as great as his was. He wasn't going to lose her.

"Where is she?"

"I'll take you to her."

Agnes looked so small in her bed. She was breathing shallowly, and her face was ashen. Her blond hair flared out on her pillow.

Hoss couldn't hold back the tears.

Tryker clasped his shoulder and squeezed. "You can do this, bro. I believe in you."

He quietly exited, leaving Hoss alone with his half-dead mate. He leaned over and kissed her stiff lips. "I won't lose you, Agnes. You belong to me. I claim you." He was too terrified to tell her how he felt. Why was so it hard to utter those three little words?

Afraid he'd fall, he sat in a chair next to her bed. His shaking hand took out the red stone. He slowly turned over Agnes's rigid wrist. Fates, this was all his fault. What had he'd done?

He placed the stone in her frozen palm. "Come back to me." He kissed her wrist, then lay his head on her hand. His tears fell on her pale skin. His dragon roared. Fire burned in his chest, and passion swirled inside him like a shooting star. Madness unhinged inside him. She was his.

Her creaky fingers moved beneath him. He jerked his head up. She was actually clasping the mating stone. Hope surged through him. He leaned over and kissed her hard, willing her to come back to him to live.

Nothing happened.

His heart sank to his toes. He push his tongue through her lips and her clenched teeth. He swirled his tongue, exploring the recesses of her mouth, hoping to ignite a spark amidst the darkness. He moved his hands up and down her arms, trying to provide warmth.

He thought he heard a groan. For a minute, he thought it was himself, but when he looked down, she stared up at him with smoky golden eyes.

"Hoss?" Her voice was so weak.

He knelt down and pushed her hair back. "Shhh."

Confusion fluttered in her eyes. "What happened?"

"I claimed you."

"I don't...understand."

He laughed. "No, I suppose you don't. You were dying."

"I was?"

"I love you Agnes Malloy. I want you with me always."

"You do? Do I have a choice?"

An arrow pierced his lungs, cutting off his breath. Emptiness descended on him, and he could feel the noose tightening around his throat. "Yes."

Her eyes fluttered shut, leaving him with a broken spirit.

He clutched her hand, refusing to let go.

"Then I choose to be with you."

Her voice was so low he wasn't sure he heard her, but he locked those words in his heart.

❧ 22 ❧

Agnes woke to the sound of beeping. Her mind was hazy. The world spun around her and her stomach swished back and forth. She shut her eyes tight, then slowly opened them. The room stopped spinning. Blurriness left her vision. Empty beds were lined up neatly against the opposite wall. Binging and dinging dashboards, right out Star Trek, hung over each bed. Dull pain throbbed in her backside, and the horrible memories of Daidhl flooded over her. The hate in his eyes... His foul breath... His icy touch... Agnes shivered.

"Are you cold?"

She turned to see Hoss on a chair next to her bed. He peered down at her with blood-shot eyes. His hair stuck out all over.

She managed a smile. "You look terrible."

"You look beautiful." He clutched her hand with shaky fingers. "Are you alright?"

He took a shuddering breath. "Now, that you're awake I am." He kissed her hand. "I thought... I thought... I was going to lose you."

His gentle kiss sent warmth through her body, chasing away the nightmares. She smirked. "You won't get rid of me that easy."

"Good. I need you. I never thought I'd need a woman before, never wanted to."

She frowned. The slight movement sent a shiver of pain through her forehead. "Why?"

"Because of my father."

When they'd had sex, he'd woken up screaming. Guilt nestled in her gut for not pursuing this further, but Daidhl hadn't given them a moment's rest. "And?"

His eyes burned gold, and a shadow fell across his face. "I always thought he was a weak man, hated him for it..." His voice trailed off as if he were lost in his own thoughts.

She remained silent. Rushing people to tell their stories always ended badly.

He kissed her knuckles. "He hung himself when I was a kid." Anguish echoed in his whisper.

She sucked in her breath. Her father had been many things, but he'd fought the bad, even when her mother died. Children remain scarred when parents abandoned them, but suicide was an ugly level she didn't fully understand. "Oh, Hoss, I'm so sorry." She moved to hug him and her pain jumped up ten octaves. She grimaced, hissing between her teeth.

"Agnes, are you okay? Do you want some pain medication?"

"No, I'm groggy as it is. I just want you at my side."

"That you always will have."

She drew on her determination not to let the throbbing consume her. Hoss needed to share his story, and she needed to hear it. "Why?" she croaked out.

"What? I didn't understand you."

She cleared her throat and a stronger voice asked, "Why did your father kill himself?"

"Because my mother left him."

She frowned. "I thought they were mated."

"Her first mate died, then she settled for my father and had me." Bitterness crept into this voice. "I don't think she loved either one of us."

"I do."

He laughed. "You don't know how glad I am to hear you say that." He stopped laughing, and his eyes turned serious. He gently kissed her forehead and stroked her hair. "Because you're my life. I...love...you."

She raised her eyebrow. "I bet that was hard for you to bust out."

He ran his fingers through his messed up hair and slumped in his chair. "You have no idea. I never wanted to end up like my father, never thought I could trust a woman not to leave me... Until now." He bent over and brushed his lips over hers.

Strangely, the throbbing pain lessened, not clouding her thoughts. "Hoss, how old were you when this happened?"

"I was six when my mother left and twelve when my father hung himself." He put both his elbows on her bed and rested his head on the top of his knuckles. "Dad and I had a fight on my birthday. Mother sent me a card every year. It was the only time I ever heard from her. I blamed him for her leaving. I left angry and went over to Damon's house."

Agnes was at a loss on what to say to him. She rubbed his trembling arm.

He raised his head. Tears glistened in his eyes. "I found him in the garden, swinging from a rope. He didn't even leave a note."

Ignoring the pain, Agnes forced herself to sit up and drew him into her arms. He lay his head on her shoulder and held her close. His heart beat pounded next to hers. She stroked his hair.

"Mother didn't send for me even after he died. Now, she's dead, too."

His voice was barely a whisper.

Anger cruised through Agnes at his mother for being so self-ish. She wasn't sorry that the Kamtrinians had killed her. His mother might not have loved Hoss's father, but Hoss was her son. She kissed his wet cheek. "I'm here. And I won't leave you."

He took a deep breath and slowly released her. "Did I hurt you?"

"No. It seems every time I touch you or kiss you, the pain lessens."

"Mates have the power to heal each other. Not necessarily cure, but heal faster."

"Well, you're doing a great job."

He smiled.

"So, you pushed women away after this, didn't you?"

"Yup. I just liked them to warm my bed. I never wanted to be mated."

"Why did you agree to mate with me?"

"Didn't have a choice. The Fates, our goddesses, had other plans. I said no, but King Greum ordered me, too. You don't say no to the king unless you want to die a horrible death."

"Smart king."

The door opened and Tryker came inside pushing Frank in a wheelchair. Dark circles were underneath his eyes, but his color was better and his eyes brighter.

"Frank!" Anges smiled.

"Hello, sis. You're looking a hundred percent better."

"So, are you. How are you feeling?"

"Like I got hit by a Mack Truck, but Tryker says I'm healing." A glint showed in his eyes. He gripped the arms of the wheelchair and stood. He tilted his head. "Thanks to him, I'll be walking soon."

"He's been trying to walk everyday until he's bone tired," Tryker said. "He's a man of steel."

"Of course, he is. He's a Malloy, and my hero."

Tryker wheeled Frank over to the other side of her bed. Frank leaned over and kissed her on the cheek.

"You scared ten years off me, sis. I'm glad you're on the up and up."

"He's been visiting you everyday," Hoss said. "Tryker had to force him to leave."

Anges swelled with love. Her brother cared. He'd proven it to her. "I never thanked you for saving my life."

"And I hear you went to hell and back to save me. I guess we're even." He sighed and looked around the room. "I wanted to apologize to you for giving you a hard time about your ability. Without it, we would have been in a world of hurt down there. Do you forgive me?"

She'd waited a lifetime to hear those words, gone over what she'd say, how she'd bawl him out, but all she could do through the tears brimming in her eyes was utter yes.

She wiped her eyes. "Okay, I think I'm done crying for one day." She took a deep breath, looking at the two men who meant more to her than anything. She asked in her best cop voice, "I know this is a dumb question, but are we on Earth or in space?"

"Earth," Tryker answered. "Our ships are still invisible, and the captain ordered us not to move you or Frank until you were completely healed."

"I think he's worried that if the space medicine didn't work"— Frank smirked—"that they would need to rush us to a hospital."

Her stomach let a rumbling roar. The three men looked at each other and burst out laughing.

"Would you like something to eat, mate?" Hoss asked.

"Obviously. Can I get a cheeseburger and fries?"

"Definitely, my sister," Frank quipped.

"Of course, you can." Hoss kissed her forehead. "I'll get you anything you want. You're my mate."

Two months later

AGNES SNUGGLED NEXT TO HOSS, LISTENING TO HIS HEARTBEAT. Her body still tingled from their love-making. He snored softly next to her. She never wanted to leave his side. It had been difficult to say good-bye to Frank, who had returned to the FBI. He was a different man, more open minded, and aware that humans weren't the only ones in the universe. He'd be an excellent ally for the Zalarians.

The one who drew the death stick had been Kathy. She was devastated over her sister's death and blamed herself. No matter what she or Hoss or Frank had told her, she said the death was her fault. If she'd believed... If she hadn't gone out for Starbucks... Lisa would have been alive. Kathy was wrong. If she'd been with her sister, she'd be dead, too.

Agnes sighed, knowing she was helpless in changing Kathy's mind. She wished she could be there for Kathy, but her place was with Hoss. He'd promised that she could visit Frank and Kathy whenever she wanted. She'd hold him to that. But as far as she could tell, her mate would deny her nothing.

She drew on his chest with her finger.

"You keep doing that, and I'm liable to take you again, mate," he mumbled.

She looked up into his hooded eyes. "Promises, promises..."

"You're such a tease."

"I know. But we're a team."

"I don't know what the captain was thinking putting you on my team." He shook his head. "You could get killed."

"He knows a good cop when he sees one. He was impressed with what I did on Earth."

"Such a stubborn wench."

He rolled on top of her and kissed her hard. He moved his hands all over her body, caressing her breasts. His thumbs brushed over her nipples, igniting a fire. She caressed his back, his muscles rippling underneath her fingers.

He left her hungry mouth and trailed kisses along her throat. He slowly edged down her body, kissing and suckling as he went until he captured a nipple. She gasped and threaded her fingers in his hair. He stroked the curls between her legs, teasing her with his strong fingers.

Another wave of passion built inside her. She wiggled beneath him as he brought her pleasure. She spread her legs, wanting to feel him pumping inside her.

He released her nipple, lifted himself up, and in one swift thrust, filled her with his cock. She gripped his shoulders as he rode her hard, stealing her breath and rushing her toward another orgasm. Her heart thundered, sending blood roaring through her, pooling between her legs. She met his rocking thrust each time, skin against skin, heat stirring heat.

She dug her nails into his shoulders, as the furious orgasm built inside her. She inhaled his fiery breath. Her dragon demanded to be satisfied, and she locked her legs around his hips, imprisoning him. Her orgasm burst through, sending her on a mountain high. She screamed out his name.

He pounded harder then followed, spilling his seed inside her. He collapsed, panting. "I'll never get tired of hearing you scream out my name."

She kissed his hot lips and broke away. "I'll never get tired of saying it. I love you."

He stared at her with possessive eyes. "And I you. You've unhinged the nightmares inside me and killed the madness. With you by my side, we can rebuild my world."

She put her palms on his sleek cheeks. "And protect mine." She caressed his buttocks with the back of her leg. "Claim me one more time."

He ran his hand down her side. "Never satisfied."

Shivers of desire pumped through her. "Not with you I'm not."

Hoss claimed her again and again, leaving her little doubt that she'd captured the heart of a dragon.

DO YOU LOVE DRAGONS? WANT TO READ MORE? CHECK OUT Madness Unmasked! The adventure continues. You'll also meet the dragons' allies—Arians. They're space bears!

In this next book, Ysam is Daidhl's brother and he's blamed for what his brother did on Earth. He's problems get even worse when he learns his mate is none other than Kathy Strong who wants nothing to do with aliens. But if they don't mate, it spells doom for the Zalarians and Earth. Will those two ever be mated or will both their worlds be destroyed?

EXCERPT FROM MADNESS UNMASKED
Vrae Galaxy

STARS WHIZZED ON THE MAIN BRIDGE SCREEN, BUT THE Kamtrinian ship was faster, leaving the Intrepid in the dust.

Nucl pressed flashing buttons rapidly on his navigation and security board. "Captain, the Kamtrinians are out of our phaser range. We're losing them!" His panicked voice matched his shaking fingers.

Tash, captain of the Intrepid, leaned forward on his command chair that had control panels on each side of the arms. The right panel readings listed the damage to the colony—buildings disintegrated, vegetation burned, and lifeforms dead. "I can see that helmsman. We need to remain calm." His heart was thundering, pumping adrenaline at ultra speed, but his voice remained in control. His bear demanded to be set loose so he could tear apart a Kamtrininan, but he drew on his training as a United Planet Confederation Captain to push back his anger and control his animal.

The Intrepid rattled as it chased after the faster ship.

Tash's intercom binged on the left control panel. "Captain?"

Tash cringed. It was his youngest brother, Ryruc, who they called Rye. He was the chief engineer, but when he was annoying, he called him by his real name. "Yes, Ryruc."

"Damn it, Tash. What the hell are you doing? The engines can't take much more of this. The Intrepid will shake apart."

Rye was the alarmist of the family and the one with the shortest temper.

"Captain," Vaughn, the Intrepid's science officer and Tash's brother, looked up from his red-colored scanner. He narrowed his green eyes. "If we enter the Chronos Star Solar System, we will be violating Confederation Command."

Knup tapped his headset and punched the smooth buttons on his blue keyboard. "The Kamtrinians are demanding contact, Captain."

Tash sank back into his black chair. "Put them on the screen."

A tall, muscular humanoid with smooth white skin and three black eyes flashed onto the soft gray screen. "I am Yagok, Captain of the Executor. You are about to enter our solar system, which is a violation between our two confederations."

Tash refused to show fear, but something about those three beady eyes reminded him of swirling, black holes and sent the hair on the back of his neck standing up. "This is Captain Tash of the Intrepid. You murdered innocent men, women, and children on Taurous. We have—"

Yagok growled, his eyes glowing darker. "They were invaders."

"Taurous and Sutois are part of our solar system. You had no right to destroy them."

Yagok smiled. "Only the strongest will survive, which you will soon discover. Prepare to be destroyed. Communications out."

Nucl turned around, sweat glistening off his temples. "We have to do something. We have to destroy them. They decimated the colony!"

"I'm very aware of what they did, Nucl."

A group of scientists had recently set up a settlement on the farthest orbiting moon—Taurous—of Sutois, which was the farthest and unknown planet of the Vrae Galaxy. Their mission had been to study the unknown planet of Sutois for possible life and development for the Confederation.

"The engines are overheating," Rye growled. He was very close to letting his bear escape. The Intrepid was his baby and his bear was fiercely protective of her.

Nucl gripped his console. "Captain, we can't reduce speed."

"She'll break apart," Rye snarled.

"I suggest, navigator," Vaugh said. "That you remain calm and not endanger the ship. Or you risk tangling with our chief engineer."

Nucl's face turned several shades of grey. Rye was twice the bear he was, and when the Intrepid was in danger, he showed no mercy.

"But..."

Tash clutched his navigator's seat, dominating the bear's fear. "Nucl, stay on course. Reduce ultra-speed to nine. I'm not sure what Yagok is planning, but we have to keep our wits together."

"Aye, aye, sir," he grumbled. He was wise enough not to argue with Tash, since Rye was still listening.

Tash swiveled his chair. "Knup, have you been able to reach Confederation command?"

Knup shook his head. "No, Captain." He furiously typed on his beeping keyboard. "Static is blocking our communications. It's coming from the Kamtrinian ship."

"Vaughn, what do we know of Sutois?"

"Not much, Captain. The atmosphere is similar to Aria—oxygen atmosphere, water, plants, minerals—and the planet can support life. No advanced civilizations inhabit the planet. However, the scientists had reported before their demise that there was life on Sutois. They were preparing to investigate when they were attacked."

Tash rubbed his chin. "Maybe that's why they were attacked."

Vaughn nodded. "Possibly."

Nucl glanced over his shoulder. "Captain, the Kamtrinian ship is slowing down."

"Be prepared. Yagok said they planned to destroy us." Tash stood. "Why wait until they reach the edge of our galaxy? Vaughn?"

Vaughn had returned to his scanner. "Unknown, Captain. But they appear to be firing up their weapons. Wait, there's a second ship."

Tash's adrenaline whisked through him, his bear demanding to be released. The hairs on his back rose and his nails lengthened. He clenched his fist, struggling to remain in control. "How could we have missed them?"

Vaughn jerked his head up. "The second ship appears to have had a cloaking system."

Tash's mouth ran dry and the adrenaline pushing through his veins spiked, making him sweat. He hit the alert button. He scrambled for his captain's voice, almost got it. "Red alert, red alert. All crew members report to battle stations."

Rather than calm, cool and collective, he growled. "Nulc, raise our shields!"

Nulc cried, "They're firing, Captain!"

Two torpedoes fired. The spinning white lights slammed into the Intrepid's shields, and she jerked.

Vaughn pushed the shields' control on his panel. "We lost shield number one."

Tash ordered. "Return fire!"

Nucl fired photon ruptors. The ruptors smashed into the first ship, but the second one disappeared.

Another hit slammed into the Intrepid from behind, and she lurched forward.

"The second ship is behind us, Captain," Vaughn said. "We're trapped."

"Not yet, we're not. Nulc, navigate to maneuver five."

Maneuver five meant the ship would move down rather than forward or backward. Just as the first ship was to return fire, the Intrepid vertically dropped, so the two Kamtrinian ships were facing each other. A crash rocked overhead.

"Captain?" Vaughn smiled. "The first ship fired on their own ship, but it disappeared."

"We were lucky," Tash said. "I doubt we will be again. Nucl, circle around to the first ship."

"Aye, Captain."

"Vaughn, scan for the second ship. Look for any unknown gas."

"Yes, Captain."

The Kamtrinian ship filled the screen. "Fire, Nucl. Full proton torpedoes."

Torpedoes blazed toward the Kamtrinian ship. Victory was at hand, but another blast slammed into the Intrepid, sending her into a spinning nose dive. Tash somersaulted, the bridge rushing around him. He crashed into a wall, dots blurring his vision.

Sparks bursts through the bridge like a chain of explosions.

"Captain!" Rye yelled over the intercom. "We're down to one shield and one engine."

Tash slowly crawled to his feet, ignoring the pain throbbing in his back. "Vaughn, what the Jiarus happened?"

"That second ship has a new weapon, Captain. I should have surmised this." Vaughn was surprisingly still at his post, his hands gripping the scanner. "We can't withstand another direct hit."

Knup snatched his hands off his flickering console. "Our communication system has short-circuited, Captain. Even if we get out of here, I can't reach Confederation command."

Phasers zapped the ship. Lights blinked. The Intrepid jolted, then slowed.

Rye buzzed. "Captain, we need to make repairs or we'll be dead in space."

Tash's gut dropped to his feet. The Kamtrinians would blow the Intrepid into oblivion. "Evasive procedures, Nucl. We have to save the ship. Set a course for Sutois."

"But Captain, we have to fight."

"Nucl, there are over three hundred crew men and women on board this ship. I'll not risk their lives to satisfy your lust for revenge." He narrowed his eyes. "That's a direct order."

His body bulked up with the bear threatening to cut loose. The navigator flinched and immediately set a course away from the two starships.

"Rye, divert all power to shields. Nucl, maneuver six."

"Aye, Captain," they both answered.

The ship jumped straight up, just as the two Kamtrinians fired, hitting each other. Explosions flared on the Kamtrinians' bridge. They tipped forward, hanging in midair.

"Considerable damage on the two ships, Captain," Vaughn reported. "This may give us the time to make repairs on Sutois. I would suggest that we land on the planet itself instead of the star port on the moon. The Kamtrinians will be expecting us to land there."

"Agreed." Tash set back in his chair, his heart slowing to a steady pulse. "Let's just hope we can make repairs before the Kamtrinians find us."

"Life forms have been reported on Sutois's surface, Captain," Rye interrupted over the intercom. "I suggest we be prepared for hostile creatures."

"They could also be non-threatening," Vaughn argued. "We need to study before we attack."

Tash glared at Vaughn. "We will be on yellow alert until I know it's safe for our people."

Vaughn huffed and whirled around. He returned to his station, muttering. Sometimes his voice of practicality and reasoning drove Tash crazy. His choices were nil. The Intrepid wouldn't survive another battle with the Kamtrinian ships. To survive, they needed to make repairs.

He rubbed his sweating forehead and gritted his teeth, hoping he hadn't made a deadly mistake.

ABOUT THE AUTHOR

\

Award Winning Author M.L. Guida loves the paranormal.
Even when she was four years old, she would watch the soap
opera, Dark Shadows, and fell in love with vampires! Who
wouldn't want a bite on the neck? But she didn't stop there.
Witches, dragons, angels, and demons are sprinkled throughout
her books.

Today, she continues to love the preternatural and watches Supernatural, Paranormal Survivor, and A Haunting. Like Dean Winchester, she loves to write alpha males who aren't afraid to face the forces of evil.

ALSO BY ML GUIDA

Dragons of Zalara Series

Madness Unleashed

Madness Unmasked

Touch of Madness

Touch of Darkness

Madness Unbalanced (Coming in June)

Legends of the Soaring Phoenix

A Pirate's Curse

A Pirate's Revenge

A Pirate's Agony

A Pirate's Obsession

A Pirate's Bane

A Pirate's Darkness